WHISPERS IN A PHONE BOOTH

A Depression-Era Tale of Danger and Deception

J. DANIEL REED

For all inquiries or more information, contact:
b.reed@terra3communications.com

First edition December 2023
ISBN 979-8-9850592-2-9 (paperback)
ISBN 979-8-9850592-3-6 (ebook)
Published by Terra3 Communications, LLC
Mount Prospect, Illinois
www.terra3communications.com

This book is dedicated to US Army Staff Sergeant Brian Michael Reed who faithfully served from August 2005 to March 2016 when he lost his battle with post-traumatic stress disorder. He saw combat in both Iraq and Afghanistan and was awarded The Bronze Star with a "V" device for heroism.

My deepest gratitude to my deceased nephew Brian, and to all the brave members of the US Armed Forces of the past and present, along with their families, for their service and sacrifice.

PREFACE

Whispers in a Phone Booth takes place in the same Chicago northside neighborhood that was the first American home to my grandparents upon their emigration out of eastern Europe. They all met and married in Chicago. I use the historical fiction genre because it allows me to share a story my father told me of a harrowing event he witnessed as a seventeen-year-old. Part of the description of the incident is based on my father's exact words.

When undertaking to write this novel, I reflected on two very different topics. Disparate ideas can inexplicably be connected in any author's mind in an instant, giving spark to a combination of themes, creating the foundation for a new story.

First, I focused on the proud and virtuous ancestors of mine that left eastern Europe at the start of the twentieth century. Hardworking people of faith, many with little formal education, struggled to build a new life in America, fighting anti-immigrant bigotry and other barriers, including language. But, they persevered. Generations followed, each built on the foundation of hard work, courage, gratitude, and faith. I am fortunate to have had such fine people as my ancestors.

Like so many other families, multiple generations of my family also served in the US military—the most recent of whom was my deceased nephew, Brian Michael Reed. This book is dedicated to him. I attempt to offer a brief, but respectful perspective on the sacrifices made by countless military heroes and the myriad damages done to them by the traumas of war. While no one can offer a completely adequate description, I strived to pay tribute to all our military members past and present within the storyline about certain fictional, heroic veterans of World War I. All who serve or have served deserve the unrelenting gratitude, support, and love of family, comrades, friends, and neighbors.

The second, disparate idea came when hearing a Catholic priest speak of one of the 613 precepts of the Jewish law. He described the obligation in The Law that one is to help a collapsed beast of burden under its overwhelming load—even if the animal is the property of an enemy or stranger.

Something clicked. Why should the innocent suffer because of their family, or clan, or in the case of the animal, its owner? Suddenly I imagined two very similar immigrant families back in the old neighborhood, living very different lives. By sheer coincidence, just as the purpose of the novel began to take shape, I was listening to a dear friend speak of his great grandfather, Max Stine, the founder of Stineway Drug Stores. It was a Chicago landmark started in the early 1930's. And where better, I thought, than a neighborhood pharmacy as the center of the novel's orbit.

This story contemplates how simple choices made, whether ignorantly, or in the full light of intellectual and moral understanding, may not be all that govern our lives. Do we know for certain that our fortune only springs from those two paradigms? Is it possible good fortune or the lack thereof is impacted from things we don't fully understand, such as invisible things in the spiritual realm? If such things exist, how does a lineage break its bonds of misfortune? Rather than exploring such mysteries in a titillating dalliance into unknown darkness, this story focuses on what virtues might defeat those negative shadows, regardless of their exact nature.

One of the main characters is based upon someone I once knew in my adult life, who should have had ample reasons to be happy, but was not. A loyal spouse, healthy children, and a comfortable lifestyle were just some of this individual's good fortune. But happiness seemed lacking, almost impossible to grasp. Why?

Sometimes one can look upon another person and sense there is something lurking beneath the surface—something profoundly grim. Rarely do we ever confirm if our sense of another's disorder is justified, let alone identify the specific cause of that darkness.

How does one so afflicted, if questioned, know if the other is perversely curious or acting out of love? Sometimes, the motivation of the inquiry may never be known until it's too late. It is only when our motivation springs from love that such exploration is truly justified. Tragically, even when motivated by love, many of us are too fearful to explore ways to help. This novel considers if the thing which damaged one person, if not lovingly addressed, may taint future generations long afterward and in innumerable ways.

While it is common wisdom to say one can't always control what happens in life, regardless, one has the ability to choose how to react to it. In this novel, I also explore if this is always true. What happens when random tragedy or evil repeatedly attempts to crush a life? How many individuals can hold up to repeated brutal attacks of cruel fate? Can those gifted with opportunity, or intelligence, or beauty be more resilient than others less fortunate? Could such a curse, if you will, invisibly carry on to future generations too powerful to be shed by the strong and the weak alike? If wealth and reputation can be passed on from generation to generation, why can't misfortune?

In contrast, sometimes a most minor twist of plans can have a dramatic impact on what happens or what might have happened. There are reports of someone missing a flight or giving up a seat on an airplane when it is overbooked and then tragedy strikes when the plane goes down, killing all aboard. How is it a seemingly minor event like being late to the airport gate or being generous to a stranger have such profound life and death consequences? How can fate be so cruel to some, and generous to others?

After brushing with profound evil, will our antihero from the lineage of the unfortunate, be strong enough to end the generations of calamity—or be destroyed? As irresistible dangers gather nearby, will the acts of kindness and charity from others be powerful enough to save him?

The reader must decide if the true redemption of our antihero will prevail. Similarly, for two other major characters, you will be left to wonder how their futures might change after going through much trauma, then experiencing the potentially transformative kindness of neighbors.

I have used the names of my paternal grandparents, Peter and Helen, and my father, Walter in this story. It is just the way it happened in the initial telling. As many authors explain, we often only know the beginning and the ending of a new novel when starting to write. In between, the characters help tell the world their stories through the author.

The young and incredibly gifted teenager in the story, Wally, has the good attributes of my father, who was smart, streetwise, physically powerful, and had an amazing bond with dogs. Whether the pets of family or random, unknown animals, they all were drawn to him. However, unlike the fictional character bearing his name, my father was also a virtuous man. It would be hard to find many men and fathers better than he. I know, would he still be alive today, he would love this story and be very amused by the use of his name.

CHAPTER 1

The flickering yellow light of the diminishing fire cast long shadows from the hearth. Stinking of the stable, Martha walked into the shack, her boots still covered in mud and blood after hours helping a young mare give birth to her first foal. Once again, she had to fill in for her father.

She entered and saw the body on the floor. It was a familiar sight. Passed out again, his face lying in a pool of his own vomit, Martha hissed, "You monster. I hate you!" as she kicked her father in the face, breaking one of his teeth. Although bleeding, the man would not awaken until later that morning when enough alcohol had metabolized to allow consciousness. The stable master to the estate of some minor Prussian prince and princess who did not matter to humanity beat his wife and daughters almost as often as he drank whiskey.

The depraved monster's wife lamented with fear and anguish, "Oh Martha, what have you done? No, Martha, no!"

Quickly summoning her maternal strength, she took control. "Martha, go wash up and change into something suitable for travel—put on your Easter finest. You too, Helen—you both must leave tonight! I have been planning your escape for months because I love you both more than anything in the world, and because you must get to safety. The evil curse on our family can no longer be fought here. It has haunted generations upon this land. You must flee across the ocean to America. There you both will find liberation from the demons that torment us."

Their mother's secret plan could no longer wait. A skilled seamstress, she often kept remnants of the finest bolts of cloth and lace after making clothes for the royals. With these scraps, she lovingly created one summer and one winter outfit each for both of her girls that rivaled what the royalty might wear on days without ceremony. She had also taken a pair of barely worn leather cases from the royal family's trash months ago which she pulled from under the bed. Opening the luggage, she pointed and commanded: "Now!" The sisters flew about the dresser drawers and closets, hurriedly stuffing two suitcases to bursting. Dressed and packed, they were ready to go as the hour of evil approached—3:00 a.m. The girls' mother gathered her daughters into her desperate arms. "I love you both more than you might ever be able to understand."

Releasing her daughters with tears still pouring down her face, she pulled a dresser drawer completely out of its tracks, turning it over to reveal a large envelope affixed to the bottom. Ripping it off the drawer's underside, she handed the envelope to the eldest girl. "Martha, take this. It contains five, twenty-mark notes and two common steerage passes on any Hamburg-America Line steamship leaving Cuxhaven to New York. I've been secretly hiding small bits of money until I could save enough to send you both to somewhere safe. Inside are also two boarding passes for a schooner from Gdańsk to Cuxhaven."

While her mother was still speaking, Martha opened it to examine the contents finding an unsealed gilded envelope. Reaching inside she removed a thick linen paper embossed with the royal crest. It was covered with calligraphy, scrolls of gold foil, and royal titles. Everything was written in German. At the top, under the royal crest was the name Wilhelm II. "Momma? What is this?" asked the oldest girl, showing her confusion.

"Martha, that is an Order of Unrestricted Passage from the king himself for the members of the royal family. Should soldiers try to question you at either the train station or the dock, you must show them this. They will also see the crest on your suitcases. You do not have to tell them anything other than you have free passage under order of the king. They will think you are part of the royal family. Should anyone doubt, speak to them like the prince speaks to all of us servants—with condescension and disdain. Give orders like a princess and you will be fine."

Astonished, Martha queried, "Mother, how did you ever come to possess such a thing?"

"Don't worry. When the war started, these letters were brought by courier to the main house just in case the prince and his family had to flee. Dozens of these were lying all about. I slipped one into my sewing sack as I worked on her royal highness's clothes. There were so many, I was certain no one would miss just one."

Reaching down, the mother pulled up a loose floorboard and retrieved a small sack. From it she handed Martha five, ten-mark gold coins along with two crumpled train tickets.

The younger girl, Helen, began to tearfully object. Her mother gently covered her daughter's mouth with her hand. "Shush, my little one. You and Martha will take the worn-out, one-horse carriage and the old roan mare." It was Lucy, Helen's favorite horse. "You'll be safe; she won't spook easily. Follow the north road to the train station. Martha, you know where it is. Leave the carriage and the mare at the station. The crest on the carriage should be all that's needed for you to have a safe ride and later for the sire's property to be returned. Should highwaymen try to stop the carriage along the way, Martha, whip them hard across the face. Don't let anything stop you, no matter how hard you must fight—use your knife if you have to."

Helen pleaded again. "Momma...I'm afraid."

"I know you are. But you can do it. You both work so hard around the stable—you are very strong girls. Listen to me; there is no other way. You must leave now to reach the station in time to catch the 6:20 a.m. train to Gdańsk. Once there, you will have to spend the night in the station, but in the morning, you will be able to walk to the port and board the schooner *Sea Angel*. There is a map inside the envelope showing the route from the station to the pier; it is only about a ten-minute walk. Your ship will depart at 9:00 a.m.—be there by 7:00 a.m. Once in Cuxhaven, you will easily find the Hamburg-America pier."

Hysterical with fear, Helen left her mother's arms and fled to her sister. "Martha, tell momma things will get better. Father can be good if we can help him to stop drinking. Tell momma no!" Sobbing, Helen begged unintelligibly as she tried to move toward her passed out father.

Martha grabbed the smaller girl's arm, spinning her around, "Shut up, Helen. Stop it! He *is* a monster. We are leaving. We must." Helen refused to comply as she tried to pull away, but the older sister held on tightly. Without warning, Martha's single, open-handed slap across Helen's face stopped the hysteria.

The eldest girl pleaded with her mother. "Please come with us. You can't stay here any longer. It isn't safe for you either!"

Their mother looked away. "I can't go. There are only two tickets and there's barely enough money for the trip. I will follow you to America soon, just not now—I am making my own plans. You both must leave before your father wakes—there isn't much time!"

Grabbing the two suitcases, she quickly led them to the smaller stable with the worn-out tack and nearly-useless animals, soon to be food for the servants. The girls stood helplessly, watching their mother place the breast strap, bridle, and bit upon the mare, guiding her into the carriage's rig. After tying the suitcases down, she turned and again grabbed her two daughters.

Stroking their faces and hair, placing kisses upon their cheeks, she stared intensely into their eyes. "Should I live a thousand lifetimes, I can't imagine I could ever be blessed with two daughters as wonderful as you. No mother could ever hope to have daughters so beautiful, clever, and sweet. While my heart will ache every moment you are away from me, you must leave this place, for your sake. I could not bear to see you destroyed by the beast I married. Now, be strong and brave. Helen, you listen to Martha; she is older and less trusting than you. She will know how to get to America safely. Now get in the carriage and go!"

Obediently, they both climbed into the carriage. Martha took the reins in hand and steadfastly reassured her maternal hero, "I promise, mother. I will get us to America safely, and then to Aunt Bernice in Chicago." As the girls left under the cover of night, they feared what horrors might befall their mother at daybreak when the monster awoke to discover her brave betrayal.

Martha cracked the whip gently. The old mare struggled to pull the carriage up the hill to the north road into the fog of early morning dew, saturated with the smell of manure—the girls didn't notice. Helen wept—she would not speak again until they reached the train station. Focused on escape, Martha refused to look back as the carriage gained speed, not seeing their mother wave her final and invisible goodbye.

Their young hearts ached for their mother, especially at the frequent rumors of the monster's clandestine meetings with any maid he could seduce. All the servants of the royal household knew his lust was insatiable. Together, the mother and her two daughters fought their miserable existence in a futile attempt to scratch out some happiness in their lives.

So, that fateful night, the two snuck from under the shadow of the stable master's powerful arm while he lay unconscious. Just fifteen, Helen was given into the custody of Martha, herself only sixteen. Martha could not help but draw attention to herself. Fair of face, tall, and athletic in a feminine way, everyone who saw her could not help but stare at her elegant beauty. Her unique strawberry-blond hair was a perfect complement to her lovely complexion and striking green eyes. The corners of her mouth were permanently turned up slightly, always appearing happy and confident, occasionally revealing an engaging smile. She already appeared to be quite the woman.

While pleasant in her greetings, Martha suspected everyone a villain, quickly planning in her mind how to kill each of them, if needed. She kept a knife with a five-inch-long blade held in its brown leather sheath concealed within her boot or in secret pockets her mother had sewn in her clothes. The razor-sharp weapon, double ground to the hilt, had never left her strong side since she was thirteen.

As the sun's first rays defeated the darkness, Martha pulled back on the reins and guided the old roan mare to a stop alongside the station master's shed. Hopping off the carriage, Helen patted and kissed Lucy on the cheek for the last time. "I will miss you, old girl."

The sisters easily found the platform for their train with time to spare. Spying a lone porter cleaning the far side of the platform, Martha instructed Helen. "You wait here. Don't go anywhere and don't get on the train. I'll be right back." She boldly approached the workman. "By the station master's shed is a horse and buggy with the royal seal. The mare will need food and water. Tend to her promptly, then see that she is returned to the prince's estate." The captivated man just nodded.

The two young women embarked upon the trip without escort, slowly growing in the courage their mother demanded of them. Traveling on the Warsaw–Gdańsk Railway, what was once a grueling and filthy four-day trip by horse-drawn carriage was now reduced to eight hours.

CHAPTER 2

Arriving at the port complex in Gdańsk, the thick crowds of soldiers and sailors held the girls in the tight grip of confusion. Martha grabbed a young sailor by the arm and cooly demanded, "Sir, take us to the *Sea Angel.*"

Entranced by her beauty he stepped between the girls and grabbed hold of their suitcases, immediately noticing the royal seal. "Your Royal Highnesses, take my arms. I will show you the way." His chest puffed out proudly, their impromptu escort led them through the crowd of desperate passengers, each waiting their turn to be interrogated by sailors at the terminal gates.

Suddenly, a rotund man in a tattered suit crashed into Helen. She stumbled but held on tightly to her escort. In a voice loud enough to echo off the ship's hull, Martha roared, "How dare you! Thou shall not touch the crown prince's niece." The sailor took a menacing step toward the lout, causing the frightened traveler to bow and apologize repeatedly as he backed away.

The three, now the object of everyone's attention upon the pier, strutted past the inspection point, all the way to the base of the gangway where the boatswain's mate bowed and then took the girls' boarding passes. Martha confidently demanded to their escort, "Take our bags aboard and leave them at the deck rail."

Royal suitcases in hand, he eagerly led the way up the rope and wooden stairway. It creaked and swayed while the brisk salt breeze tangled the girls' hair as they followed behind. Once on deck, Martha offered her hand to the young sailor who eagerly kissed it. "Thank you, good sir." The young man's now flushed face beamed with satisfaction as he bowed to his temporary charge. Martha and Helen waited at the rail for his return to the pier, waving a relieved thank you to the infatuated sailor below.

The girls quickly found the cold metal stairs leading below deck, descending into the stench of saltwater bilge and rusting metal. In the shelter of their berth, the excited and fearful girls held onto each other for reassurance, as they received their first introduction to choppy seas. But it would not adequately prepare them for the raging swells of the Atlantic Ocean.

Soon relieved to disembark from the short journey on the *Sea Angel,* they easily made their connection in Cuxhaven, Germany, the steamship port opened in 1900. This time there would be no handsome, young sailor to escort them. Martha and Helen shuffled along for at least an hour within a crowd countless in number. The scene was overwhelming and chaotic. Finally nearing the boarding gate, they could hear sailors yelling at each would-be passenger, "Show me your papers!" They poured over the documents and suitcases, demanding answers to questions as if each traveler was guilty of some soon-to-be-discovered crime.

Now, only two back in queue, the girls observed the would-be traveler at the inspection point under intense interrogation suddenly surrounded by the shore police. "Spy—traitor!" one of the sailors called out. Martha and Helen watched as the men began to struggle. With the blow of a police baton, the struggle ended as quickly as it started. The shore police bound the traveler's wrists and dragged him off, semi-conscious.

Helen pleaded with her sister. "They'll know we aren't royalty. We need to leave before they catch us."

But Martha was ready. "Be quiet Helen; we aren't turning back. Everything will be fine. You just keep your mouth shut."

Reaching the inspection point, Martha was ready. She flung her suitcase onto the table revealing the royal seal, then flashed the Order of Unrestricted Passage, demanding, "Have someone take our bags to our berth immediately." Helen did her best to copy her older sister's bravado, barely hiding her trembling.

The inspector at the gate looked at the crest on the suitcase and then her fine clothing. Martha shoved the crest-bearing letter closer toward his face. "Now!" she barked.

"Very good, your Royal Highness," the inspector bowed and quickly growled orders to one of his subordinates. Their mother had thought of everything—except her own escape.

Once upon the ocean liner bound for Ellis Island, the sisters never lost their dream to find a place without welts and the stench of whiskey puke, even while riding the great ocean's own waves of vomit. The formerly three-month journey on ships under the sail was now only three weeks by steam on the Hamburg-America Line. At the beginning of the twentieth century, steerage was a miserable way to travel, but was all most immigrants could afford.

While being tossed to and fro, the younger girl tried to keep them distracted with dreams of the happiness and riches America would bring. Helen fantasized aloud: "Life in America will be so wonderful. We will find money, and live in a large house, and someday we'll have servants of our own. I understand Chicago is a place where everyone finds great success. And Martha, you are so smart, bold, and confident, especially you will find success. Do you believe this?"

Martha replied, "Helen, you will drive me crazy with your daydreams. I have read all the letters from Aunt Bernice. Don't you know America is a perilous place? Chicago is big and dirty.

It smells of factories and stockyards. You dream of wealth and servants; I'll keep us alive!"

Unfortunately for Helen, every conversation always started with the same speech: "Mother told me to watch over you at all times. She made me promise that I will be a responsible older sister without exception. When we arrive in America, stay next to me. If the crowds are large, walk behind me and hold onto my belt with your hand. Wrap your fingers tightly around the leather so that you can't be lost."

Beaming a loving smile, Helen replied, "I know Martha; you are in charge. I will listen to you."

But the older sister was not cut from the same cloth as the younger. Martha, always quiet, did not speak of the past or the future, even to her beloved sister. While Helen's childlike innocence gnawed at Martha, she did not falter in her commitment to watch over her younger sister. Helen knew her role as well. She never stopped her loving expressions of optimism, hoping that one day Martha's demons would be evicted.

With each day of the ocean crossing, they slowly began to realize they were now actually free. The girls wondered if their mother's unceasing prayers might have been the only thing that made escape possible. When sober, their father might have spoken of the Lord God Almighty once in his life. But their mother constantly pleaded for God's final justice, even upon the man with whom she shared her life. Thus Helen, a tender soul wrapped in a body equally pure and beautiful, narrowly escaped the shadow of the monster under which another year might have destroyed her. While all souls are eventually crushed under relentless domination, some have a resiliency that allows survival well beyond what the average person might endure. The younger sister was that kind of soul.

For months after their arrival in America, letters from the girls—like a pack of scent-tracking hounds—tirelessly searched for the fate of their courageous and selfless mother, but failed to pick up the trail. The sisters never stopped writing and waiting for a reply.

CHAPTER 3

To truly understand the absence of color, you only need to spend a few weeks in Chicago during the winter. Gray becomes both the canvas and the paint to an invisible hand that wields a filthy brush, splashing snowmelt and slush onto everything it can reach. Cloud cover more powerful than the frigid season's low-hanging sun slowly thickens and descends so that one day you think you might reach up and touch it, should you dare to test its bleakness with your own flesh. All the time within this chilling monochrome immersion, a bitter wind makes you aware that it too has an indefatigable heart of filthy gray.

In this desolate place, days after the winter solstice, Wally was born, the first child of Peter and Helen, two of the countless Polish immigrants in pre-Depression Chicago. Beginning life on a street with houses standing side by side with nary room for their elbows like an elevator packed with strangers, they dared not touch, dared not look in any direction but forward, as somehow each structure sought the chance to breathe freely one day. In such a building, on that dreary day with a bitter, howling wind, Wally entered the world, a descendant of monstrous ancestors he could not know.

Helen had met Peter shortly after her arrival in Chicago. It was love at first sight. Helen and Martha, living nearby with their aunt, sat in the church pew near Peter the first Sunday following their arrival in Chicago. After Mass, he followed the women outside, approaching Aunt Bernice. Tipping his hat, he spoke in perfect English with little accent, impressing the girls' aunt. "Excuse me, miss. I think your girls might like to know about the English classes in the church basement on Monday and Thursday evenings at seven o'clock." With his charming smile, he shot a quick glance at Helen. Shyly she replied with her own smile. Peter thought he had just glimpsed the face of an angel. From that moment on, Peter could only think of Helen. Aunt Bernice sent the girls to English classes as suggested by him, and Peter was there to help them with their lessons every time. It would be only six weeks before he proposed marriage and Helen accepted. Aunt Bernice was thrilled; hiding her jealousy, Martha was not.

A gritty young man of the Warsaw slums, Peter had arrived at eighteen years of age, just a couple of years prior to Helen. Reaching Chicago as World War I was erupting across Europe, he found work at one of the sprawling industrial factories known as a foundry. Constant heat from furnaces liquefying iron at 2,600 degrees Fahrenheit had not only kept Peter warm during his shift, but kept him always looking like he had just come in from the hot summer sun regardless of the season. He rented the bottom apartment of a two-flat from an elderly widower, Mr. Feherty, who would one day become his benefactor. Peter's income, frequently supplemented by overtime pay, allowed him to pay his bills, support his parish, and save more than a few dollars, too. Confident and affable, Peter always greeted strangers or friends with a charming, charismatic smile, and a cheerful word. His personality also won him his landlord's favor. After almost three years as a tenant, when Peter had saved up a substantial amount—enough for a down payment—the recently widowed man agreed to seller-finance Peter's purchase of the building. It was perfect for raising a family.

Wally, Peter and Helen's first born, was as handsome as his mother and Aunt Martha were beautiful. Growing up as a man of action, he always seemed to know the right thing to do. Having a last name impossible to spell or pronounce to non-Poles, he learned to use his fists at a young age when local boys teased him about his Polish name and heritage. Intensifying his rejection by his peers, was every teacher's fondness for Wally, for his charm, and good looks, but especially his brilliant ability to excel at every subject.

The school playground served as the favorite place for his antagonists to tease and taunt him. He suffered frequent verbal abuse year after year until the start of seventh grade, when two boys cornered him against the playground's chain-link fence. As they called him dumb Polack for the umpteenth time and teased him that his mother was too stupid to read or write English, something snapped in the boy's mind. Feet kicking and fists punching he threw himself at the boy nearest him, knocking him to the ground after delivering several blows. The second villain tried to tackle Wally. But he sidestepped the charge and grabbed his attacker by the hair, forcing his face downward with his left hand and repeatedly punching the boy with his right. After several punches, he let go. Nose and mouth bleeding, the second kid ran away.

The next week it would be four kids who confronted him against the fence. Wally took a beating, the first of many, but he felt little pain, each time punishing his attackers a bit more than the last. By eighth grade, as his body began to mature, growing larger than almost all his classmates, no one seemed to want to fight him anymore. He had become hardened—the way only adolescent prejudice and fists can do. Unwittingly the young bigots had formed their own dominator.

By his second year in high school, to match his near-adult physique, Wally also developed the street smarts most boys in the neighborhood could only wish for. His two sisters and two brothers looked to him whenever their father Peter was not there for guidance, which was often.

CHAPTER 4

A stocky man with broad shoulders, massive hands and forearms, with a core as stout as an oak tree, Wally's father Peter was up for the physical demands of any job in the foundry, but it was especially his innate ability to observe and learn quickly that made him stand out to management. His devotion to the faith of his homeland placed him in Saint Joseph's Catholic Church every morning of the week for Mass at 6:00 a.m. Afterward, Peter ran five blocks to the entry gate, always arriving no later than 6:50 a.m. For the first year of his life in Chicago, on two weekday evenings each week, he returned to his parish for English tutoring from one of the Sisters of St. Francis. For Peter, just as it was for immigrants all over America, parish life among people with a common national origin and religion formed the critical social fabric holding each ethnic neighborhood together.

With his power, charisma, and ability to think on his feet, Peter found himself summoned to the shop foreman's office on a Friday afternoon, a time which usually indicated termination of employment. Perhaps too, it was his irresistible personality that cracked open to Peter an unexpected opportunity. He was greeted warmly by Fritz as he entered the sooty office. It was this man—the metallurgist and production foreman whom everyone respectfully called the melt-man—who had earned every employee's admiration for his reliability and skill. When charging the great furnace with ferrous material, the presence of too much excess moisture could result in catastrophe to the melt-man and everyone nearby. Just a small amount of water would turn deadly, expanding several thousand times its size in an instantaneous steam explosion of incredible power. Everyone trusted Fritz as the one who managed the processes with the utmost caution and skill. All actions around the furnaces ran with precision and safety thanks to him.

For more than a decade and a half, Fritz held this key position on the furnace floor, unlike the man he had replaced, who after only three months on the job, met his maker in a cloud of supercharged steam. By the extent of the explosion's damage, it seemed miraculous that only one man died that day.

In fact, another man stood near the victim at the moment fate played its hand. Propelled by the explosion, a massive iron plate, taller than a man and weighing nearly one ton, launched through the air. At an incredible speed, it headed directly toward the second man and should have cut him in half, but somehow it clipped against a steel column, tumbled and pivoted around him, deflecting most of the blast and its deadly debris. Sadly, one corner of the heavy object glanced across his face from his jaw, cheekbone, nose, and forehead, inflicting damage everywhere, including his left eye socket, and crushing much of his facial features. In spite of the horrible damage, the survivor did not lose sight in the eye, which now sat bulging in a bed of facial horror. With a partially-shattered lower jaw and several missing teeth, the man would need to learn again how to speak clearly.

This unfortunate soul became the hideous living reminder of another man's death, an odd and mysterious fellow everyone thereafter called Joe "Metal" Harpy. That fateful day was his first day on the job. Joe, many reasoned, had brought bad luck and death to the foundry. No one there on the day of the explosion would ever forget the blood and shredded body parts of the foreman strewn about the walls and floor. The survivor's unfortunate nickname derived not from the flying steel shield, but from the stainless-steel plates and pins that patched together his devastated face. Reconstructive surgery was primitive at the time, and the result left a once handsome man grotesque. Every worker wondered whether it was out of pity or loyalty, that management of the foundry did not abandon Joe. After three months of surgeries and recuperation, he was allowed back on the furnace floor.

The steelworkers were a close-knit group, many of whom had worked together before and after returning from the Great War. Newcomers were not accepted until they proved themselves. The death of the furnace floor foreman kept the maimed young man an outcast undeserving of friendship, in spite of the miracle of the iron plate. Although isolated, Joe's work was always above and beyond the foreman's demands, and ownership's loyalty never wavered.

Also standing with Fritz in the dingy, poorly-lit office was a man donning an ill-fitting suit, a hard hat, and round spectacles—the kind of glasses that expanded the size of his eyes to anyone looking in from the other side. The crown of his hard hat simply read "Schmidt." Peter knew who he was, everyone did, but they had never been formally introduced. He wondered why the owner of the foundry would want to speak to him.

The kindness of the man's face was not interrupted by the long, jagged scar that traversed his left cheek from the center of his chin to his ear lobe and up to his temple. His calmness seemed palpable. Neither did the scar detract from the benevolence in his eyes and pleasant formation of his lips when he started to speak. "Peter, my name is John Schmidt. My father started this foundry over forty years ago. Fritz has said many good things about you. As a matter of fact, he believes you are the best man on his crew."

With a controlled flicker of a smile, Peter replied in perfect English, "Very nice to meet you, Mr. Schmidt. You know, Fritz is a man of great skill on the furnace floor, but he may be lacking as a judge of character!" All three men burst into laughter as the foundry owner extended his hand to Peter. The size and strength of Schmidt's hand surprised Peter, who was accustomed to engulfing another man's hand with his own when the requisite social ceremony occurred.

"Peter, we need a man to train under Fritz to one day become the leader of the furnace floor. We have bigger plans for him. Our enterprise will be expanding our line of specialty alloys. We need him as Chief Metallurgist to ensure the success of our growing venture. Peter, would you be interested in such an opportunity—taking Fritz's place on the furnace floor one day soon?"

Without hesitation, Peter replied: "Mr. Schmidt, every man in this place would feel it an honor to work as an apprentice to Fritz. But why am I worthy of consideration?"

Schmidt continued: "I have watched you from the catwalk leading to the bridge cranes. I have reviewed your work record. And I have spoken to others. To a man, everyone believes you are smart, hardworking, cautious, and completely reliable. I have noticed that you have never once missed your shift and have never been disciplined." He paused and then continued: "Furthermore, I am told you have never been in a fight with another steelworker. Now that says a lot!" Again, the three men laughed as men in dangerous endeavors must do, be it waging war or making steel. Laughter is often the first bridge to friendship and respect in perilous places.

Not trying to contain his smile, Schmidt elaborated. "I believe you are ready, but this will not be easy. It will require you to attend metallurgy classes on your days off or evenings. You shall work side by side with Fritz whenever he beckons and perform all other work regularly assigned to you. But should you complete your coursework and satisfy Fritz that you are ready, you too will join the management team, be provided a significant salary, and one day train your own apprentice. How does that sound?"

Peter had attempted to support Helen and their five children on his laborer's pay of $40 per week plus overtime, but at the end of some weeks, a bit of lard and sugar spread on stale bread would have to satisfy his growing family. If such fare was necessary, it was he who fed off the greasy loaf. It was inconceivable to Peter that his wife and children would suffer such gastronomic catastrophe.

With only a momentary glance at Fritz, who returned the look with a confirming nod, Peter responded, "Thank you, sir. I will do my best to justify your faith in me."

Schmidt looked at Fritz and said, "He is all yours now." Then, placing a powerful hand upon Peter's shoulder, he remarked, "Peter, starting Monday your base pay will be increased by fifteen dollars per week as apprentice metallurgist.

If your work and studies are satisfactory after four months, it will increase by another twenty dollars. As a member of the management team, you will also qualify for an annual bonus, based on our profitability. Come to the office and speak with Millicent on Monday morning. She will provide you with instructions on beginning your coursework...oh, one more thing." Suddenly intense, Schmidt pointed directly at Peter. "I heard a few men have been threatening Joe Harpy. You need to nip that in the bud. I want you to keep an eye on him. This is a condition of your promotion. Got it?" With that, the man with the ill-fitting suit turned and walked out. Peter noticed a slight limp, apparently on the same side of his body as the scar.

Fritz extended his hand, "Congratulations, Peter. Why don't you hurry home—Helen will want to hear the news. I will see you after Mass on Sunday and we can talk about your first day as my apprentice." As they shook hands, Peter used his left hand to add to the heartfelt doubled-handed shake with Fritz, holding on just a bit longer than men find comfortable. But Fritz did not mind; he felt truly happy for his new apprentice.

Racing home to his beloved, although they'd already shared seventeen happy years together, Helen appeared just as lovely as ever. With a joyful hug, Peter, not fully letting go, called out to his children to join them around the kitchen table. Soon releasing one of his mighty arms from the embrace, he kept the other around his wife's shoulders as he relayed his news to the table full of his loving family. Only the eldest, Wally, and his beautiful mother Helen, would fully grasp the economic implications of a significant raise during the time known as the Great Depression—when the national unemployment rate exceeded twenty-four percent at its worst. In Chicago, heavily reliant on manufacturing, immigrant and minority unemployment likely approached fifty percent. Helen's heart silently brimmed with profound gratitude knowing she had truly found love and happiness in America.

CHAPTER 5

In Warsaw, in a neighborhood not far from where Peter grew up, David and Miriam raised five children, Alvin being the oldest. Three years after Alvin was born, his father, David enrolled in the first class of the Tzar Nicolas II Warsaw Polytechnic Institute, eventually receiving a degree in chemistry. Fluent in Polish, German, and Russian, he quickly applied his newly-gained knowledge to the burgeoning field of pharmacology.

When fourteen years old, Alvin wanted nothing more than to imitate his father by studying chemistry. Once he completed his chores and homework, the ambitious young man spent every free moment reading any chemistry book he could borrow, asking questions of his father well into the evening. David and Miriam marveled at their oldest child's determination, especially his unwavering intellectual focus.

Alvin's family prospered, staying within their own neighborhood as Jews often did at that time. But within the tight-knit family and an equally tight-knit subculture, life seemed normal to Alvin. At the latter stages of the nineteenth century, reforms by both Austrian and Russian empires that had dominion over the former Polish homeland, slowly resulted in more Jewish political rights and social acceptance. Regression of those rights and much worse would come soon thereafter.

Alvin accelerated past his peers, qualifying for the Polytechnic Institute at just sixteen. Continuing his dizzying academic pace, in only two years the determined young chemist finished number one in his graduating class. But after a year of working with his father, Alvin began to hear the call of America. Growing obsessed, Alvin calmly approached his parents on his nineteenth birthday and informed them of his decision. He would go to America. David and Miriam knew better than to doubt their boy's resolve.

The very day Alvin purchased his tickets for the trip, June 28, 1914, profound disaster unfolded on the European continent. While Alvin's brain swirled with his exciting plans and dreams of a glorious future, Archduke Ferdinand, heir to the throne of the Austro-Hungarian Empire, and his wife, Sophie, were assassinated in Sarajevo, the capital of the province of Bosnia and Herzegovina. With increasing rumors of war and the drawing of battle lines, the continent hurtled toward an uncontrollable explosion. Oblivious, Alvin joyfully packed his bags.

His parents sorrowfully watched as their eldest son made his final preparations. The first step in his trip would be a long train ride to Berlin, and then another to Hamburg, and finally to the seaport complex at Cuxhaven.

On July 4th, Alvin began his journey to America. Miriam hugged her precious firstborn saying, "My dearest boy, you have always been the most remarkably gifted and obedient child. Your father and I know you shall find success and happiness in America. But you must promise us you will be careful at all times. There will be danger along the way."

Alvin would not let go of his mom. "You and father have been so good to all of us that my heart feels as if it might burst. I am both happy and sad, excited and afraid. But look at me, I am strong and clever, and I have saved all that I could. Uncle Myron and Aunt Ruth are waiting and will take good care of me. Please don't be afraid for me, mother...I love you." He held on just a bit longer as both broke into tears. There always was a special bond between these two souls that would never be broken, neither by time nor distance. Until the day his mother died, never a week went by that they did not write to each other.

David put his hand on his son and said, "Alvin, you will follow all the precepts of The Law you have been taught. Promise me this, for should you faithfully follow them, you shall flourish. You shall also honor your mother and me, and all our ancestors. Remember, the habits we develop in youth are what we follow in old age." Alvin nodded his yes. His father continued, "You know I love you, and we will eagerly await your letters. Now gaze upon your brothers and sisters. Do not forget those who look up to you with such respect and admiration. While you will not be here to lead them by your good example, they will be counting on your every correspondence."

Alvin lavished each of his siblings with hugs and kisses as tears streamed down everyone's cheeks. Then, with the most emphatic final "I love you all" he could muster, Alvin stepped between his bags, picked them up, jumped onto the train and hurried into his compartment. The iron wheels creaked into forward motion as he threw open the window of his compartment. He forced his upper body out of the window as he waved goodbye to his loved ones left behind on the platform, just like other riders did from every window of the train.

Three and one-half weeks after his departure, on July 28th, 1914, Alvin's feet now on American soil, Austria-Hungary declared war on Serbia. Soon Russia, France, Belgium, Great Britain, and Serbia had sided against Austria-Hungary and Germany, and the Great War, as it came to be known, exploded upon Europe. By August 4th, American President Woodrow Wilson spoke of the war and America's desire for isolation: "...must be neutral in fact as well as in name during these days that are to try men's souls." But the very ocean that carried immigrants like Alvin to safety eventually served as the gateway to America's involvement in the war.

Quickly mastering English and overcoming his eastern European accent, with his Uncle Myron's help, Alvin voraciously consumed the content of Chicago's newspapers—international news was his greatest interest. Far removed from the great conflict devastating Europe, safe within America's heartland, Alvin read of the torpedoing of an American cargo ship, the USS *Gulflight* on May 1, 1915—it would be the first of many. He instinctively realized the murderous assaults at sea would increase, somehow knowing it was only a matter of time before his new country would join the conflict.

Month after month, more painfully with each news account, Alvin spoke of his fears. "This nation cannot tolerate the increasing murder at sea. First, the *Gulflight*, then the *Lusitania*, and just weeks ago, the *Sussex*. These ships were not navy vessels. They only carried goods and people. It is only a matter of time until the whole world is at war." Staring blindly, perhaps overcome by fear or heartbreak, Myron said nothing. Alvin could not help contemplating if he might feel compelled to enlist when the inevitable American commitment came.

When, on the first day of March 1917, the story of the Zimmermann Telegram became public—Alvin cried out, startling his aunt and uncle. "The people will take no more!" Alvin read aloud the reports about the Zimmermann Telegram—the headline story in every newspaper across the country. The

Germans were secretly trying to enlist Mexico and Japan against the Allies if America joined the war. Thank goodness, he thought, British spies had intercepted the telegram.

Alvin's precognition of America joining the war was ful-filled when, one month after the news of the Zimmermann Telegram broke, on April 1, 1917, a German U-boat sunk the American cargo ship SS *Aztec* off the coast of France, killing twenty-eight. The next day, on April 2, 1917, President Wilson addressed a special joint session of Congress seeking a decla-ration of war against Germany, including the famous words; "The world must be made safe for democracy." The US Senate and House approved the declaration of war on April 6, 1917.

CHAPTER 6

On the day the United States formally declared war, Alvin immersed himself in the memories of his arrival in America. Eyes closed, he could recall every detail—starting with the chills of excitement and awe that electrified his entire being as Alvin caught his first glimpse of the Statue of Liberty. He grabbed hold of the ship's railing to steady the weakness in his knees and offered a quiet prayer of gratitude, realizing the best part of his life was only beginning.

From his studies, he knew all the words of the poem "The New Colossus" by Emma Lazarus, placed in bronze on the statue's great masonry pedestal. He softly whispered it aloud:

Give me your tired, your poor,
Your huddled masses yearning to breathe free
The wretched refuse of your teeming shore,
Send these, the homeless, tempest-tossed to me.
I lift my lamp beside the golden door.

A stocky, young Polish man nearly his own age stood next to Alvin at the ship's railing. "Excuse me, sir. What is that giant statue?" the stranger asked while pointing at Lady Liberty.

Alvin, knowing much about the great lady from his studies and recalling the reasons for the gift of the statue, explained: "It is called *Liberty Enlightening the World*. It was a gift to America from the people of France—the idea of Frenchman Édouard de Laboulaye. He loved the promise of America."

Without taking his eyes off the statue, the young man nodded. "It's magnificent—tell me more!"

Alvin gladly continued to teach. "The Frenchman, Laboulaye was a great lover of liberty. He, like the assassinated American President Abraham Lincoln, believed every person was born with a sacred right to freedom. Ten years after the statue was conceived, the sculptor Bartholdi, built that beautiful lady. It was shipped across the ocean and erected in 1883. On her pedestal, she stands three-hundred-five feet tall!"

The young passenger's stare jumped from Alvin to Lady Liberty and back again. All he could utter was, "Amazing."

Alvin smiled. "By the way, where are you going to live, now that you've reached America's shores?"

"I'm going to Chicago. And you—where are you bound?"

Alvin laughed with the joy of coincidence. "That must be a wonderful place, because that's where I'm going too." They both laughed, sharing the unspoken thought they might meet again one day.

Opening his eyes to exit his happy daydream, on that Monday, the day of America's commitment to defend Europe, Alvin became obsessed with concern over how many of the people from his homeland now desperately fit the poem's description but could no longer follow him to freedom. In his mind, he fearfully contemplated would America's involvement expand the devastation wrought upon Europe or hasten its end? What would happen to his parents and siblings?

Three years prior, at the outbreak of World War I, Alvin had arrived at Ellis Island as part of the third great wave of old-world immigrants to America. He was more fortunate than many for soon, the United States would apply severe caps on immigration, even more so on the Jews of Europe.

At the recently constructed Ellis Island, four hundred or more government employees processed thousands of migrants per day. Alvin, like countless bewildered newcomers, found himself shuttled through twelve corridors of iron bars under soaring ceilings of the Grand Hall, leading to interpreters, social workers, doctors, nurses, and immigration officers. Patiently shuffling his feet on the floor of granite pavers, proceeding ever so slowly, Alvin, like everyone else, chatted among companions and strangers alike. With hushed voices, they spoke in fear and reverence at the introduction to their new home as sunlight streamed through clearstory windows.

At the end of his second day on American soil, Alvin boarded a train for Chicago. He was no different than countless economic refugees, all bound for industrialized eastern and midwestern cities to find work in dangerous places like steel mills, foundries, tanneries, meat packing plants, and stockyards. They traveled to join family members who were expected to help their relations adapt and survive. Government social services for immigrants were virtually nil and their sponsors shouldered responsibility for the newcomers.

These third-wave immigrants—the Italians, the Poles, the Slovaks, the Russians, and the European Jews—found barriers to work, housing, and education as xenophobia grew commonplace among the prior citizenry. Ignorance of strangers was fertile ground for prejudice, which throughout human history seems to be the natural order of things. Therefore, communities of their own ethnic origins and religious affiliations formed, creating neighborhoods with pejorative names—like Little Warsaw—where new Americans could find a feeling of home. For Chicago's rapidly growing eastern European community, churches and synagogues sprung up in new immigrant neighborhoods all over the city. Alvin's aunt and uncle had settled in a small northside Jewish enclave within a neighborhood called Lakeview—this would become Alvin's American home. On days with a strong south wind, the air carried the thick industrial odors of Schmidt Foundry north to their home and beyond—it was just part of living in the city.

CHAPTER 7

In 1914, the year of Alvin's arrival, not far from Myron and Ruth's home, the city constructed a baseball field at the intersection of Clark and Addison. Called Weeghman Park (now known as the famous Wrigley Field), it first served as home field for the Federal League's Chicago Whales, soon replaced by the Cubs in 1916. Uncle Myron walked to the ballpark to take in ballgames as often as he could find time. His influence on Alvin was undeniable as he too became fascinated with the game of baseball. As a scientist, Alvin found the almost unlimited potential for statistical analysis particularly interesting, although after his second year in America, he rarely could attend baseball games in person, instead only reading about the results.

Grand entertainment aside, all the residents of this rapidly expanding city needed the basic necessities of life. Corner grocers, tailor shops, clothing stores, and especially taverns, populated every ethnic neighborhood, becoming part of the unique fabric of the city. Old-world style apothecaries, now called pharmacies, slowly became a neighborhood staple as well. Thus, Alvin's dedication to his father's gift of love for pharmacology would eventually make him a man of accomplishment and bring him happiness in helping others. With his impeccable scientific credentials, Alvin easily found work at the largest pharmacy company in the city.

In this exciting urban growth environment, Alvin enjoyed his new Chicago lifestyle of entertainment and culture. He also dutifully followed the required protocols from the family's American patriarch, Myron. He continued his studies of the Torah and Talmud and carefully kept the Sabbath. And every week Alvin wrote to his family in Warsaw, receiving their correspondence weekly as well.

It was after Alvin's second year in America, 1916, when Aunt Ruth stumbled and fell down the front steps of their home. She lay unconscious only a few minutes before Alvin's return from work. He sprang into action checking her pulse and breathing. Relieved she was alive, he called out for help from the neighbor next door. The two men rushed her to the hospital leaving word of the accident for Myron with others. Her loving husband arrived at the hospital shortly thereafter as Ruth awoke.

Myron called out, "Ruth! Ruth, are you okay? Is anything broken? Alvin, what happened?"

"Quit your fussing Myron—I'm fine," she replied. "It was just a little tumble down the stairs." But when Ruth attempted to get out of the hospital bed to prove her resiliency the damage to her spine was discovered. Having taken a class in anatomy, in the back of Alvin's mind lingered a painful thought—did he harm his beloved aunt's spine by moving her? The personal guilt of this thought would haunt him for the rest of his life—an emotional plea for forgiveness he never shared with anyone—other than The Omniscient Recipient of Prayers.

With his aunt now partially paralyzed, Alvin would unselfishly embrace many new and time-consuming responsibilities. He never shrunk from them, helping Uncle Myron care for his beloved and their home. One year later, his thoughts of enlisting in the American Expeditionary Force would be impossible.

Every waking moment of every day, when not working as a pharmacist, Alvin devoted himself to caring for his aunt and uncle. A determined woman, Ruth quickly mastered the use of her wheelchair, refusing to accept being a burden to others, but there was much she could no longer do. Alvin filled the void. Aunt and nephew shared their evenings together with Alvin summarizing the day's newspaper stories for Aunt Ruth. But the conversation always switched to the same topic, with Aunt Ruth insisting, "Alvin, you are a young man. You must get out of the house and make friends—and find a wife."

And Alvin always ended the conversations the same way, "Yes, Aunt Ruth. I will get out more next week." But next week did not seem to exist for more than a decade and a half, until to Alvin's surprise and delight, his employer gave him Friday afternoon off and a box seat ticket to a Chicago Cubs' baseball game. Coming home after the game in time for Shabbat, he appeared a changed man.

On a particularly beautiful September weekend in 1933, Alvin addressed his uncle as they sat in the dining room: "Uncle Myron, you and Aunt Ruth have been so generous to me, more than I might have the right to expect. I can never thank you enough. While you have refused to accept my attempts at paying rent, I am very grateful that you have allowed me to contribute to our grocery expenses."

Myron interrupted his nephew, "Alvin, you are my brother's son, we are of the same flesh as if you were my own. That Ruth and I have not been blessed with children has been our shame, but you have filled that void like no other could. I would never accept rent from my own child. And should I have been blessed with a son, I could wish for no finer a young man than you. It has been many years since Ruth's accident and you have never once done a selfish thing. This is why you are listed on the title to our home. When we are gone, this and everything else we own shall be yours."

He moved across the room, taking the seat next to his nephew, leaned close and continued: "I suspect you have met a special young woman. I can see it by the distraction on your face. This is not like you—you have changed. She must be very special. Please ask her and her parents to our home so we might meet them with all proprieties met."

Alvin felt his intended speech completely derailed. He wanted to tell his uncle that he wished to find a place of his own after thanking Myron for all his generosity. Alvin grappled with his concern about leaving them on their own, but decided it was time—today he would tell them.

Uncle Myron was right. Although he had only just met Lois, Alvin's heart was now on fire. Slowly, the young man regathered his thoughts and respectfully replied, "Uncle Myron, I must say that you are correct, there is a young woman who is my distraction. I will invite her and her uncle to your home...I mean our home. Her uncle, with whom she lives, is her only family. I shall let you know when arrangements can be made." Regaining his composure, Alvin returned to his original intent: "Uncle Myron, I believe it is time for me to make a very important step in my life."

Myron, raising his voice a little, again interrupted, "Do not speak of marriage until our families have met! I don't even know if she is Jewish."

But Alvin quickly clarified, "No sir, the important step is my hope to purchase a small building nearby, not too far from the Schmidt Foundry. It has a wide retail presence on Fullerton Avenue with three apartments above. I wish to buy it to start my own pharmacy. I shall live above the store and rent out the other apartments to help make expenses. The kindness you and Aunt Ruth have shown me made it possible for me to save enough money to reach for this dream of mine. I deeply desire your support and advice; more importantly, I seek your blessing. But I shall not do this thing should you advise against it. My first responsibility is to you and Aunt Ruth."

Uncle Myron considered what Alvin said for an uncomfortably long time. Finally, he called out, "Ruth, come join us. Alvin wishes to discuss important things with us."

His aunt rolled into the room in her wheelchair. She went to her husband and greeted him with a kiss, then turned to Alvin and kissed his cheek warmly as he bent to receive her affection. "I've seen your distraction, have you met a girl?"

At this, Alvin threw up his hands exclaiming, "Yes, Aunt Ruth, I met a girl, but I want to buy a store and apartment building instead!" His answer hung in the air. Finally relieved of his stress, he started to laugh aloud at the ridiculousness of his response, causing the others to join him in joyous laughter.

Myron retrieved them from humor's distraction back to more serious things: "Ruth, I have not given this fine young man a chance to speak what is on his mind. Let us listen to all he has to say. Alvin, please tell us everything about this building you have found."

Ruth would not hear of it. "You men speak of buildings and business later. I want to know about this young woman who has captured your heart."

The young man, full of love and respect for his aunt and uncle offered, "Yes, Uncle Myron, of course she is Jewish. Her name is Lois and she's from France. She is a bit younger than I, and more beautiful than I might believe is possible. Her smile is warm and loving and her eyes are captivating. When the ninth inning began, I asked her uncle François if I might see her again. He briefly spoke to Lois in French and couldn't have been more respectful when he handed me his card and suggested I join them for dinner. It's scheduled for tomorrow afternoon. I don't know how I know, but without a doubt, this is the woman for me."

Thrilled, Uncle Myron reassured his nephew. "Your patience and your dedication to us will be rewarded, I am sure. If this woman is the one, all things will fall into place. Now tell me about the building you have found."

Ruth sighed as she rolled out of the room, calling out to Alvin, "My dear boy, tomorrow evening you shall confirm what your heart already knows to be true. Then you shall bring them here to meet us. You will always be able to find a building, but there will only be one chance to find true love."

CHAPTER 8

The building on Fullerton Avenue represented an ideal opportunity for Alvin. Residential buildings filled the surrounding area, and some enduring businesses like the Schmidt Foundry, provided employment nearby, despite the Depression. The density of residents and workers surrounding the storefront made it seem to Alvin a viable place for business. But Uncle Myron found himself bothered by the distance between his home and the place of his nephew's dreams. Although it was only eleven blocks (about a mile and a half), it seemed too far from their synagogue and the people of his faith. While less than a thirty-minute walk, Myron knew from his childhood in Warsaw how quickly one neighborhood can end and another, mostly hostile one begins.

Early the following Monday evening, Myron and Alvin walked to the Fullerton Avenue building where the real estate agent was waiting to give them a tour. The hot, south wind filled their nostrils with the burning smell of Schmidt Foundry the entire way. As they walked, Myron brought up his concerns. He knew the building would be what it would be, but the neighborhood was paramount in his mind. "Alvin, you will be much too far from our synagogue. Ruth and I will not be able to carry on if you are not with us for Shabbat. We don't know anyone else this far south. Will the people in this area accept you, Alvin? Did you look closer to our home?"

Alvin reassured his uncle. "It is not too far. Don't worry."

As they continued walking, they passed the crowded soup kitchen on the corner of Belmont and Racine operated by the Schmidt family. Uncle Myron pleaded with his nephew: "Look at these men, belts cinched tightly upon pants pleated to deformity. Worn-out clothes hang pitifully upon their skinny frames, their faces gaunt with hopelessness while they beg to be fed. Why, of all times, would you want to start a new business now? Many people have no money, Alvin. It has been just five years since the Wall Street crash, and things have only gotten worse."

Alvin replied with confidence. "I need to pursue my dream before I get too old. Somehow, I just know this is the opportunity I've been seeking."

But Myron would not relent. "Alvin, your employer must see you as irreplaceable. Your skill and hard work have earned you the respect of your peers and management—everyone.

You are trusted and you earn a good living. You now supervise other pharmacists. Why would you risk such security?"

Slowly, he considered his uncle's concern. "You and I do not know the future. I have lived with you for many years allowing me, by your generosity, to stand ready for this day. But I cannot help wonder if a perfect day would ever arrive, or if I would know when it did. Uncle Myron, people will always need medicine. My craft can help countless people struggling to get well."

The elder man still objected. "Alvin, you are helping plenty of people now—with a job that also gives you security."

Smiling patiently, the pharmacist continued. "Yes, I am, but I wish to do more. For some, what I do represents their only hope in the face of infirmities they do not understand. I must move forward as providence and your love have provided. For those who cannot afford what they need, I will find a way to help them as well. Now it seems that since I have met Lois, a future of happiness, love, and success has been presented to me. I must seize it." Without breaking stride, Alvin put his arm around his uncle's shoulder. "*This* will be the place."

Again, Uncle Myron objected. "What do you know about this neighborhood? For all you know the people will not welcome you!"

Confidently, Alvin reassured his uncle. "Sir, most of them are from Poland just like us. I will speak to them in Polish, German, or English—even Russian if I must—whatever helps them understand their medicines. They will NOT reject me. One day my store will be a neighborhood fixture—a place not only to purchase one's needs, but to socialize and help build community."

Suddenly, Myron stepped in front of his nephew, forcing him to stop. "You are intelligent, but more importantly, you are wise beyond your years, and your motives are virtuous. If you, the man who accepts the risks is not frightened in the face of uncertainty, why should I be afraid for you? If anyone can overcome hurdles put in his way, it is you. My dearest boy, you are right and—I give you my whole-hearted blessing."

"Thank you, sir." Alvin sighed in relief, knowing his plans for his life would now accelerate.

Grabbing Alvin's shoulders as he spoke, Myron hugged his nephew, kissing him once on each cheek, as a tear of joy fell. "You have my blessing and my prayers. Now you must do what you have set out to do. Know that Aunt Ruth and I will always be here for you." Myron then turned and began to walk on with new determination, now taking the lead, setting a rapid pace to their destination.

Upon arrival at the building on Fullerton, Myron jumped into action like a mother bear with a cub: "Tell me Mr. Mc-Carthy, why is this property for sale?" The salesman replied, "I am representing the heirs of the owner who passed from a protracted illness. His family will be willing to sell the store fixtures at an additional price."

Myron found this particular business term unsettling. "Mr. McCarthy, if they are affixed to the building, they are part of the building. That is why they are called fixtures, because they are affixed. What are you trying to pull?" He continued his attack. "The apartments appear vacant. Is that because of the owner's neglect or because of these hard times?" Not giving McCarthy a chance to answer, he continued. "Either way, we are likely buying a bucket full of problems. Anyone can see that, even you."

Alvin had never seen his uncle operate in this way. He felt both impressed and a little embarrassed since his work as a teacher and language tutor never brought out that side. Then just as quickly as his surprise attack, Myron changed tactics. "Mr. McCarthy, little details like this can be worked out. I did not mean to question your motives. Let's discuss how soon the family wishes to complete the sale. I think we can accommodate any timeframe they need, and without seller financing. Did you hear that? *Cash!*"

McCarthy looked at Myron, and then at Alvin, asking, "What do you think of the property, Alvin? You are the one who first spoke to me about it at my office last Friday morning. I thought this property was for your own interests, no?"

Myron jumped in before Alvin could reply. "You are dealing with both of us. If Alvin is not happy with something, I am not. And if I am not happy, neither is Alvin. We will ask the questions, and if satisfied, we will offer you a contract today.

With this, you shall satisfy your duties to your seller, and you will establish a relationship with a businessman who will have future need of your services. Let's not play games." Smiling and diplomatically answering all their questions, McCarthy did not want a fight, he wanted to close the deal.

The building seemed perfectly suited to Alvin's vision. He planned a soda fountain counter in the front portion of the store, with excellent visibility to the large, street-facing window. Shelves and cabinets lined part of the store providing ample sales displays for sundries—the rest of the first floor would be his pharmacy. There was even substantial room for storage in the rather surprisingly clean and dry basement. Trying to take advantage of the tension creating by his uncle, Alvin took his chance. "Mr. McCarthy," Alvin began confidently, "this deal must include cleaning and inspection of the boiler. It must be in good working condition. The coal bin shall be full. The store and the apartments shall all be thoroughly cleaned. All bills and liens associated with the property shall be satisfied as of the day of closing—we must have clean title. All of the store fixtures shall be part of the transaction. Then I will pay seventy-five percent of your asking price—no more." It was virtually all the money Alvin had saved. "Additionally, the price must be discounted by the amount equal to three months rental for each of two apartments. I shall occupy the third, and for it, I expect no discount. The extra months are my contingency in case no qualified tenants are quickly found.

The funds are ready. Will you present this offer to your clients immediately, please?"

While Myron beamed with approval, McCarthy said, "Alvin, it's late—too late to write a contract. Please come to my office on Belmont Avenue tomorrow morning and I will have a purchase and sale agreement ready for your signature. You two might skin a leopard and walk away with the pelt before the beast even knew what hit it."

It was an unrehearsed tag team of smart men looking to be tough, yet fair. They wanted to leave no change on the table, but neither did they wish to leave blood in the street. There were no appraisals to be had and the former boomtown market was now languishing under economic calamity. No one really knew what property would be worth from one month to the next. But Alvin knew he had found the foundation for his dreams, hopefully at a price that he could afford, with rental income to aid the ramp-up of his business. Somehow, he knew this would be the first of many stores.

The family selling the property rejected Alvin's initial of-fer—they had become comfortable in their patriarch's ability to fund their lifestyle. But after his passing, they did not un-derstand the direness of their circumstances—and their sale price expectations had been puffed up by their agent. After the expiration of his first offer, Alvin was steadfast. He submitted it again, emphasizing the ready availability of his funds. As a bleak and brutal Chicago winter fell upon the city, the sellers eventually realized how much they had spent on coal to heat the building with no rental income to offset expenses. So, on the first day of March, upon submission of Alvin's sixth identical offer, the sellers accepted his terms except the for the nearly empty coal bin and filthy apartments. Alvin agreed.

On the day the sale was closed, as they walked to the building Alvin now owned, Uncle Myron presented him with a copy of a business article. It described how Willis Haviland Carrier had the year before developed a compressor-based cooling system. It would soon become the standard technology of the industry. "Alvin, Ruth and I wish to help you succeed. We will pay for this new thing called 'air conditioning' for your building. You will be the first pharmacy in Chicago to have it!"

Alvin was more than shocked with their generosity. "Sir, I don't know what to say. Can you and Aunt Ruth afford paying for such a luxury for a property that isn't even yours?"

Smiling from ear to ear, Myron replied. "It was Ruth's idea. She loves you so. And don't worry, we have ample savings. Nothing would make us happier than to see you own the best pharmacy in the city."

By 1935, nearly one thousand Carrier-designed cooling systems had been installed in Chicago commercial buildings.

CHAPTER 9

Peter and Helen's home stood several blocks south and west of Uncle Myron and Aunt Ruth's humble frame, two-story home and about two blocks from Alvin's new store. Between the new baseball field and the Polish Triangle bounded by Milwaukee and Chicago Avenues and Division Street, their home lay just east of the Chicago River. Along both sides of the river, industry sprouted like uncontrollable weeds in an untended field. Within factories, both big and small, waves of eager but mostly unskilled men sought work in often dirty and dangerous conditions while labor unions continued to expand their ranks and political power.

The local Polish boys, including Wally, all liked hanging around near the corner of Fullerton and Racine, a few blocks east of Alvin's building. The boys often played in an open lot there, and wandered around the retail storefronts on Fullerton. They especially liked to race across the train tracks when a locomotive lumbered slowly by, near the end of the industrial rail spur, playing chicken with the iron goliaths.

When brown paper was placed upon the storefront windows of Alvin's new store to hide the remodeling, the boys, led by Wally, tried to peek in to see what was happening. One spring weekend afternoon, the first weekend Alvin did not keep Shabbat, Wally stepped to the front door and threw it open saying, "Come on in guys—you never have a problem if you act like you own the place!" And with that, five teenagers met Alvin.

"Come on in, men. Any of you looking for work? I have some heavy lifting that strong fellows like you might be able to handle." Alvin spoke excitedly, anticipating his first true entrepreneurial endeavor. The boys found his enthusiasm contagious, except for Wally.

The young leader spoke for the want-to-be crew: "We are not working for anybody until we see the cash."

Alvin chuckled and replied. "Of course, I can see you are astute men of business. Here is my proposition; I will give you each four bits upon your handshake. Then you shall carry in from the alley the truckload of boxes and crates just dropped off for me. When you bring them in and place them where I direct without damaging anything, I will pay you each another buck. Anything broken or anything placed in the wrong spot, no second payment. That's a buck-and-a-half each for being at the right place at the right time—if you do a good job." Alvin then walked up to Wally, extended his hand and asked, "Do we have a deal?" Before Wally could answer, all the others rushed to Alvin with their hands out, maybe to shake or maybe to collect. Wally pushed the others aside and extended his hand to seal the deal. He squeezed Alvin's hand just to let him know how strong he was.

Alvin appeared a bit surprised, and hiding how much his hand hurt, burst out, "Hey there big guy, take it easy on my hand. Look at the size of your paws! You are quite the powerful young man, and a talented leader. So, it appears we have a deal. Good!"

With that, Wally released his grip and collected the first payment for the entire team. Then he spoke up for the group. "Show me where you want everything to go. I'll make sure the boys do what you want." Turning to his friends, Wally barked, "Screw up and I'll keep your first payment, too. Now do what I tell you and we'll take this Jew's money and split."

The teens did exactly as Alvin requested. Quickly, Wally figured out how to treat the task with production-line efficiency. He directed them to form a line, passing the boxes from one boy to another until the last one in line placed each parcel where directed. Dozens of boxes, some large and others small, found their proper place until the team shifted to the basement stairs to repeat the process. Wally carefully read the label on each. With the innate gift of spatial aptitude, he surveyed the basement and considered how to best organize the items remaining. Then Alvin directed them to move the larger wooden crates, mostly containing the specialty furniture and fixtures of his trade. Some were so heavy it took four of the boys to move them safely. Quite pleased with the speed and efficiency of Wally's team, Alvin was nevertheless glad to see them all break a sweat.

Soon the truckload was fully handled without damage to anything. Wally, without Alvin's prompting, then directed the others to break down the shipping crates and neatly stack the debris in the alley. Smiling broadly, the impromptu movers eagerly watched as Alvin paid the balance to Wally. "Well done everyone! Wally, here is an extra dollar for refreshments. I have nothing here to give you to drink, so why don't you go over to Thompson's Town Liquors next door and buy a pop for everyone?"

Change in their pockets, each having received their first and second payment from Alvin through Wally, they headed to the door without even saying thank you. Self-satisfied, the boys left the store knowing they had made a dollar-and-a-half for less than two hours of work. Their fathers as steelworkers, blacksmiths, and foundrymen received only around one dollar per hour, or maybe, if lucky, one dollar and twenty-five cents per hour. For the children of recent immigrants to earn this much money so easily was unheard of.

The last to leave, Wally lingered a moment. He stood in the doorway and looked back at Alvin. Not saying anything, not even thank you—he paused just long enough to thoroughly scan the store. It was the stare of a young tyrant, calculating his future triumph over one of *them*.

After his temporary crew left, Alvin tirelessly worked on the final preparations of his establishment, bolting together and leveling cabinets, setting countertops, and installing the metal bins for the soda fountain. The day the local plumber completed the installation of all the plumbing fixtures, Alvin pulled down the brown paper from the windows and hung a white paper sign, perfectly centered upon the window with large red letters, Opening Soon. The second line said in royal blue, Lincolnway Pharmacy. Alvin named his business after his hero, President Lincoln. Enthralled with the sixteenth president, the young entrepreneur had read the transcripts of all his major speeches while a young student in Warsaw. In fact, Mr. Lincoln's words had ignited Alvin's burning desire to arrive upon America's shores. The great leader's commitment to fairness for the abused and downtrodden, even at the price of civil war, filled Alvin with hope for mankind. If the French could give America a magnificent statue, naming his store after Mr. Lincoln was, he thought, the least he could do to honor the man who freed the slaves and saved the world's first constitutional republic—and lost his life to an assassin's bullet in the process.   The view from outside disclosed a gleaming Thásos white marble floor uniquely surrounded by a border of blue Calcutta marble with heavy, dramatic veins. Like a picture frame, the blue color contrasted against the purity of the Thásos. Together they provided a soft and pleasing feeling, creating a peacefulness that embraced every drugstore customer. Weeks ago, Alvin had spent days stripping the filth and grime from the now glistening floor, revealing an attribute he could not have seen when buying the building. He was amazed that anyone would use such a fine marble for flooring—Thásos was the highly prized stone often preferred by the great sculptors of Europe. Sitting upon such a pleasing base was the new soda fountain, complete with seven seats. Opposite from them towered the original quartersawn oak cabinets and shelving running along the side wall, all the way to the pharmacy area in the rear, terminating against the public telephone booth.

A single series of ceiling light fixtures with integrated fans ran a straight line perpendicular to the street, from the storefront to the pharmacy counter. The globes of the fixtures were perfectly round, translucent, white glass, hanging on long bronze pendants from a ceiling that was twelve feet above the floor. They illuminated the space with the kind of warmth that also beckoned entry. A trio of miniature versions of these lights hung above the pharmacy's counter at a right angle to their larger cousins. In perfect balance, they led the way to the approachable dispensary. Matching oak crown molding was highlighted by the freshly-painted walls and ceiling, together providing the finishing halo to the interior's charm.

Alvin couldn't have felt more pleased with the way his store balanced efficiency with beauty, proportion with comfort. He turned to gaze upon his future, feeling that chilling combination of excitement and fear. He would ignore both for now—only action mattered. After months of cleaning, repairing, and remodeling the store and apartments, the time had finally arrived to launch his enterprise.

Alvin walked up the long staircase and placed the For Rent signs, one in each of the front-facing apartments he had finished cleaning late the previous night. He would live in the inferior rear unit. As he descended the stairs to the foyer's entrance, signs installed only moments before, he was startled by a strangely gruesome figure who suddenly appeared, blocking his path.

"As I walked by your establishment, I saw you hanging the for-rent signs above. I am in need of an apartment. My name is Joe Harpy. I work for the Schmidts at the foundry." Joe always spoke plainly.

Having processed Joe's disfigurements and regained his composure, Alvin extended his hand with a warm and sincere handshake and said, "Let's head upstairs and see if you like the apartments, Mr. Harpy. You are my first prospect, so you may pick which suits you best."

The two bounded up the wooden staircase, with risers and treads creaking underfoot. Alvin swung the door open to the first apartment, stepped back, and politely offered Joe entry first. "This looks much larger than I would have expected from downstairs. The light pouring in makes this feel like a warm and private sanctuary. Is the other the same?" asked Joe.

"It is identical to this one," Alvin explained, "except the floor plan is reversed—it's a mirror image. What do you think?" Before Joe could answer Alvin added, "The rent is only $30 per month including water, electric, and heat from a common boiler. And the workers are just finishing the installation of a cooling system just like some movie theaters have."

Joe, delighted with the reasonable rental, looked at Alvin and asked, "Air conditioning? Really? This apartment is perfect! May I move in this weekend? Next Tuesday is the first of the month. I was hoping to have several days to move. I have no one to help me."

Alvin nodded, saying, "I have a simple lease. Let's fill in the blanks together back in my store. You may then have the keys and full use of the apartment as soon as I confirm your employment. Rent will not be due until the first of the month. You are welcome to take advantage of the few extra days at no charge but I will need your first month's rent paid before you move in.

Reaching into his pocket, Joe replied. "Of course, here is sixty dollars. I want to always be paid up one month in advance. You may call John Schmidt's executive assistant, Millicent to confirm my employment. Here is the phone number." He handed Schmidt's business card to Alvin.

Alvin smiled broadly. "The extra month of rent is not necessary." Pushing half the cash back to his new tenant, Joe refused to accept it.

Not wishing to start out on the wrong foot over a minor item, the landlord smiled again. "I am delighted to have you as my first tenant, Mr. Harpy. I will give you a receipt, of course. We will call the extra amount your next month's rent. Now, if I can help you with your transition, please don't hesitate to ask." With that, Alvin led the way back down the chattering staircase and to the consummation of Joe's leasehold. He called out loudly so the man behind could easily hear: "I know a few neighborhood boys that might be available to help."

CHAPTER 10

Wally's father, Peter, like all those who worked for the Schmidt family, knew little of Joe Metal Harpy. Although he faithfully obeyed Mr. Schmidt's direction, keeping certain steelworkers from threatening Joe, his charge absolutely refused to engage in any conversation. Peter did not have time to force socializing, especially with an outcast who refused to speak. It was all the more confounding that an outcast like Joe plainly refused his offers of friendship.

Peter worked hard at the foundry, attended metallurgy classes, and during the few remaining free moments of each week, lavished attention on his beloved Helen and on his children. Even though English was his newly-learned second language, he excelled in his studies, surprising his teachers and his employer with his speedy mastery of all subjects. Somehow, even with a full load of responsibilities, Peter always attended morning Mass, arrived to work on time, completed his regular duties, and worked tirelessly for Fritz. At night and on weekends when not at class or studying, Peter entertained his family with stories about the physical properties of certain elements. Fascinated by all the things their superman father would make possible, four of his children loved hearing about how elements were combined to create alloys. While the chemistry was beyond their understanding, the children proudly knew that only by his work could other craftsmen ply their trades.

Wally, on the other hand, grew tired of the wonders of science repeated night after night. That seemed to be the only thing his father cared much about. This did not put money in Wally's pocket, nor make him more popular with the cool kids—the children of the previous wave of immigrants who now enjoyed control over everything that mattered. Fortunately, Wally held one advantage over the exclusive crowd—they understood the power of his fists and dared not taunt him to his face.

Most evenings Wally met up with a couple of his Polish friends, Ziggy and Bobby. They were part of the moving crew that helped Alvin. The former was the only kid on their part of the north side more physically intimidating than Wally, but without his intellect or charm. Bobby was the clever, quiet one. While not a big bruiser like his friends, he was square and stocky. Bobby had a certain look in his eyes that made people fear him. Would he flip into a rage in an instant? Could his impulsive rage even lead him to kill? No one knew, and no one wanted to find out. This boy's dangerous reputation expanded after an incident in the school hallway. Bobby punched another junior, breaking his jaw, knocking the victim unconscious. Word spread quickly. Those nearby told others of the sound of breaking bone, shattering teeth and the loud thud as the unfortunate one crumpled to the floor.

Together, the inseparable, fearsome trio ruled their neighborhood, fearing no one except the Chicago Police, with their guns, billy clubs, blackjacks, and saps. These three athletic young men banded together to counteract the anti-immigrant vitriol they faced almost daily.

One night, like so many others, they hung around the corner near Weber's Billiards Hall and Thompson's Town Liquors at Fullerton and Southport, just west of the rail spur and vacant lots near Racine Avenue. Both establishments served as occasional sources of distraction and amusement—loitering inside, then roaring with laughter after eventually getting chased out.

The liquor store was a bit of a neighborhood legend. Soon after Prohibition was overturned in February 1933, Town Liquors opened and quickly became a very successful business. The proprietor was a first cousin of William "Big Bill" Thompson—Chicago's Mayor from 1915 to 1923 and again for a third term from 1927 to 1931. The liquor store stood ready to open just one week after the law changed, and miraculously without interference from the city government or the infamous Chicago mob. Rumors abounded about the mayor's cozy relationship with Al Capone, including accepting campaign donations from him. When Big Bill passed away in 1944, newspapers reported millions of dollars were found stuffed in his desk and safe deposit boxes.

Wally and his friends, like all the kids in the neighborhood, heard rumors of dead bodies encased in concrete hidden under the basement floor or behind the walls of the vaulted sidewalk. Most of the neighborhood kids dared not even make eye contact with Town Liquors' owner, but to Wally—who fearlessly stared him in the eye any chance he got—the man was nothing more than just another anti-Polish bigot.

With the way a teenage idea can defeat boredom, no matter how simple, Wally called out to his buds: "Hey guys, you know that Jew-boy with all the money we helped? You know, Alvin. He just finished up his pharmacy yesterday. Let's walk down there and check out his place. He's such a freak—wonder if he'll be wearing his funny hat."

Bobby calmly answered, "It's called a yarmulke. He probably wears it to hide his bald spot." All laughing, they headed east.

While Opening Soon still hung on the window, they bounced through the entrance, laughing as they elbowed their way in, muscling each against the other. Alvin stood behind the pharmacy counter carefully organizing the medicines and other constituents of his craft. He did not break his concentration.

Sitting at the first seat of the soda fountain and far from Alvin was Joe Metal Harpy. The boys stared at his disfigured face, then started to laugh. Boldly, Ziggy called out, "What's wrong with your face?" Joe considered answering when Ziggy continued, "Kissed a train?" The boys hooted again as they elbowed their way back out, amused with themselves and blind to their ignorance and insensitivity.

Alvin was embarrassed for Joe. "Unfortunately, those were some of the boys I had in mind for your move. They are hard workers and aren't usually so disrespectful, but maybe I can recruit a couple of the others; I will let you know. If not, I will be happy to help you myself. If you can wait until Sunday to move the large things which require both of us, I might have access to a small truck if you think we will need it."

Joe looked at Alvin without speaking for a few moments— the kind of delay that makes one wonder what's on another's mind that they choose not to say. But Alvin's patience was more than adequate, where another's might not have been. Finally, Joe answered: "John Schmidt has offered me a vehicle to use; coincidentally he said I could borrow it on Sunday. I would greatly appreciate your help with only five large pieces of furniture. If you can help me, I will pay you for your time."

With an inflection of new friendship in his voice, Alvin replied: "Mr. Harpy, you are thoughtful, but payment will not be necessary. I have another idea. Perhaps, you might help me hang the new store sign after it arrives. It is large and heavy and will require two men to install it safely. This would make us even."

Again, Joe's mind drifted off for a moment completely lost in his thoughts, providing no timely reply as Alvin watched—until he snapped back to the present. "Your kindness is most appreciated. Why would you treat a stranger so?"

Alvin grinned ear to ear and chuckled warmly, "You are not a stranger, Mr. Harpy. You are my neighbor and my tenant. Perhaps from this day forward we shall also be friends. Please call me Alvin. May I call you Joe?"

Joe replied. "Thank you, Alvin, yes, please call me Joe."

"Great!" Alvin replied, "Why don't you step behind the counter and help yourself to a phosphate? I would be grateful if you would test the equipment and ingredients. I've been too focused on my pharmacy to do it myself."

Immediately realizing he might have improperly imposed on Joe, Alvin added, "Or, if you like, I will prepare one for you in just a moment. I am almost done here. Actually, I need the practice on the fountain. Yes, I definitely need practice. But soon I will have my new bride here to run things. This Tuesday will be our two-month anniversary! Mr. Harpy, I can't wait for you to meet Lois. She will operate the soda fountain and most everything else. I will have my hands full with my dispensary."

Those who first ventured inside Lincolnway were immediately captivated by the beautiful environment inside. But mostly it was Alvin's almost unlimited knowledge of pharmacology that would soon make the store a success and guarantee unwavering customer loyalty. Word would soon spread like wildfire through the neighborhood and beyond. Thanks to Uncle Myron's and Aunt Ruth's gift of air conditioning, the soda fountain often grew busy enough that people had to wait for a stool to clear. Those with a spare nickel could buy a few minutes of sweet distraction from the grim realities of life while seated at the fountain. Alvin loved that the business represented both a place of healing and a neighborhood gathering place. Some days the crowd was so thick, it was hard to pass from the front door to the rear counter.

Alvin's hopes and dreams needed only one more thing for complete perfection—Lois. After a few months of courtship, the two married. They agreed that she would quickly finish her nursing degree started in Paris. When not in class or waiting on customers, Lois studied her books behind the soda counter. She attended DePaul University; their Department of Nursing Education was organized at St. Mary of Nazareth Hospital just six years prior. Several years younger than Alvin, she adored him and was incapable of even noticing the handsomeness of other men. Her magical, twinkling blue eyes and ready smile lit up any room she occupied. Her irresistible French accent paired with a sincere concern for others ensured every customer felt welcomed.

Alvin's friendliness touched Joe deeply. "Congratulations on your marriage. I can't wait to meet your bride. May your life together be filled with good health, much joy, and many children. You are a very lucky man." With the conclusion of his words, Joe's mind seemed to wander off again to that mysterious place, this time the length of Joe's mental departure was painful to Alvin.

The pharmacist quickly set down the tools of his trade and raced to the soda fountain. He mixed the phosphoric acid, carbonated water, and cherry juice; a bit of ice and Coke syrup completed the recipe for Joe's just-discovered favorite beverage. He pushed the glass toward Joe. "Congratulations, Mr. Harpy. You are the first to sample my handiwork."

Joe silently finished his satisfyingly tart beverage and placed two nickels on the counter. "That was quite refreshing and delicious. Thank you. And I too hope we shall become friends."

Looking at the change on the counter, Alvin frowned. "Joe, keep your money. I have a better idea. Why don't you and I try all the other flavors? Like I said, I really need the practice."

With only a moment's pondering, Joe sat back down. Alvin grinned widely. So, the two men began their friendship tasting every item in the soda fountain, one after another until they became almost drunk with sugar. Alvin laughed. "My Uncle Myron, sweet tooth and all, insisted I offer as many different flavors as possible. He demanded the quality of the fountain offerings should be equal to that of my pharmacy."

Alvin grabbed his now bloated stomach. "Why in the world did I listen to him?"

"Ha Ha Ha!" Joe bellowed. "Alvin, I think your uncle was right. Just to be sure, I think we should try them *all* again!"

Laughing, Alvin shot back. "Never! I don't care if I ever have another soda!"

The taste testing session ended with a refrain of childlike laughter. Joe slid the two nickels off the counter and into his hand, dropping them into his pocket. "Alvin, I can't thank you enough. I feel like a spoiled youngster tasting all those sweet drinks, but I should be off now. I have packing to do."

As Joe grasped the front door, Alvin called out. "Of course, Joe. By the way, where do you live now?"

Pretending not to hear his new landlord, Joe kept walking away. Deliberately, he quickly headed to the stairs for another peek at the apartment—his next, new beginning. Intentionally, he avoided telling Alvin his prior landlord would not renew his lease, nor the reason why. Should Joe have been pressed to answer, as a gentleman, he would have been loath to explain how his landlady simply refused to look at him even one day longer than necessary. His personal code of honor abhorred the idea of criticizing his landlady, even for her hateful shortcomings. Joe felt the pain of rejection—not being known for the man he was, the things he had done, and how he lived by a higher moral code, but instead, unfairly judged for his disfigurement.

CHAPTER 11

The three boys wandered back toward their homes for the night after the brief taunting of Joe. Finding no other amusements, they parted company with a chorus of "see ya's." Wally walked alone, south down the alley toward home. The neighbor's two dogs stood at the fence to greet him. They had picked up his scent while he was quite a distance away and patiently waited.

The beasts could smell the lack of fear the first time Wally approached them a year ago. Sticking his face on the top rail of the fence, oblivious to the danger of the powerful canine bite, he spoke softly, feeding them bits of chicken, pinching small pieces tightly between his fingers, forcing the dogs to take the food gently from him. Permanent and loyal friends were made that day.

Never letting any of his friends see his way with dogs, now safely out of sight, Wally hurried to the fence and reached over the top rail to pet his secret canine pals. Vicious animals, too aggressive for anyone else to approach, leaned against the fence, almost begging the boy to scratch and pet them through the chain-link barrier. He spoke in a soft voice while digging his fingers into the beasts' thick fur, telling them, "You are good dogs. I don't know why your owner beats you. One day we will stop him. I know what it's like to get beaten, but don't worry. I promise you, one day we will stop him." Their tails wagged all the harder as he spoke with a tenderness belying a neighborhood tough guy.

Leaving his canine friends, Wally, bored as usual, sulked into the kitchen to find his mother opening a letter. After sixteen long, painful years of silence, a letter postmarked from Indiana had arrived. Helen eagerly devoured the correspondence. She still regretted her inability to help her sister years ago when Martha had needed her most, but remained unable to hold a grudge at her sister's last words, *go to hell*. Seeing her son, she burst out with excitement; "It's from your Aunt Martha. She's coming to Chicago soon. Wally, you'll get to meet your Aunt Martha! Aren't you excited?"

"Okay, mom," said Wally. His mind working quickly, he rattled off a series of questions. "How come she's never come around before? What does she want? How long will she be here? What's she going to do all day when you're sewing, cooking, or taking care of the little ones? Just don't make me be her tour guide or something."

Helen overlooked her son's disrespect, for she would soon be embracing the one who brought her to America, and to Chicago, where she met Peter. The sisters had been through a lot together.

After Helen's quick marriage, Martha had remained with Aunt Bernice. Seven months after Helen's marriage to Peter, Martha met a man from out of town who was visiting a friend at a nearby factory. He stayed for a week, spending as much time with the beautiful Martha as the somewhat protective Aunt Bernice would allow. On the last day of his visit, he promised to return soon. One week later, with a nearly-flawless one-carat diamond set upon an elegant gold ring, and on bended knee he proposed. She had never seen a piece of jewelry so beautiful since her life of servitude to the royal household. Martha, too, was deeply in love and joyfully accepted marriage to the handsome and charming fellow everyone called JJ. But Aunt Bernice urged caution. "Martha, you barely know him! Why didn't you tell him it was too soon?" But the beautiful young woman had made up her mind and no one could change it.

Although Peter and Helen had only met JJ a couple of times, they both adored him and tried their best to assuage the fears of Aunt Bernice.

When Martha's wedding date came, Helen, struggling and bedridden in her eighth month of pregnancy with Wally, could not travel to her older sister's wedding. As much as the younger sister wanted to serve as the matron of honor, it was impossible. Later, she and Peter could only contemplate Aunt Bernice's shared memories of the wedding day. "Your sister Martha was so statuesque and beautiful. She made the perfect bride. When she embraced that stunningly handsome man after the wedding vows were complete, I burst into tears as did every woman in the church!" Helen felt certain that Martha had fallen into the romantic dream life every young girl longs for and imagines.

Helen recalled how the heartache of loneliness poured forth from Martha's first letter to her sixteen years ago. It was as if the letter was engulfed in flames burning in the younger sister's hands. It did not contain the details of why the whirl-wind romance ended almost as soon as it started, only that Martha's beloved JJ left. She revealed nothing else. Instead, she pleaded with Helen to come to Milwaukee to console her. But with a colicky infant on her breast and a midwestern snowstorm raging, Helen could not travel once again. Soon Martha's second letter arrived—her life had changed forever. She found a roommate and was moving to Indiana with her. And *Helen could go straight to hell*. Reading that second letter, a chill suddenly ran down Helen's spine, fearing the family curse might have followed them to America.

But now, after sixteen years of estrangement, this third letter arrived. Helen couldn't help harboring the loving fantasy that the relationship could be repaired, and they would be best friends again. The letter told of the new fellow. Handsome and dynamic—Jack was now her life. He traveled about the Midwest for his work and visited Chicago from time to time. He made lots of money and lavished Martha with gifts and even showered her with spending money from time to time. Martha hoped to tag along the next time the man planned to deliver merchandise to his Chicago garage, or maybe even travel there on her own. Either way, Martha would return to the old neighborhood soon. The older sister closed the letter with the hope they could reunite.

While Helen read, Wally stood quietly, staring out the dining room window. When she finished, Helen asked, "Wally, come over and sit down next to me. What did you and your friends do this evening?"

Her oldest boy answered, "Nothing."

Helen, delighted in his answer, informed him, "Walter, this seems to be your usual answer whenever I ask. You must be very bored. Now that school is out, it's time for you to take a part-time job, if you can find one. But first, you will help me by showing Martha all around our neighborhood—take her to the place where they play that game of baseball, and treat her to the soda fountain at Lincolnway Pharmacy. Everyone's talking about it. I've heard that it is beautiful inside."

Wally knew this was coming; it was inevitable. His mom had the young ones to look after and she was busy with the seamstress work that always found its way into their home, possessing most of her free time. Always in demand, Helen had learned the craft from her mother as a youngster in the old country. At least, Wally thought, the extra income was making a difference in their lives during such sparse times. He knew any more objections would be as ineffective as his first complaint, so Wally simply said, "Yes, mother." Hoping to change the subject he asked, "Is dad at metal school again tonight?" He did not want to think about being saddled with an aunt who he did not know, at least until the task was upon him.

Helen looked up at Wally saying, "Yes, Walter he is. Did you know that Mr. Schmidt told Fritz that he has never seen an apprentice as brilliant as your father? I heard it from one of the ladies who knows Mrs. Schmidt really well, so it must be true. He may just be as smart as you!" And she grabbed her boy, hugging and kissing him just the way most teenagers detest. Breaking free of the maternal smothering, he smiled and stared at the rear door.

"I think I'll go out back for a little bit. It's still too hot in the house." Wally said this in perfect sequence with his steps—one syllable per step until he was out the door and halfway down the back porch stairs. Having no real destination, he thought of the dogs, named *Ziemniak* (Polish for potato) and *Marchewka* (meaning carrot). God, he hated those names. Walking through the backyard to the alley gate, he saw a silhouette of a man approaching the fence with the two canine guards. Chuckling to himself, he thought, what's that idiot think he's doing? I hope they scare the crap out of him! But he watched with amazement and a little jealousy as both animals leaned against the fence for attention as they often did for him.

"Who the hell are you? Get away from those dogs; they are dangerous." Wally called out, still a few lots away to the south. The silhouette tipped his hat toward Wally and walked away, slowly like one who has nowhere to go. Incredulous, the boy raced toward the dogs, but they did not turn to watch him, instead they remained focused on the stranger as he disappeared from sight.

Wally reached the fence as the dogs leaned against it for the anticipated scratching and petting. Still looking for the once-present stranger, they only glanced at their young fan. "Hey, you big mean dogs, why didn't tear him to pieces?" Wally asked, as if he expected them to speak. "Who was that? Did he bring you treats like I do?" Petting his canine friends a few minutes more, Wally then headed back home.

Entering the back door, he called out, "Hi mom, I'm back. There was some weird guy in the alley petting Potato and Carrot. I think it was that *jot* (local slang for Polish *zadek*, meaning rear end, or ass) who roams the alleys at night. I don't know why they didn't bite him." No sooner did he speak to his mother, than he heard yelling and the yelping of dogs he knew too well. Bursting out of the house, he ran to see the owner of the dogs beating one with a thick, long ax handle.

He had hooked Potato's collar to an eyebolt in the wall of the house so the animal could not run or fight and was striking as if he meant to kill him.

Carrot was pulling mightily at the rope that held him against the garage, wanting to rescue his littermate. Again and again, he pulled against his restraint, the frayed rope unraveling a bit more with each powerful lunge. Surely the rope or the garage wall could not hold back the muscular dog much longer.

Wally threw the gate open and ran to his friend's rescue. Seeing the dog bleeding and cowering, suddenly filled with the rage of his own beatings, he grabbed the club as the cruel owner raised it again. Ripping the weapon from the neighbor's hand, Wally whipped it across his skull—the man stumbled. Then Wally drove the butt end of the handle into the owner's stomach—the villain keeled over. With one upward swing, Wally split open the skin of the cruel master's chin and cheek, as the scoundrel fell to the ground unconscious. He finished the assault with a kick to his neighbor's jaw. It happened in an instant, so quickly that Wally might not even have realized what he had done. The uncontrollable rage washed over the boy, almost like it was part of his very DNA.

Unhooking the whimpering dog from the wall, attempting to comfort it, Potato broke from his grasp and ran toward the gate. Wally had left it open. The rope holding Carrot finally snapped under the power of the straining dog, and the two canines ran through the gate. Wally called out, "Carrot, Potato, come!" But they ignored him as they turned south and headed down the alley. About to call again, he saw a woman with two young children, all hand in hand walking toward the dogs, oblivious to the imminent danger. Wally yelled. "Those dogs are vicious, run!" Now twenty-five feet from certain mauling, the defenseless threesome stopped, frozen with fear.

Before Wally could exit the yard, a single, loud, shrill whistle emanated from up the alley, as the silhouette appeared again. "*Platz*" rang out in a powerful voice. Both dogs dropped to the ground, laying down immediately, not more than ten feet from their terrified targets. "*Kommen*" the voice called, and the beasts stood, turned and ran back north. As they approached their yard the stranger pointed and called out, "*Geh Rein,*" and the dogs went into their yard.

It all happened so fast. Wally barely reached the rear gate, as the dogs reentered the yard at the stranger's command. The silhouette now directed Wally: "Take the dogs to your yard and stay there. Do not let anyone enter. Tell your father or mother you rescued the dogs and to summon the police." Wally hooked up a rope to Potato, grabbed the one still tied to Carrot and led both dogs to his yard as the man instructed. Meanwhile, his bloodied victim tried to stand. Wally waited in his own yard.

When the cops arrived the neighbor, who was bleeding profusely and stumbling from a likely concussion, screamed,

"He tried to kill me! I want him put in jail!" With that, one officer approached the victim, grabbed his arm and spoke to him. The other cop walked to the gate of Wally's yard to hear the boy's side of the story. "Get your ass over here, kid. I'm not coming in the yard with those vicious beasts." But the dogs were remarkably calm as the second police officer spoke with Wally from the alley side of the backyard fence. The cop rested his right hand on the handle of his holstered revolver just to be sure, his potbelly hanging over his utility belt.

Before the officer asked his first question, Wally pleaded, "It's been a year since that asshole has owned these two Alsatians. I think they were trained as army dogs. Sometimes when it's hot he leaves them in the yard all day and night, and I have to bring them water so they don't die. I watched that pig sit in his backyard and get drunk. Sometimes he throws things and sometimes he hits them with that stick." Reading the cop's name tag, Wally addressed him properly. "Sergeant Fitzgerald, tonight's beating was the worst ever—I could not take it anymore!"

The cop responded, "You committed assault and battery; it will be up to the prosecutor to determine whether a more serious charge is in order. You also stole two valuable dogs after committing the first crime. If the prosecutor links these two crimes as a premeditated act, you may very well face felony charges—and jail time."

The dogs waited patiently in the shade where the rear yard met the side gangway at the back of the house. The sergeant ordered Wally to leave the yard and join him on the alley side of the gate. With his billy club, Fitzgerald suddenly shoved the boy against the garage door, placing the length of the club just below Wally's chin in such a way that he could collapse the boy's trachea with just a twitch. Now his tone grew threatening. "Big strong punks like you are the kind I most like to hurt. You think you're tough, huh?" Releasing just a little pressure the cop continued, "How old are you?"

Wally evaded the question. Instead, he said, "A man up the alley ordered the dogs and they obeyed. They were about to attack a lady and her two children. He told me to bring them to my yard. I didn't steal them. I was trying to save them."

Helen frantically watched out the back porch window, trying to see exactly what was happening, her vision partially obscured by the garage. With Peter due home any minute, she called out, "What are you doing to my son?" And then called to her boy, "Wally, are you okay?"

Ignoring his mother's question, Wally, choking from the pressure on his throat, finally answered the policeman, "I am seventeen."

Again, increasing the pressure on the boy's throat, the cop looked at him, eye to eye, and said, "Oh, so you can be charged as an adult—good. Now keep your mouth shut until

I tell you to speak." Fitzgerald then called up to Helen, "How old is this boy of yours?"

She replied, "He will be seventeen in six months."

"Is this Peter's boy?"

"Yes, this is our oldest child, Walter. What do you want from him?"

A big grin appeared on the officer's face as he yelled back to Helen. "Never you mind, just let me do my job." Then he laughed in Wally's face. "You are quite the man, aren't you? With that stubble on your face and the size of your arms, shoulders, and chest, I would have guessed you were in your early twenties and working at the foundry. No wonder. You are Peter's son. Why else would you be such a monster at sixteen? I am releasing you to the custody of your mother and father." Sergeant Fitzgerald eased the pressure from the boy's throat but never relented in his dominating stare.

With the billy club released, Wally was able to relax from standing on desperate tiptoes. He protested: "What about Potato and Carrot? What's to happen to them?"

The cop abruptly took his billy club and drove it into Wally's stomach. His wind only partially knocked out of him, the boy did not buckle over like his drunk neighbor. He stood strong, and easily catching his breath, he repeated, "What is going to happen to the dogs?"

The cop, impressed with the boy's ability to take a blow that should have dropped him to his knees, taunted him, "You stay here with them, someone else from the city will be here soon to shoot them and take them away. You make any trouble and they'll shoot you, too."

"Shoot them? Shoot them? No, they did nothing wrong!" Wally cried out. As the cop moved further away, Wally screamed all the louder, repeating his plea. Ignoring the boy's demands, Wally's interrogator walked to join his partner to compare stories.

Rejoining the Alsatians in the yard, Wally called up to his mother: "Don't let anyone out of the house. Can you bring me something to help Potato? I need some hydrogen peroxide, and some food and water for them. Put a bunch of ice in a rag. You can drop everything to me from the window."

CHAPTER 12

The neighborhood dog catcher knew of the two Alsatians and told Fitzgerald he refused to collect them. "Shoot them and do the neighborhood a favor," was all he said before he hung up the phone on the cop. Sergeant Fitzgerald marveled at his own clairvoyance in taunting Wally—perhaps the other cops would actually shoot the two dogs. If not, he certainly wouldn't mind doing it himself, if it came to that.

Wally waited in panic caring for Potato and Carrot. He successfully soothed Potato's wounds with peroxide, a bit of petroleum jelly, and a rag stuffed with ice. Slowly he coaxed the battered beast to take water, then chicken scraps from the icebox. Carrot, desperately hungry, would not interrupt the care its littermate received. Wally called him to take his share of water and food. Carrot obeyed. Tormented, as the dogs lay at his feet waiting for their destruction, Wally urgently began to plan their escape. But before he could act, his father, Peter, called to him from the porch window.

"Son, there were two policemen at the front door—Sergeant Fitzgerald and some other cop whose name I did not get. We spoke at length about the abuse inflicted on the dogs and the drunken rage of their owner. They spoke to other neighbors who confirmed your story and told them of the viciousness of the two dogs. Apparently, while answering the policeman's questions, the dogs' owner started to threaten them too. This was unwise on his part. You will not be going to jail. But you will have to deal with me. Your behavior has brought shame upon all of us. After the dogs are destroyed, we shall discuss the repercussions of your inability to control your temper."

Despondently staring at the dogs, Wally replied, "But they did nothing wrong! That asshole beat Potato so severely that if I did not stop him, he would have killed the poor thing."

Peter gathered his thoughts for a moment, mostly to temper his own anger. Finally, he answered, "There will be repercussions for your vulgarities as well. You are my son and I love you. But you will follow the ways of our home or you will no longer be welcome here. Do you understand?"

The mostly one-sided conversation was interrupted by the noise of the dilapidated 1927 Ford Model AA Chicago Police Department paddy wagon coming down the alley. Its black steel cab had exposed fenders protruding from the sides of the engine's hood. A matching black steel box sat upon the rear portion, forming the cage that usually carried men, but would tonight carry the remains of Potato and Carrot. Just above the ground, the space between the front and rear wheels on each side was filled with running boards, wide and flat so that extra policemen could stand safely on the boards, hanging onto the doorframes of open windows or any other suitable handle when responding en masse to mob shootings or riots.

"Come in the house, Wally," Peter demanded. "I will not have you there when the police put the animals down...come in NOW!" Wally squeezed through the rear porch door, slamming it behind him quickly as the dogs tried to follow. They began to bark and whine at the back door for the return of their savior. Climbing up the stairs he was met by his father at the first landing. "You do not need to watch this son. Go into the kitchen. I will come inside after it is done."

Peter leaned out of the porch window and watched as the two officers exited their vehicle, grabbing two snare poles from a side-mounted equipment box. One donned a heavy arm pad. They had been warned about the two Alsatians. The cop without the arm pad leaned his snare pole against the garage and drew his .38-caliber revolver from its tanned leather holster. Confirming the contents of each chamber of the six-shot cylinder, he slid the weapon back into its holster without snapping it shut. He picked up the pole—it would prevent them from having to shoot moving targets.

Before they entered the gate to perform their intended deed, Peter saw a man, his collar turned up and wearing a cap, striding toward the two officers. All three now stood frozen in intense conversation, the stranger gesticulating until one of the officers reached out to shake his hand. Then with a whistle, the stranger opened the gate and called out, "*Kommen*." The animals ran to him. "*Geh Rein,*" he ordered, pointing toward the paddy wagon's rear cage. Peter watched as the beasts leaped inside. Then the stranger climbed into the cage with them. Without placing the padlock upon the hasp, the policemen shut the door, hopped into the cab, and drove away.

Peter entered the kitchen to find Helen, Wally, and the four little ones at the table. He looked at Helen, ignoring the children. "The police have not destroyed the dogs. They and another man took them away in the paddy wagon. I do not know their fate, but thank goodness they did not shoot them in our own backyard. It is very late; I want you all to go to bed now."

"Where did they..." Wally began but was interrupted by his father.

"Silence! Go to bed. It is better we not speak of these things until tomorrow. Not another word from your mouth or you will surely spend the night on the streets."

Having never seen such aggression from their father, the younger children trembled, doing as they were told without sound or protest. Immediately, Wally climbed up the rear stairs to his attic bedroom. Helen and Peter then held each other in the firm embrace of the fearful seeking reassurance. Helen spoke first: "What has become of our beautiful son? How could Wally beat another man with a club? Why didn't they shoot the dogs? Who was the other man, a policeman, too?"

Peter placed his cheek against hers and whispered, "Our boy is strong and wild. We must insert new things in his life that will aim him toward good. We have no other choice."

"You are big and strong, but you are pleasant and wise. How have we failed?" as tears now flowed freely.

But Peter refused to allow his beloved to slide down despair's treacherous slope. "We have not failed; we are in the process of molding an adult. This is not easy work, especially in these desperate times. We shall do all we must to bring him purpose, happiness, and success. Tomorrow I will ask Fritz if he thinks I might approach Mr. Schmidt about a job for Wally. A young man of his physical and mental gifts needs to work hard among men stronger than he. He needs to face danger and intentionally defeat it with his determination, intelligence, and fortitude. Our boy has these traits; he just needs more direction than most. Now, my love, let us rest and pray for our son's productive future."

"What happened to the dogs?" Helen persisted. "Wally will not rest until he knows. And who was the third man, a detective?"

"I will find out about the dogs tomorrow. And I'm pretty sure the third fellow was that *jot*—you know, the one who is always picking through the garbage cans late at night. He probably knows how to get along with the dogs in the neighborhood since they must scavenge the same places together from time to time," Peter reassured his wife in his most soothing tone. "Now it is time to close your eyes and dream of tomorrow's promise. All will be well." He scooped her up effortlessly and carried her to their bedroom, gently placing her on the bed as he had done many times before. Reassured, Helen sighed in guarded relief.

Upstairs, Wally laid in his sweltering attic bedroom, his mind in an emotional swirl that he could not understand or control. Staring at the rotating blades of the window fan, he contemplated the actions he could take to find and save *his* dogs.

CHAPTER 13

The early morning darkness found Peter standing in Wally's room, stroking his eldest child's arm with a gentleness not often displayed by a man of his strength. The Baby Ben clock read 4:45 a.m. "Son, wake up now. This is the best time for men like us to discuss the important things of manhood."

Jolted awake, as if jettisoned from a bad dream, the boy sat up, startled to find his father there so early and speaking so tenderly. "Good morning, father, why...what...?" But Peter did not wait for Wally to complete his questions.

"Son, every boy becomes a man differently. Some first mature physically, others emotionally, yet there are some whose intellectual development leads the way. You are rapidly growing in two of these areas, and the third is lagging. Can you tell me how you see yourself?"

Such a surprise visit, dumping complicated questions about adulthood was nothing Wally was prepared to handle upon first awakening. "Father, I don't understand. Why are you asking me this?"

Firmly, Peter continued: "You, like every adult, are responsible for your choices and for your actions. Yesterday, you tried to protect an animal from abuse which is most commendable but you also assaulted a man, a neighbor. Instead of only stopping him, you chose to punish him—while I don't believe you made a premeditated decision to do so. It is most likely that you lost control of your temper. Either way, it is bad; and either way, there is no justification for such aggression. Do I correctly understand what happened, Wally?"

The boy looked at his father, unsure. Finally, he responded: "Yes, I lost my temper. I am sorry, daddy."

Peter had not heard his boy use the term daddy for many years. While touched by its use, he pressed harder. "Wally, of all the ways a man can mature, it is your kind of development that is most dangerous. You have the strength and intelligence of a grown man, but you are emotionally immature. This was clearly exhibited by your actions yesterday. You must learn to use your intellect to control your emotions—but it will not be easy. You must learn to be thoughtful and deliberate." Peter let his explanation hang in the air for Wally to absorb.

Wally sat quietly, internally angered by the blunt assessment of his immaturity. Deciding neither to accept nor reject his father's thesis, but feeling compelled to say something, he let his juvenile emotions take the lead. "You must know best. I can only assume you are correct. Now what?"

Disappointed at the immature reply, Peter remained hopeful that some of his criticism would sink in. Changing from his attempt at reason, he shifted to punishment. "Son, I want you to think about what I said. We can revisit it later. Now, you are not to leave the house or the fenced portion of our yard. You may not invite friends over to visit, not even to talk over the fence. You will start your punishment by washing the walls in each room of the house. When done, you will wash the floors in each room. Then you will wash the walls and decking of the interior of the rear porch. The quality and speed of your work will determine the balance of your punishment. We will revisit this topic when I return from work, so be ready." With that Peter exited the attic and prepared for morning Mass and work thereafter.

Wally wanted to use the words he only used on the street to reply to his father, but fortunately for the boy, he did not. Seething, he waited for his father to leave the house. While the others were just beginning to stir, Wally dressed, grabbed some food from the first-floor pantry, and even drank milk directly out of the bottle—a forbidden practice in the household. The boy helped himself to several dollars of his mother's seamstress pay from the cookie jar and prepared to leave. He slammed the door shut without saying anything, completing a trifecta of disobedience. His father's words from last night rang in his head, "...or you can live on the streets."

Wally aimlessly meandered the early morning streets until the neighborhood started to come to life. The milkmen were finishing their early deliveries. Water from melting ice poured out of the trucks and wagons of the icemen. It was going to be another sweltering day.

In the gangway of his first destination, he called out, "Yo, Bob-by!" Such was the way the city's young beckoned others. Moments later, the boy with the dangerous eyes jumped down the last four risers and treads of the back porch stairs before bursting out of the door to join his buddy. "Bobby, let's go get Ziggy."

The two friends walked briskly south, then west, across Clybourn Avenue, stepping onto the short block of residential properties engulfed by the industrial behemoths on three sides and bordering the river. In the shadow of Schmidt's Foundry, these apartments appeared to fit in with the industrial set-ting—shabby and neglected—the worst in the neighborhood. The ritual calling was not required, as Ziggy had been watching for his friends from the window and stumbled through the doorway when they came into view.

"Ziggy, I need someplace to stay for a few days." Wally asked, "Do you think your mom will object if I come home with you for dinner? My father says I am no good; I need to live on the streets. Your mom is kind of nice when she's not drunk. I have a few dollars I can give her if she'll feed me and let me stay over a couple of nights."

Wally's two friends were stunned; Peter always seemed like the nicest man in the neighborhood.

Ziggy reassured his friend. "Sure, you give her five dollars when we come back here around dinner time and she'll probably let you stay for at least a couple of nights."

"Why did you get thrown out?" Bobby asked. "What did you do, Wally?"

"That's crazy! Your dad wouldn't do that!" Ziggy added.

"What the hell did you do?" repeated Bobby. "It must have been so bad! I love it. Tell us everything."

The man-child explained, almost reliving the anger of the attack. "You guys know that drunken slob with the two vicious dogs who lives five houses up from me? Well, early last night he started to beat Potato with a club, so I took it away from him and split his head open. I laid him out cold, then I kicked him in the mouth." The rage in his voice became palpable as he continued. "That son of a bitch better not mess with me again or I'll kill him."

Ziggy stood dumbfounded, but Bobby was thrilled. "That is so good! I wish I would have seen you do it! If you want to beat him again, let me know and I'll join you. What happened to the dogs?"

Wally relayed the entire story in great detail. It ended with the mystery of two vicious dogs in the back of the dilapidated Ford paddy wagon with a *jot* they seemed to like.

CHAPTER 14

All over Chicago and other American cities, motorcars and light-duty trucks were replacing horse-drawn carts at an ever-increasing speed. The number of cars on America's streets had increased to more than twenty million by 1929, nearly quadrupling over ten years. Of course, Black Monday—the day Wall Street crashed, and the subsequent Great Depression slowed this growth rate for more than a decade. Still, it came as no surprise to Helen to see a 1933 Oldsmobile Sedan parked in front of their home. From her window, she strained to see inside of the vehicle, wondering who was blowing the car's horn repeatedly. It was big, black, with whitewall tires on copper-colored wheels, and it contained her sister.

"Martha! Martha! Oh, my goodness, is it really you?" Helen shouted as she ran across the front yard to embrace her sister with a hug that might have lasted all day if Martha hadn't wriggled out. "Is it really you? I have missed you so!

Oh, my goodness—look at you. You look like a movie star! You're more beautiful than ever. Why didn't you tell me what day you were arriving? Oh, how I must look!" she exclaimed, running her hands over her disheveled hair.

But Helen's preoccupation with her missing son was all consuming. "Come in the house, Martha. We have so much catching up to do. But first I must tell you about Wally. Martha, my oldest boy is missing! Wally left the house yesterday morning and never came back. We don't know where he is."

Just like when they were teenagers, Martha acted when called to duty. Instinctively, she put her arm around Helen, determined to lead. "Let's go inside and you can tell me all about it," she reassured her younger sister. They sat down in the kitchen—there was no time for bitterness or dredging up old wounds. The younger sister had need of help, and Martha automatically reverted to her childhood commitment of leadership and protection. Helen explained that her four younger children were at church summer school, and Peter was at the foundry, so she freely released to her sister a desperate stream of fear-filled consciousness.

Martha encouraged Helen, "You say he's sixteen and smart for his age. Don't worry, I don't think he would do anything foolish or put himself in a dangerous situation. Tell me what happened the day before he left?"

Helen conveyed the entire story of the dogs and the brutal neighbor, the police who didn't shoot the dogs, and the *jot* who could control the vicious beasts. "Wally will soon be seventeen, Martha. He is so much like his father, big and strong, handsome and charming. Why would he leave? We never did anything to make him want to leave us."

Martha started to probe in greater detail. "Tell me about Wally's interaction with the police. Did they arrest him? Did they rough him up? Did he ever have trouble with the cops before?"

"No Martha, I don't think he ever had trouble before. The one officer held him against the garage wall with his billy club, but didn't hurt him. Wally was so kind to those poor dogs."

Martha pressed further. "Who are his closest friends? Tell me their names, tell me where they live. And tell me why your husband hasn't found him yet. What's wrong with him?" The undercurrent of Martha's jealousy over her sister's marriage when asking about Peter's ineptness in this situation would have been apparent to anyone else, except for Helen.

The younger sister's desperation grew more intense. "Martha, you have to help me. I can't sleep. I can't eat. Peter works all day and is in school in the evening; I don't know how much more he can do. Last night he walked the streets past midnight, just barely getting any sleep before going to work this morning. Wally is too young to be on his own this long. Where would he sleep, how would he eat?"

Martha, again in control, confidently shared her plan with Helen. "You stay home, wait for the other children and for your husband. I will find your boy, but if he is in jail, I won't be able to help. Only his parents will be able to bail him out."

Now Helen's agitation was out of control. "In jail? Why? Martha, don't tell me you think he is in jail. He can't be! He's too young. Someone might hurt him!"

Helen's tears seemed only to strengthen Martha. "Did I not get us from that awful stable to Chicago safely? Didn't I protect you, and was it not me who was with you when you met your husband? I have a car, Helen. I know how young men, struggling to become real men, behave. I will bring him home. Now tell me about his closest friends. What are their names and where do they live?"

Helen complied. "Here is a picture of my boy. Look at him Martha, he's so handsome. You just have to find him."

Pinching the photo of Wally between her two fingers and other necessary information received, Martha gave Helen a parting hug, still the elegant athlete—still in control.

First, Bobby's house; then Ziggy's, but the determined aunt did not find any of them. Slowly she cruised the neighborhood, keeping to the alleys more than the streets. She knew her nephew would not stand in plain view on a busy street. More likely she'd discover him lurking in gangways or alleys trying to avoid detection.

Martha drove around the neighborhood using a right turn protocol until she felt certain she had not missed a single street or alley. Chicago's grid system of street design made that easy.

She did not bother going into Weber's Billiards or any other hang out. She knew Wally, like most vagrants and petty thieves on the run, would lay low, never venturing too far from his usual haunts—too ignorant and fearful to move into a totally new environment.

Failing to find him during her first tour, Martha returned to the house on Southport and started the process all over again. Soon idling slowly through the alley behind Lincolnway Pharmacy she saw three late-teenage boys—one very handsome, one hulking, and one plain. It would be too risky to stop her vehicle near them; it might send the boys running. So, Martha turned right, down the perpendicular alley before getting too close to where they stood, then drove around the block to a spot near Alvin's store. Parking her Oldsmobile about one-half block away from his front door, she went inside. Joe Metal Harpy was sitting on a fountain stool and Alvin was behind the pharmacy counter. Lois energetically wiped the counter. A slight hint of bleach filled the air.

As Martha elegantly glided along the row of the fountain's stools, Alvin could not help looking up. To him, Martha's movement appeared sheer perfection. She had nearly reached the public phone booth that separated the fountain from the pharmacy along the aisle, when the proprietor called out, apologetically, "I'm sorry miss, but we are not yet open for business. We have our grand opening tomorrow morning."

"Something is wrong with my car," she replied pleasantly. "It stopped working right behind your store. I just need to use your phone." Joe turned too late to see any more than her back as she entered the booth and shut the door. Pretending to make a call, Martha wrote down the phone number of the booth's telephone on a matchbook cover as she faked a phone conversation. As she exited the booth, she continued the deception: "Excuse me, sir. My brother will be coming to help me soon. Do you have a back door that I may use? My car is in the alley behind your store. I don't want to walk all the way around the block again."

"Of course. Just follow the hallway past the bathroom and you will see the rear door," Alvin explained with a smile.

Joe stood up, intending to offer his mechanical skills. He turned to speak as Martha looked his way, saw his disfigured face, grimaced, and turned away in horror. Joe froze, unable to move. Alvin observed the tragic moment, feeling painful sympathy for his tenant and friend as Martha hastened out of the store's back door.

As she hoped, the boys saw her come out, unescorted, no vehicle nearby, so they approached her. Bobby took a long drag on his cigarette, dropped it, stomped on it, and moved toward her in one easy movement. He found the mystery woman's looks and walk captivating. "What's a pretty dame like you doing in an alley? Can we help you find your cat or something?" They all moved closer to her, donning the eager smiles of boys well past the age of innocence.

Unintimidated, Martha took an aggressive step toward Bobby. "Maybe you boys need to find little girls your own age. My brother, a Chicago copper, is on his way. If I were you, I would get your skinny asses out of here." Two of the boys howled with delight at her audacity. The third did not. Martha couldn't help noticing the handsome, quiet one held a remarkable resemblance to the monster who tormented her as a child—there was no doubt in her mind. She split the space between her two new fans, grabbing Wally by the arm. "Wally, I'm your Aunt Martha. My car is out front. Send your friends home; you are coming with me."

Wally stared dumbfounded at this gorgeous creature claiming to be his aunt. He had heard of her beauty and courage from his mother, but could not believe his eyes—she was more beautiful and courageous then he imagined. Finally, he turned to Bobby and Ziggy and simply said, "Ya, my mom said my Aunt Martha was coming to visit. You guys get lost. I'll see you later." Then he turned to Aunt Martha and asked, "Why do we need your car? The house is just a couple of blocks away."

Martha, still firmly holding his arm, replied, "Who said anything about going home? We are going for a ride. I'll decide when, or if, it's time for you to go home." His friends, still in earshot, were astounded. They couldn't wait to find out

about this feminine powerhouse and what she was going to
do with Wally.

CHAPTER 15

It was nearing 6:00 p.m. when Martha cleverly snatched Wally from the alley behind Lincolnway Pharmacy. He had spent the previous night sleeping on the floor at Ziggy's place but wondered if his mom would let him stay another night. They drove west on Fullerton, then turned north on Milwaukee Avenue until Wally had no idea where they were as the cityscape turned to rural emptiness.

During the entire drive Martha interrogated Wally. The runaway could not resist the force of her personality. Martha asked questions with some mysterious authority. Sitting in the passenger seat, he kept looking at the perfect features of her face and how her tight-fitting dress highlighted her feminine shape, slowly becoming disarmed by her charm, questions, and stunning looks.

She learned about the boy's boredom, his temper, and his angst. Soon internal rivers of his anger were released as he told Martha about the Irish and German kids in school who teased him about his name and ganged up on him—until he responded by using his fists. The prejudice— whether for a name, for a nationality, or for a language—painfully cut to the depths of his soul. The young man would forever bear the internal scars of hate and rejection.

With a soft and soothing voice, Martha offered, "I understand how you feel, Wally. Some scars are hidden on our hearts, never to heal. These make us who we are."

He continued his cathartic rant. "I was never accepted. I didn't do anything to them. They were just cruel and hateful. Eventually, I taught them all a lesson."

A bloody nose, a black eye, a chipped tooth, a face ground into the playground's gravel, were the prices they paid. Now none dared to speak badly of him; they held their tongues, wanting nothing to do with him.

Wally, having bared his heart, was now falling under the control of Martha's intense and sincere interest. "I'm glad you stood up to the other boys and fought. Sometimes you have to fight...I think we're going to get along just fine." She flashed a sympathetic smile at the boy.

After nearly an hour of driving, long after sidewalks ceased, Martha steered the Oldsmobile to the right, onto the river road. The pavement turned to gravel and mud as the road grew pocked with grooves made by wheel after wheel, forcing Martha to skillfully avoid bottoming out the car on the high spots. Suddenly, she turned onto a long dirt driveway, weaving through trees and underbrush that hid the property and its structures from the street. Carefully she guided the vehicle through the woods until they reached a clearing. There, Wally saw a modest, single-story house with a large garage behind it. Perhaps it was a small barn, but Wally saw no animals or crops. They were well outside the city, somewhere that made Wally feel alone. Martha turned off the motor and threw open her car door. Before sliding out, she explained, "A friend of mine owns this place. He uses it when he's in town. The Des Plaines River is just a hundred yards through the woods that way. Take a good sniff—you can smell it."

Wally suddenly regained awareness of his olfactory sense. "Wow, I can smell the woods and the dampness of the river's air. This doesn't smell anything like Chicago."

Chuckling, Martha directed her nephew. "It's nice around here, except for the mosquitos. Let's go in and find something to eat. It isn't much of a house, but it's clean, and the garage is big enough for Jack's needs. Anyway, after we eat, we can decide if we take you back home or bivouac here."

"What does that mean? What's biv-whack?" Wally asked, interrupting her as they walked to the front door of the house.

With a broad smile she replied, "Wally, it's a military term for an impromptu campground, usually with little gear. I don't know where I learned it. But don't worry, we have plenty of supplies and all the comforts inside."

The boy repeated the word again and again, enjoying the way it sounded and the adventure it promised. "How do you spell it, Aunt Martha?"

"B-I-V-O-U-A-C" she replied. Then Wally repeated the spelling, repeated the word, now delighted with having learned something new.

Amazed at how his aunt could make his day change from one of fear and uncertainty, to feelings of safety and adventure, a barrage of questions swirled in Wally's mind. As she slipped the key into the lock, he put together a cohesive query: "Aunt Martha, if you live far away in Indiana, how did you find this place? And how come you have a key for the front door?"

Martha chuckled warmly in a way that did not convey amusement at Wally in some derogatory way, but made him feel welcome. "My friend, Jack, had me bring some things here for him—that's why I came to town. Wally, you are a delight. I wish I had not waited so long to visit."

Inside, she lit an ornate steel oil lamp, one with a large wick and equally large hurricane glass that instantly illuminated the room in a flickering light. Before closing the glass, she lit a cigarette with the lamp's yellow flame. Martha instructed, "Wally, throw open the windows. Then look through the cans in the upper cupboard. Pick some meat; I prefer the Polish ham. Grab some sort of fruit or vegetable, or both. I don't care what you choose. Open the cans and put out two plates. Get the bucket from under the corner cabinet and pump some water into it. You know how to use a well with a hand pump, city boy?" The smile on her face let Wally know it was a simple phrase of smart-ass-fun and affection.

"I don't see a bathroom with a toilet. Where do I...go?" Wally asked with embarrassment.

Martha pointed out the back window to the miniature shack. "Hey, you're lucky to get a nice outhouse when we bivouac." Wally now understood they were going to stay there until the morning. And that would be okay—he had become captivated by his aunt, the legendary, beautiful relative he had only heretofore heard about.

She then asked, "Ever use an ax to split wood for a cooking stove?"

"No, Aunt Martha, but I've driven spikes into railroad ties. It's pretty much the same, right?" Wally asked, hoping to let loose and swing away.

"Pretty much the same. Let's step out the back before it gets dark and the mosquitos eat you alive. All you'll need to do is place a log onto that tree stump over there by the woodpile. Stand each log, one at a time, on end and swing the ax directly at the center of the log. If you keep your hips and shoulders square to your work, any misses with the ax will not hurt you. You need me to show you how?" She grabbed his arm. "Split the wood so the pieces aren't any larger than your forearm." The boy grinned indignantly and squared himself in preparation to swing.

Later, as Martha sat inside sipping some vodka she kept hidden for herself, no longer hearing the crash of steel splitting wood, she peeked outside. Wally stood proudly, drenched in sweat amid a pile of split firewood that could heat the house for more than a couple of winter nights. "What a great job!" she called. "Oh, did I forget to tell you, you have to stack it too?"

Undaunted, Wally had his freshly split face cord of wood perfectly stacked minutes later.

Back in the house, Wally dumped an armful of wood into a metal scuttle next to the stove and quickly pumped a bit of water into the sink, rinsed out his shirt, and hung it to dry. He took a fresh bucket of water into the next room to sponge himself off as Martha stared at his powerful body. "Aunt Martha, does your friend have any clean shirts I could borrow?"

"Sure. Look in the closet." She called from the other room. He helped himself. The short-sleeved cotton shirt was not quite adequate for his physique but he was now suitable company for dinner.

Martha lit a couple of smaller lamps as night fell. The two sat and talked a bit more after eating, all the while she marveled at his manliness. Staring at him she thought of JJ and Jack, until the recurring nightmare of the Monster of Warsaw stole her fond memories, as usual. Though she and Helen named their father thus long ago, she never repeated his surname or used the term father in any conversation—even within her own head. She only used monster.

It was a perfect evening. A cool breeze slid through the screened windows offering the river's sweet woodland air to the interior of the house. Wally learned a bit about his mother and aunt's leaving Poland when they were young, but nothing about why. Martha consistently directed the conversation to Wally's young life and feelings and away from her own. His aunt was enchanting—irresistible in spite of her subtle interrogations. Her queries seemed sure signs of interest and affection, so he talked freely. Soon they were like lifelong friends catching up after a long separation.

Feeling loved, Wally purged his soul completely, sharing Peter's harsh words and subsequent punishment. Martha listened sympathetically, consistently offering empathy and reassurance. Finally, the two could resist slumber no more. "Wally, I could listen to you forever. You are the sweetest and smartest young man I have ever met. I would love to listen to you all night but we should get some rest. We'll need to return to your home first thing in the morning."

Martha showed the boy which bedroom to use. As they said good night, she hugged her nephew fully. Not one of those, 'just touch the arms' type of hugs, but an embrace of the body. She felt firm and strong. Wally wasn't expecting that. Releasing him, she said, "Some men are pigs, Wally. But you will never be one—I'll make sure of that."

He swung the door shut but it did not latch, the creaking old hinges refusing to complete their journey. Peeking through the crack, Martha carefully watched the boy strip to his briefs, staring long and hard until she went into another bedroom, locking the door behind her.

CHAPTER 16

The second night of Wally's absence, just like the first, the occupants of the house on Southport found it impossible to sleep. But a bittersweet comfort crept into Helen's mind, giving some hope. She reasoned that in the worst-case scenario, Martha would return without her boy. Therefore, Helen firmly believed that as long as her sister remained out, there was a good chance Wally might be found. She was confident that any minute she would hear the front door open and her childhood hero would return with her son.

At dawn, Martha and Wally made the drive back to Chicago's north side. Initially, the two remained mostly silent as Martha anticipated every turn, making each seem smooth and effortless. Eventually, the young man broke the spell, but not without some trepidation: "Aunt Martha, what are we going to do when we get home? What should I tell my parents?

They'll want to know where I spent the last two nights, and exactly when and where you found me."

Martha reassured her nephew. "Wally, the only way you can make the best of your stupidity is to make up a really good story. We have less than an hour to come up with it and rehearse it. Do you understand what I am saying to you?"

Wally's first reaction was shock at the ease with which his aunt suggested lying. "You don't want me to tell them everything, right? What parts should I include and which shall I leave out?"

Martha laughed loudly and her words poked at the boy. "You better learn to think like a businessman. Like a man of the city, like a tough guy. Figure it out in your head and explain it to me. I'll give you five or ten minutes." She spun the car into the next turn, accelerating and throwing Wally against the inside door panel, laughing with callous delight. The pair grew silent again.

Eventually, Wally offered, "Okay, I hitchhiked out of town and you found me. How does that sound?"

"How the hell could I find you if you were already out of town? Come on, use your head. You can do better than that," Martha barked. More silence.

"Please help me, Aunt Martha. I don't know what you want me to say," Wally pleaded.

"Okay, let's try this on for size," Martha offered. "Last night you told me quite a bit about your two best friends. Bobby is a wild and dangerous boy. Everybody knows it. If you blame him for being out for two nights, he'll never have a chance to tell your parents what really happened. Your parents will shun him. He will never be allowed in your house again. You can still hang with him, though. They won't know the truth as long as you don't bring him around. Does that help you come up with something? Remember, at some point if you make the improbable sound absurd, no one will think it's a lie."

Wally felt really surprised by the ease with which Martha turned deceitful, but the thrill of creating a fabulous tale also excited him. "Okay, how about this? The first night I stayed with Ziggy, just like I really did. The next day, Bobby showed up with a car and we drove around into the evening. I don't think it was his car—I don't know where he got it. He was being really reckless and I begged him to stop. But he drove a long way north of the city. Eventually, we parked in the woods along the Des Plaines River to sleep. I was really scared. When we drove back toward home just after dawn, he saw a police car and started to flee. He pulled into an alley, but crashed the car into a telephone pole. So, we jumped out and ran. I don't know where Bobby went, but I ran in the opposite direction. I ran for blocks until I figured I was far enough away from that car to be safe. That's when I left the alleys and gangways. I stopped running and started to walk out in the open, on the sidewalk. I was on Ashland, near Irving Park Road, when you found me. You told me you had been looking for me all night."

Martha's voice turned chillingly serious. "Not only are you handsome and strong, you are clever. You have a knack for storytelling. Don't worry about anything. This is what is called a white lie. It will be better for everyone if you tell that story. When telling the truth in a situation like this, you can only hurt yourself and me. And if you hurt me, you won't live long enough to regret it."

Incredulous, Wally pondered this sudden change in his aunt, hoping to get a sign or a word to indicate the threat was a joke, but she made no acknowledgment. In the same cold and mysterious voice, she continued. "Your story will work—follow it," she commanded. "And don't you ever betray me, understand?" Dumbfounded, Wally stared at her, wide-eyed, as she concluded. "They would never believe Bobby over you, should they ever have a chance to talk to him. And I don't have to remember any part of the story except I drove all night until I found you walking on Ashland, near Irving Park. Perfect. You did good." She reached over and gently stroked his thigh, repeating "You did good."

As they approached the house on Southport, Martha sounded the horn over and over. She intentionally raced the car up to the curb at an unsafe speed as if she had no intention of parking accurately. She slammed on the brakes and screeched to a halt, sending dust and gravel flying. In a cloud of dust, the car stopped perfectly parallel to the curb, only inches away from contact with it. Wally was amazed how she skidded the car into a perfect park job. As Martha planned, it became the boisterous Saturday morning arrival of a hero and her recovered, innocent victim.

Helen, near the front window as Martha exploded on the scene, began to scream: "Peter! Peter, Martha is here with Wally! Oh my God, it's Wally! It's Wally!" She burst through the front door with her husband right behind. Throwing herself at the car as Wally opened the door, he nearly struck his mother with it. Helen threw her arms around her wayward son as she flooded his checks with kisses, never breaking her hug. Wally dragged his mother from the curb and into the front yard. Peter just stood back and watched.

Then he called out to his spouse, "Helen, he looks fine. Let him go...stop drooling all over the boy." Slowly she released her arms from around Wally's neck, then grabbed him again. "Helen, let the boy go! Son, go inside." Peter looked at Martha. "Thank you. How did you find him?"

"I kept driving the neighborhood in bigger and bigger concentric circles. Then I came back to your block and started again. I lost track of how many times I did this. Anyway, about 2:00 a.m. or 3:00 a.m., I stopped in front of Alexian Brothers Hospital and dozed for a little while in my car. I just needed a little time to close my eyes and figured I'd be safe there near the hospital's entrance. At first light, I started looking again. I was northbound on Ashland when I saw him walking southbound." The white lie launched successfully, as planned.

Peter stepped back slightly, gesturing to Martha with his hand to proceed into the house before him. He walked in last, shut the door, and gruffly called out, "Wally, sit down at the kitchen table. Helen, my love, please join him. Martha, you are welcome too." The three took their places, with Martha selecting the chair nearest the wall where she leaned back against it just enough for the front legs of the chair to float above the floor. She looked perfectly relaxed—and self-impressed. Peter stood a couple of feet from the group, filling the doorway to the next room. Staring at the eyes and body language of his oldest child he instructed, "Wally, start from the beginning. Tell me every single thing you did from the moment I left the house, the morning you ran away."

The boy was not ready for this. The whole story was not what he rehearsed with Martha. He looked to her, not knowing what to say, when she snapped at him, "You big dope. Don't stare at me with your mouth open. You're damn lucky I found you. Now answer your father. Don't look at me like I know where the hell you were for a couple of days and nights."

The stress-filled family dynamics, complicated by the white lie approach, began to screw down on Wally's composure. He had never done this before and his compatriot in creating the lie was suddenly not only abandoning him, she was attacking him. Not knowing how to deal with more pressure, Wally, looking at his aunt, snapped back, "Don't talk to me that way.

Who do you think you are? You're crazy. No, you're bat-shit crazy!"

With that, Peter, holding back his anger, stepped up to the table and ordered the two women to leave the house. "I don't care where you go, but I want you to leave for a while. Take a walk, take a drive somewhere. It is time for me and the boy to spend time together, alone. It's 7:30 a.m.; don't come back until 8:30 a.m. Understand?"

Both sisters screamed simultaneously, Martha at Wally, and Helen at Peter. "Wally, don't you ever talk to me that way again, understand?" Then she repeated herself with almost deafening volume.

Helen, who rarely ever raised her voice, blustered at her husband. She had never seen him so angry. "Why do you want to be alone with Wally? What do intend to do? Don't you dare hurt my boy!"

"Silence, all of you!" Peter lifted up the unoccupied chair remaining at the table. With one hand on its back, he placed the other on the seat, slamming it to the floor; the chair's metal legs bent out of shape from the force.

Terrified by Peter's rage, the sisters made a beeline for the front door.

Suddenly, Helen changed course toward the backdoor. "The other children are playing in the yard. I can't leave them."

Peter, unmoved, replied. "Take them with you and drive to the lakefront. All of you go to Lincoln Park. If they don't want to leave, drag them to the car. There has been enough disobedience over the last two days—enough to last for the next ten years. I want you to leave now, and better yet, don't come back for at least two hours!"

As the rear door shut behind them, Helen and Martha collected the four younger kids. They exited via the gangway along the side of the house and to the front yard. Raised voices from inside the house could be heard as everyone climbed into the Oldsmobile.

Out of the corner of her eye, Martha watched with silent glee as tears ran down Helen's cheeks. "My Peter is gentle and kind. But he's so big and strong that no one ever challenges him." She feared that Wally would be the first to try.

CHAPTER 17

The steelworker who purportedly never had a fight with another, suddenly thought logic and reason needed serious reinforcements as he impatiently listened to his son's heated defense. His anger soon reaching the boiling point, Peter yelled, "That's enough lying! Shut up."

The uncontrollable wave of rage again washed over Wally. He stood up and stepped toward his father. Peter reacted, striking his son in the face with his closed fist, knocking the boy out of the back door and onto the porch. Sprawled on his back, rubbing his face and jaw, barely conscious, he found his father towering over him. Peter took hold of his son, grabbed him under his armpits, and lifted him in the air. "I haven't felt the need to strike you since you were three when I paddled your bottom for trying to eat lye. You needed it now much more than then."

Slowly he set the boy back on his own feet. Wally stumbled into the kitchen and onto a chair. "You harmed your mother with your disappearance; you disrespected both her and me. This morning you disrespected your aunt. Two days ago, you beat a neighbor senseless. When we spoke in the early morning you would not engage in an adult conversation. Your selfish and immature behavior must change immediately, and permanently. If not, we will make other arrangements. You will not have a second chance. Perhaps the army will be what you need."

The flesh around Wally's eye swelled and blackened. Blood poured from his nose and from the skin of his split-open cheek. "Go to the sink and rinse your face with cold water. I will get you something from the icebox. If your nose won't stop bleeding, shove a handkerchief inside each nostril for a while." Peter sat down at the kitchen table and waited for the boy to tend to himself. As his breathing slowed along with the tempest inside of him, Peter called Wally back to the kitchen chair. He then gently placed four butterfly-style bandages across the wound on Wally's cheek, tightly closing it up—but not enough to prevent the inevitable scar.

As if a switch had been flipped by his father's right cross, the whole story just flowed from Wally's lips like sweet cream butter on a hot plate. The young runaway explained how he went to Bobby's house, then to Ziggy's. How he spent the first night at Ziggy's, but his mother got drunk, and before she passed out, told him he better be gone in the morning and never come back. Wally laid out everything as it really happened, except Martha's appearance—it was Bobby who drove a stolen car. Effortlessly he maintained eye contact with his father, not even blinking. He even described the smell of the woods along the river and how Bobby sat on the front bumper to take a crap. "Dad, you should have seen how Bobby drove, he was like a madman. And when he saw the cop car do a U-turn to follow us, he cussed and took off. I thought we'd go to jail. I am so glad I ran the other way. I don't ever want to be around that maniac again."

For the pièce de resistance of his white lie storytelling, Wally reached into his pocket and handed his father most of the money he had taken from his mother's hiding place—two singles and a fin. "I left something out. Here daddy, I took seven dollars from the cookie jar, but felt terrible about it. I just could not spend it. I'm sorry. I will never do it again." In as much as Peter had no idea that the boy had taken the money, or how much, it made the whole story and the boy's false regret all the more believable, amplified by again using the endearing term he had used just a few days before.

After ten minutes of silence, both sitting at the table staring at its patinaed surface, Peter broke the ice: "While you were gone, as I walked the neighborhood looking for you, I spoke to a couple of guys drinking beer at the Greenwood Inn. One told me that *jot* who jumped into the paddy wagon set up an army dog training camp—that's how he knew what to do and why the animals obeyed him. All police and army dog trainers use some foreign language for the commands so no one else would know how to do it. Those dogs must have been trained by somebody. Once the police captain learned the dogs had some training, he told my friend's brother they might be adopted by the Chicago Police Department. And the funny thing was, when the paddy wagon arrived at the police station the *jot* was gone. He must have jumped out along the way. Thankfully, his detailed explanation to the two officers, those sent to shoot the dogs, was complete enough for the captain to believe it. One of the police lieutenants had trained dogs in the army during the Great War. Your friends Potato and Carrot will be fine."

Wally looked up. "Thanks dad, that's great." As the ice pack slowed the swelling and his nostrils stopped bleeding, he walked to the rear porch and sat on the bottom flight of stairs. Peter stayed in the kitchen. Neither man had any more words to share.

CHAPTER 18

Returning to the house, Martha and Helen walked through the gangway to the backyard so the little ones could play. Helen did not want them in the house for fear of what might have happened. "Oh, my goodness!" Helen shrieked when she entered and saw Wally's face. "Wally? Peter? What happened to my boy's beautiful face?" Helen had to repeat her question twice before Peter spoke.

"Wally now understands the rules of our house, don't you Wally?" Peter asked with just a little more shame than resolve—he knew what he had done hurt Helen deeply.

Helen tried to take Wally in her arms, but he resisted, gently pushing his mother away. "I'm fine. Dad explained everything to me. I am sorry I troubled you so, mom. It was never my intent to hurt you or scare you. Please forgive me." He turned to his aunt. "I'm sorry, Aunt Martha." Wally delivered this apology as smoothly as he told his father the white lie—maybe more so.

Martha just stood back and watched, knowing Wally was now capable of telling stories like a practiced con man, oozing with such sincerity that no parent could detect any falsehood. And the beating was just what she hoped for to increase her control of the boy. Breaking the tension in the kitchen, she called out to her nephew, "Let's take a walk over to Lincolnway. We'll check out the soda fountain. Maybe the pharmacist will have something for the result of your father's handiwork too." Looking at the boy's scarred and bruised face, her mind flashed back to the hideous man she saw during her first time in that store. She looked away from Wally, hoping to banish the memory.

Helen, more grateful for her sister than ever, felt pleased and relieved that Martha was taking Wally under her wing. As she watched them walk out together, Helen now believed not only was the sisters' past rift finally behind them, their relationship was now possibly better than before.

Walking to the pharmacy, Wally offered his apology to his aunt and she shook it off as less than important. Instead, Martha asked Wally, "I'll bet you wanted to punch him back, didn't you? It was smart you did not; don't worry though, you'll have your chance. A man of the street always plans revenge patiently, carefully. You will see what I mean."

Wally looked at Martha in amazement: "How did you know I wanted to fight back?"

Martha replied, "I know you, Wally, better than you could ever guess. You are like your ancestors. Powerful men, some of whom drank too much. Men who sometimes couldn't control themselves. Tough men who were fearless and vengeful. You even look just like your grandfather. Why should you be any different from him, the Monster of Warsaw? The curse of your mother's family hangs over you. You can't avoid it, but I am here to show you how to master it like I have. I will show you how to dominate others not just with your brawn, but with your brains. You will someday get everything you want and no one will be able to stand in your way. I promise." She reached out and took his hand, like young children or infatuated couples might do. Wally did not immediately pull away, allowing their arms to swing in unison for a few steps before gently disengaging from Martha's grasp. Her affection and promises helped comfort him.

They turned the corner, and headed east to Lincolnway Pharmacy. Entering the cool atmosphere of white marble wrapped in its peaceful, blue-streaked border, and the halo of wood high above, Martha grabbed Wally by the arm and led him to the pharmacy's rear counter. "Hey, you with the shrunken hat." She called out, "You got anything for this boy's cheek? I don't want it to get infected."

Ignoring Martha's disrespect, Alvin walked around his counter and right up to Wally. "Hi, Wally; what happened to you? Let me take a look. Oh my, somebody closed that gash up very nicely. I have some salve that will speed your healing and protect the cut from infection. Come, sit down here on the last stool. If you feel up to it, Lois can stitch it up, but it will hurt a lot even if I apply a topical anesthetic."

"No, sir. I don't need any stitches or salve. I'm fine."

Alvin wasn't impressed by the boy's attempt at stoicism. "Yes, you do need something. Tell you what, I'll dress your wound with the salve and give you the rest of the tube to take home. The instruction are on the tube." The boy nodded. "Good. Now, who is this beautiful woman who brought you in?"

It was time for Martha to turn on her charm. "Sorry for the comment about your yarmulke; I was just trying to be funny. When I stopped in here to use the phone the other day, I was so impressed with you and your store. I thought you'd remember me and laugh—sorry. Anyway, now I can see that you are a true expert in your craft as well." Martha stood up and started to walk around, closely examining the cabinetry, continuing to pour on the *schmaltz*. "This is magnificent woodworking. Did you build these cabinets too? You must be a man of many talents."

Lois watched her husband struggle between his concern for the young tough guy of the neighborhood and the lavish praise from a stunningly attractive woman who seemed to be coming on to her spouse.

Walking quickly from the register, Lois greeted Wally warmly, though she had an ulterior motive for inserting herself into the situation. "Hi, Wally. I heard about the dogs. Everyone is talking about how you saved them. Whatever happened to them?" Wally just stared at Lois, saying nothing.

Lois pressed for more information: "Nobody likes that old drunk who beat those dogs anyway. I'm sure glad you didn't get in trouble with the police. Or did they give you that shiner? May I take a look at your cheek—oh my, someone did a fine job closing up that gash."

Wally, not wishing to endure any more questioning, stood up snatching the tube of salve off the counter and started toward the front door. "I'm fine; the cut will be fine. I don't need stitches."

Meanwhile, Martha went on flattering Alvin, unimpressed by the fact that Lois' eyes had locked on her. Realizing Lois only came close to him to check on Martha's behavior toward her husband, Wally walked toward the door and barked out, "Aunt Martha, come on. Let's go or we'll be late for your appointment."

Taking hold of Alvin's hand just for a moment, Martha cooed, "It was *so* nice to see you again. I'm sure we'll be seeing more of each other soon." Ignoring Lois, she strutted from the counter, all eyes watching as she followed her nephew. "Thanks for reminding me, Wally. I might have lost track of time and stayed here all afternoon if you hadn't spoken up." Joining her nephew as they neared the front door, the boy stepped to the side, gesturing to Martha with his right arm for her to go first, as he used his left arm to hold the door open. "Beautiful ladies, first."

Once on the sidewalk, Martha chuckled "Wally, you are going to be as smooth as silk one day soon. You have the potential to become a first-rate confidence man."

"What do you mean, confidence man?" Wally asked, innocently.

"Wally, you have got so much talent, but I am going to have to teach you a lot. You sure aren't going to learn how to live large in that home of yours, with a steelworker as your teacher. He's never home anyway. He loves his job more than you. But with your looks, charm, and brains, you should not have to work hard. You'll learn how to outsmart the other guy. That's part of what a confidence man does—outsmart the other guy. It's knowing how to be good at the right kind of business. No more roaming the streets. You'll be driving nice cars, dining at fine restaurants, and wearing fine clothes, all with plenty of money in your pockets. How does that sound, my special nephew, MY young man?"

In only three tumultuous days, Wally went from being a normal teenager to committing battery, to rescuing dogs, and finally to a runaway. Now he was learning how to lie, courtesy of his dynamic, but mysterious aunt.

The two returned to the house, entering quietly through the back door, but Helen immediately accosted them. "How are you feeling, Wally?" she asked. "That cut on your cheek doesn't look too bad. Did the pharmacist give you something?"

"Yes, he did, mom. His name is Alvin. He started an account for us. Aunt Martha paid him for the medicine, though," Wally answered as he and Martha walked through the kitchen into the front room with Helen right behind. "Wally's all the buzz at Lincolnway," Martha informed her sister. "Everybody thinks he is a hero for teaching that drunken neighbor a lesson. And they think he got the shiner and split cheek from the cops. Nobody has to know your husband beat him. You know, Helen, at only sixteen, the cops and the local prosecutor would not look too kindly at a grown man beating a child so severely. You know it wasn't just a swat on the bottom. He could have put Wally in the hospital!" Inside, Martha brimmed with delight in criticizing Peter and emotionally subjugating her younger sister. "Wally did not say much to anyone. He was quite the stoic and discrete young man. You're lucky he kept his mouth shut."

Once again, Wally was confused by his aunt's behavior. He wondered, was she taunting his mother? No longer having much regard for his father, he spoke up for his mother's sake, "Don't worry mom, I won't talk to anyone about anything."

"Martha, I'm sure Peter regrets what he did—I know he does. Let's just drop this!" Still quite flustered, Helen looked at her wristwatch and excused herself to begin preparing supper. Martha, ever the ungracious guest, reveled in not lifting a finger to help her sister. She just sat down at the kitchen table and said nothing.

Helen forced herself to change the subject. "Martha, I know you're a very private person, but I've been wondering what has gone on in your life all these years? I want to hear all about it—whenever you're ready."

Staring at the tabletop, Martha refused to share. "I'll let you know when I'm ready. Okay? Please don't ask me again." Helen knew it just had to be that way.

CHAPTER 19

That night, after tending to Wally and later closing up shop, Alvin and Lois reviewed the events of the day, quickly turning their focus to Joe Metal Harpy. "There is a kindness and brilliance within Joe," Lois observed. "His eyes reveal a wise and ancient soul, but there is a profound sadness that I believe obscures a hidden greatness. Why do we stand back and allow him to flee anytime other customers arrive? Isn't there something we can do to befriend him?"

Lois, especially, took a liking to Joe Metal Harpy in spite of his disfigured face and reluctance to remain in the store whenever others were there. He had mastered the quick exit out of the back door at the sound of the front door's latch set being activated, even before its little bell would ring. Perhaps it was because he regretted not doing so the day Martha used the phone booth, cringing with revulsion and running out the back door when she saw him.

Lois lamented. "I am worried about Joe—I'm worried one day he may not come back. Call it my intuition, but I can't help thinking there is so much more behind those eyes."

As they lay in the near silence of midnight's darkness, both staring at the ceiling of the bedroom, Alvin suggested, "Might we consider inviting him to dinner one day per week? Somehow, we need to make time for him to feel someone cares about him and appreciates him, a time for him to escape his loneliness. While the laws of our fathers instruct us to treat him well, I personally like him too. Lois, I'm not sure why, but I do—a lot."

Lois rolled closer to her mate, embracing him, saying, "Alvin, I am proud of you, and so lucky that we are wed. You have made me very happy. I wish Joe could find even a fraction of our joy." And with that Lois drifted to sleep with her head upon Alvin's chest, his arm under her neck, gently wrapping her shoulder. His mind persistently considered their lonely and mysterious friend. Alvin, eventually distracted by the smell his wife's hair, immersed himself in the joy of their love. Filled with gratitude that Lois fulfilled the longings of his heart and the Fullerton Avenue building provided the ideal start for his entrepreneur's dreams, he drifted to sleep.

In the morning, Alvin heard the sound of Joe leaving his apartment at 6:25 a.m., as he did every workday without exception. This time, Alvin cracked open the door of his apartment at the exact moment Joe shut his own, and softly called out,

"Good morning, Joe." The tenant returned his landlord's grin, albeit with a smaller, twisted version. "I know you are on a schedule, so I won't keep you, but Lois and I would like you to be our guest for dinner one night next week. We close the store early on Tuesdays, Wednesdays, and Sundays so maybe you can pick which of those days is best for you. You can let us know anytime, but be warned, Lois will not take no for an answer." Nodding yes and offering a cautious smile, Joe bounded down the stairs and out the lobby door as Alvin closed his apartment door.

His forehead pressed against the door in thought, Alvin recalled the day the store's sign was installed. When it had arrived, Joe was there immediately after the end of his shift with a toolbox in hand, spools of electrical wire, fasteners, ladders, and a bag of decorative stainless-steel chain. He explained to Alvin how it should be installed, its weight permanently supported and secure, centered in the storefront window, at the exact height he wished. Alvin marveled at the skills and practical knowledge of his new friend as the installation was free of even the slightest struggle. Installation complete, Alvin eagerly pulled the chain. He recalled how the two men raced outside to assess their work as the sign illuminated its message to the world as only neon can—brightly, but with a unique ethereal glow.

Alvin recalled Joe's pausing before reentering the store, having noticed the small sign in the corner of the window nearest the entry door. It contained four words painted in opaque white. Joe read them aloud. "Family Credit Accounts Available." Alvin smiled remembering Joe's next words. "Alvin, your offer of credit will certainly help many in the neighborhood who are struggling. You're a *mensch* (Yiddish for a man of integrity)." Smiling at this fond memory, the pharmacist returned to the kitchen, soon bringing his wife coffee in bed—the way he began his morning routine every day. "As Joe headed out this morning, I asked him to dinner, just like we talked about last night. He nodded yes." Lois beamed.

Joe arrived at the foundry and was greeted at the gate by the CEO, John Schmidt. Peter arrived just a few seconds later and watched as the two other men walked off to an isolated place against the outside of the building, obviously wishing to speak in privacy. He watched John repeatedly put his hand on Joe's shoulder, not in a way of consolation but of affection. Suddenly, Schmidt stepped back intensely focused, taking a rigid pose. How odd, Peter thought. He knew John Schmidt was a committed listener, but what, he wondered, could the peculiar and isolated Joe have to say about anything that could make Schmidt react that way? After all these years, John Schmidt must still feel guilty for Joe's accident, Peter reckoned.

As the private conversation continued, Peter headed inside to find Fritz to discuss possible opportunities for Wally. He found his boss in the foreman's office, as always, working well before the morning crew obeyed the factory's whistle. "Fritz, can you spare a minute? I'd like to talk about my son, Wally,"

Fritz looked up from the papers detailing the production runs for the week. "Yes, I heard about how he 'rescued' those dogs. What about Wally?"

"The boy is growing fast, gaining strength. I was wondering if he might find any menial jobs here? He turns seventeen in a few months. My goodness, he is starting to get as strong as me."

Fritz laughed out loud at the question. "Peter, first off, *nobody* is as strong as you. And I have to say, you are very politically astute as well. I appreciate the courtesy and respect you show by asking me first, but you know John Schmidt is in charge. But don't worry, if he asks my opinion, I will be all for it."

With its shrill ejection of steam, the whistle announced starting time as steelworking men obediently hurried inside. Peter and Fritz remained in the shop office for just a few minutes more, reviewing the plans until they could no longer postpone joining the men assembled on the furnace floor. Parting company with John Schmidt, Joe Metal Harpy joined the group of workers last—he was usually the first. Schmidt headed to his office.

With Fritz at his side, Peter reviewed the week's production assignments with all assembled, then had each team leader repeat them. Once confident his instructions were understood, he handed each leader the written version of their assignments. He had learned from Fritz that the three-phase instruction was highly effective for accurate production. Finished, he asked, "Fritz, they all have their assignments. I would like to head over to the main office, if you think it's okay to leave the floor for a few minutes. I won't be gone long. Is that okay with you?"

"Well done, Peter. You did a fine job explaining things to the crew. Take your time, I will try to manage the floor without you for a while." Peter smiled at his boss's sarcasm, quickly making a beeline to see John Schmidt.

Shyly cracking the office door open, feeling a little out of place and not wishing to disturb all of the important things that occurred in the office, of which he knew little, Peter spoke cautiously. "Good morning, Millicent. Might I speak with Mr. Schmidt for a few minutes, or do I need an appointment? It won't take long."

While the secretary smiled at Peter's polite ways, the inner office door swung open and John Schmidt beckoned. "Come in, Peter. Nice to see you this morning. What's on your mind?" Then he turned to his assistant: "Do not disturb us unless it is urgent. Thank you, Millie."

"Thank you for seeing me, sir. I wanted to speak to you about my boy, Wally. He will be seventeen soon," Peter began. "Is it possible for him to do some minor work around the foundry? No work on the furnace floor of course, but maybe some groundskeeping, or some janitorial type of work?

Something to keep him busy. You don't even have to pay him much. I'd like him to understand this place and meet the men here so that when he is old enough, he might work on the furnace floor." Pausing briefly to assess the foundry owner's reaction, he continued. "Is it appropriate for me to ask you this, or have I exceeded what is proper?"

Schmidt smiled, which reassured Peter, but replied without answering the question. "Peter, let me tell you about the war. I served in the Battles of Cantigny, Belleau Wood, St. Mihiel, and Argonne, under a man who was brave, intelligent, and a natural leader. He was someone every man under his command would follow to hell and back if he gave them that order. His greatest skill, however, was his ability to quickly and accurately judge the motives and attitudes of others with just a question. He had an uncanny ability to know what was in the heads of all the soldiers in his company. While I learned much from him, it was his dedication to always listening carefully, focusing on every word, every inflection of voice and facial expression that was his genius. Everyone in the five platoons he commanded knew he respected them enough to listen. It was an honor to serve under him."

Barely understanding the intensity of the war experience or what it had to do with his son, he was growing confused and a little impatient. Peter only nodded.

John Schmidt was just getting started. "While many soldiers were torn to pieces by bullets and artillery, others huddled in the safety of trenches. While most soldiers suffered horribly from the deplorable conditions of the trenches, he demanded we follow his instructions to keep ourselves clean, dry, and healthy, while the rats, trench-foot, and dysentery plagued most everyone else. Sometimes the conditions were so disgusting, men would rather 'go over the top'. Peter, that means they left the relative safety of the trenches to face likely death from enemy fire. It was that bad sometimes."

Now Peter was completely confused and unable to conceive an appropriate reply. Perhaps, he wondered, his inquiry about a job for Wally was misplaced. He thought about excusing himself and leaving without delay. He stood up.

"Peter, sit down please!" Like a man compelled to speak by some greater force, the foundry owner went on. "Every day I wish I could pay him back for the times he bravely led us in battle, and for the times he knew when to regroup or retreat—he was both fierce and fearless. We enjoyed more than our share of successful battles and endured unusually low casualty rates, all because of him. But I am eternally grateful for the time he saved my life. His courage and brilliance turned the tide in many battles. He held the greatest number of awards for valor in our division, and probably even the entire First Army. Had he been from Chicago, the city would have held a parade for him."

Peter stared at John Schmidt, seeing the great admiration he held for his former commander, but also detected a sense of sadness. "It must have been quite an honor to have known him."

"Yes, it was, but that man is no more." John took a long, deep breath. "And I'll bet you are wondering why I am telling you this. It's simple Peter—he also could tell who was lying, who was too frightened to think clearly, and who was properly focused. Since returning from the war, I have tried to emulate his leadership and listening skills."

Growing uncomfortable in his exasperation, Peter blurted out: "With no disrespect to your former commander, sir, I still don't understand what this has to do with my son."

"I'll tell you why, Peter." Schmidt replied. "It seems to me you are a man of pure motives and dedication to our business—that's why your son may see Millie Friday morning to fill out an application for part-time work in the office. He will not be allowed near the foundry operation until he is older and has proven himself reliable. Now, during the summer break, he can work several hours a day. When school starts, he can work two hours a day on weekdays, and on Saturdays, longer. Those details will be up to Millie. Peter, please understand that since he is your son, I will hold him to the highest standards. I will not dishonor you by expecting anything but perfection from him."

"Thank you, Mr. Schmidt," Peter replied, shaking the man's hand. "I should get back to the floor. I don't want to take advantage of Fritz's generosity." Then he quickly made his way out of the office and back to a more comfortable environment of intense heat and danger.

CHAPTER 20

While Peter toiled and Helen sewed, Martha and Wally spent considerable time together, often away from the house on Southport Avenue. As his mother had requested, Wally became the local tour guide for his aunt. Helen was grateful, it gave her one less thing to worry about, and she expected Martha to be a good influence on her oldest boy. While it didn't mitigate her fearful reaction to Peter's violence, at least it kept father and son apart. She hoped their relationship would smooth over with time.

Wally found spending time with his aunt thrilling. The first day after the confrontation with his father, Martha offered her nephew an unexpected opportunity. "Wally, let's take my car and explore the city. I love adventure. We can just drive and discover things."

And so, their week together began. She drove down Michigan Avenue, revealing more of the city than the young man had ever seen, all the way south to Jackson Park, including the Museum of Science and Industry. Housed in the repurposed Palace of Fine Arts Building from the 1893 World's Columbian Exposition, it amazed Wally. Only a few weeks before their visit, on May 27th, the city launched A Century of Progress International Exposition all along the lakefront from Soldier Field south to Oakwood Boulevard. There was much to be discovered.

The next day she paid for their entry to a baseball game. His mercurial, but very cool Aunt Martha expanded Wally's world, impressing him with her fearlessness, regardless of the adventure. Everywhere they went, people stared at the stunning Martha and handsome Wally. The little house on Southport would never again be satisfactory to him—Wally wanted more.

On the last full day of Martha's visit, she made an unexpected proposition while they completed yet another driving tour of Chicagoland. "How would you like to go back to Indiana with me for a few weeks? Your school is out for the summer. We could have a lot of fun together." The woman's hand rested on the teen's thigh. He felt unsure how to interpret this sign of her affection. He removed her hand. "Oh, Wally!" Martha continued. "We are becoming so close. Don't worry about my little signs of affection. Even with that scar, you are perfect in my eyes. I know it's sometimes difficult for young men to get comfortable with women, but I can't help touching you sometimes—I just love you so much!"

Wally could not tell exactly what she meant. A bit uncomfortable and confused, he directed the conversation back to Indiana. "What would I do there? Where would we go?"

Martha laughed loudly. "Where would we? What would we? You're funny! I want you to meet Jack. He's the kind of man who can teach you about living large. Maybe he'd take you on one of his business trips. Sometimes he comes back with a lot of money. Anyway, it was premature for me to suggest it. Let's forget about it for now. I'll be heading back tomorrow morning. I'm sorry. Let me make it up to you just a little bit." Then Martha pulled over and announced, "Wally, you are going to learn to drive. I'm going to teach you to take sharp corners fast, just like when I teased you in the car. You know, when I spun the wheel hard and it threw you into the door." She continued. "I'm going to show you how to do certain things with a car, and then you can try them out for yourself."

Wally was exhilarated by the impromptu driving lesson. He watched Martha's every move until he took the wheel. Martha explained how *her Jack* was an incredible driver and how he had taught her everything. Excitedly, Martha told Wally about the adhesion of a tire on pavement versus loose gravel. She illustrated with her hands the apex of a turn, then taught Wally what understeer and oversteer meant. Next Martha explained engine rpm and when to upshift or downshift based on carefully listening to the motor. She explained how maintaining maximum torque would make for ideal acceleration. The curving roads of Jackson Park were the perfect testing ground for the boy's newly-learned skills.

After a couple of hours, Martha declared the lesson over. "It's time for us to go back, and you're going to drive us home! Use everything I just taught you and apply it. Let's see how fast you can get us there. Just be careful at intersections. You don't want to run anybody over, or crash the car." The aunt proved an excellent teacher; her nephew drove home masterfully. As they roared past the factories along the river, Wally heard Martha mutter softly, "You definitely could drive for Jack."

While stopped at an intersection, Martha lit a cigarette and began to enjoy the buzz of nicotine. Wally, having watched his friend Bobby smoke but never before tried, asked Aunt Martha if he could have one. Taking her cigarette from her mouth Martha gently placed it between Wally's lips. He could taste her lipstick—it felt intimate. He responded as if they had done this sharing thing a hundred times before, gently grasping the tobacco roll with his lips like an expert. Feeling a little dirty, he took a drag, then another.

Driving on in silence, except for a couple of coughs as the boy learned how to regulate the amount of smoke he inhaled, eventually Martha spoke about Indiana again. "Wally, I'm sorry you won't be able to come with me this time, but I'll tell Jack all about you, especially your talent for driving. I expect he'll agree with me, that you can help him with his business. But I can't promise you anything for certain. Tell you what, I'll get back here just as soon as possible and then take you back with me after I've squared it with Jack. You'll be sick of your place just as soon as I leave anyway, won't you?" Her confident laugh made Wally wonder how she knew so much about him and about...well, everything. Wally couldn't help but compare his aunt and his mother; one so worldly-wise and dynamic, and one so loving and sweet, but innocent and naive. He began to realize which type of woman he now preferred.

Rounding the corner to home, Wally blurted out, "I think I would be happier with you, Aunt Martha. I need a place to live away from that tyrant."

As Wally carefully guided the Oldsmobile to the curb, the now late afternoon sun hid behind the house providing a cool parking spot. Wally made a final request: "Please tell Jack about me as soon as you get back there. Tell him I'm ready to go to work for him right now."

"You can count on it, Wally. You have so many qualities and you have a natural talent for driving, too. Jack will like that. Maybe you can be his driver and apprentice. But you'll have to wait until I talk to him—and again, it will be up to him to decide. Just know that I want you with me, and I want you to get away from your parents, this terrible house, and the boys you told me about. When we're together in Indiana, you will be so much happier. I promise." Martha let her words sink in, then added, "Wally, you know another word for tyrant? It's monster." Martha's previous use of that term to now describe his own father was not lost on Wally.

Nephew and aunt slid out of the car and walked up to the front door of the home Peter worked so hard to afford. That place where the complete devotion of two parents deeply in love should serve as an ideal environment for the growth and happiness of all family members. But that was changing for Wally.

Martha opened the front door, yelling "We're back! We had such a great time!" She led the way through the living and dining rooms to the kitchen. All four younger children were at the table with Helen, strips of newspaper and tubs of gooey stuff covering the surface, with one partially finished creation in the middle.

Helen, beaming with pride and happiness said, "Martha, the children are making you a present. It's a papier-mâché Chicago Water Tower! Look at it, isn't it beautiful? The children knew how much you liked seeing the real thing with Wally, so they wanted to make you one to take home."

Her older sister looked upon the work, praising the children. "It's beautiful, kids. You are so thoughtful and artistic. I will cherish it forever." Smiling at them, she gently patted and kissed each head. Then looking at her sister, she blurted out, "Helen, guess what? Wally smoked a cigarette today! He is becoming such a man."

Helen's heart dropped. Neither she nor Peter smoked or drank, and Peter forbade these behaviors in his home. In fact, they demanded Martha smoke outside during her visit. Only Martha could take Helen from lofty joy to sadness with just a phrase.

CHAPTER 21

Wednesday, the day Wally learned to drive, the family rushed through dinner so Peter could be on time for his evening metallurgy class. The rest of the family then moved to the backyard to enjoy the pleasant evening sunset. It was the first cool evening in a week. While playing toss with his siblings, Wally looked up to the second-floor windows of the back porch where he noticed the one-time owner peering out upon the happy family. He saw the man quickly pull his head back inside when noticed. Wally gave little thought to the hermit upstairs, as he called him.

Old Mr. Feherty, home alone after his wife's sudden passing from influenza in April 1918, put on a friendly demeanor to all the first month. But when his son, Brian, a sergeant in the American Expeditionary Force died in May 1918 in the Allies' victory at Cantigny, France, he began the slow slide into silent despair. Selling his two-flat to his tenant, Peter, seemed a helpful tonic for Feherty. Peter, Helen, and Feherty enjoyed countless pleasant conversations sitting together in the first-floor kitchen evenings after a shared dinner. Mr. Feherty embraced them both, like his own son and daughter-in-law.

At first, observing the young couple's love brought him joy—but it would not remain so. For as he watched Wally grow up in the same yard where he raised his own son, eventually he could take no more. Peter's expanding family became only a painful reminder of his own loss. Feherty's invitations to visit ceased, and the couple's offers to dine on Helen's excellent cooking were rejected with various excuses until they knew to ask no more.

About the only time thereafter that Helen or Peter caught sight of Mr. Feherty was when milk was delivered two times a week to the first-floor apartment. They always promptly carried his single glass bottle up to the second floor, setting it next to his back door. Sometimes Feherty peered through the crack of the barely opened door, just as it was set on the threshold. Rarely did he allow his eyes to meet theirs.

For the six days of Martha's visit, she noted frequent visitors in suits, carrying groceries and briefcases up to the second floor, but gave it no thought. She remembered hearing something from Helen about some tragedy, but never cared enough to recall the details. To her, he was just some quirky old guy who never bothered anyone and some relatives brought him food. But his visitors always overtly stared at Martha, looking her over carefully like a bachelor sculptor, eyeing every detail of her face and body, in the hope to create perfection in marble.

Early Thursday morning, Peter bustled around the kitchen, humming while putting on the coffee pot. Martha, also awake, lay quietly in the rear bedroom listening carefully. Moments later, she heard Helen join him, stirring the kitchen to life. Then Martha's ears perked up at Helen's gentle sobbing. "What will we do with Wally when Martha's gone? How will we keep him occupied and out of trouble?"

Thinking everyone was sleeping, Peter whispered: "Wally will be fine, but something else is on my mind. Helen, we barely know anything about your sister. What does she do? Where did she get her car and all the money she flashes? I'm glad Wally's been sightseeing with her, but something isn't quite right."

"Oh, Peter. Please don't be suspicious. Martha is a very private person. She's just not ready to talk right now. I've asked and she promised to tell me soon. But now that she's leaving, what's Wally going to do all day?"

Peter groaned, then reassured his wife. "Tomorrow Wally has an appointment at the foundry to apply for some part-time work, maybe some groundskeeping, or filing, or cleaning up around the office. Don't worry. He won't get near the furnaces. I plan to tell him tonight. There was just too much going on around here to bring it up last night—the kids' gift for Martha, the cleanup of their mess, and then our rushed dinner as I hurried to school. Tonight will be peaceful, and I can discuss things with Wally without distraction. But please don't say anything to Wally—I want to surprise him. After I lost my temper, maybe this is the right opportunity to begin rebuilding our relationship."

Helen embraced Peter. "I hope so," she sighed.

"Since your sister is still in bed, say goodbye to her for me, please. I'm sure she'll be gone well before I return home." Looking at the clock on the kitchen wall, Peter kissed his innocent and patient wife and headed off to daily Mass and then the foundry.

Martha heard the front door shut firmly, which jarred all the others out of slumber. She joined Helen, Wally, and the little boys in the kitchen. The girls followed closely behind her. To Helen, everything seemed right with the world as her home fully sprang to life.

Martha started the conversation. "Helen, Wally should be kept busy while school's out. I don't know why Peter doesn't make him get a job." She let her words churn in her younger sister's mind. "You know, he might really benefit from joining me in Indiana." Wally assumed she was laying the mental groundwork for her next trip when she promised he could join her.

"Why don't you let him come with me this morning?" she urged. "Hey, that would be great. He doesn't have anything to do except hang out with that car thief and the big ox. There is brush to be cleared, trees to be felled, and firewood to be cut and stacked. Then there is always something to do with Jack's cars. Wally could learn a bit about auto mechanics, too. Helen, please say yes."

The younger sister sat speechless. Noticing Wally might be thinking the trip was possible, Helen spoke softly to her son. "Wally, no decision like this can be made without your father being involved. I'm sorry, Martha, but that's just how it is."

Martha zeroed in for the emotional kill. "I'm not sure it's safe for Wally to stay here. Why do you think I took him around town every day? I didn't want the tyrant to hurt him again. Don't you love your son enough to protect him?"

Helen began to panic. It wasn't her decision to make alone, and Peter was going to surprise Wally tonight—but her sister had just said horrible things about Peter in front of all the children. "Stop it, Martha! Peter loves Wally. I won't have you speak about him that way." Turning to her children, she continued. "Mommy and daddy love you all very much. Aunt Martha loves all of you too, she just doesn't know how much daddy loves all of you. Your daddy always knows what's best. He is the best daddy any child ever had. Now go wash up and get dressed." Slowly the four now confused younger children left the room.

His optimism primed, Wally tested his mother's resolve. "Mom, Aunt Martha said she would be coming back here soon.

She could bring me back in a few weeks. I could go with her, keep busy, and you would know I'd be safe. Just like she looked after you when you both came to America. I've got nothing to do around here anyhow. There doesn't seem to be any reason not to go. Anyway, I could just leave regardless of what you say. You can't stop me."

Martha could scarcely keep from grinning ear to ear as Helen blurted out, "You can't go, Wally! Your dad has a job lined up for you at the foundry. He was going to tell you all about it this evening after dinner. He wanted to surprise you. He doesn't have class tonight so you two can have a long talk. Tomorrow morning, they are expecting you to come to the office and fill out the job application."

Martha's clever little trap sprung, she forcefully directed her comments to Wally. "Listen to your mother, Wally. You can visit me in Indiana after you graduate high school. You'll be too busy working at the foundry or in school until then. What a shame, I so wanted you to spend some time with me there. But it's okay, you can do that later." With that she turned and walked to her temporary bedroom, taking her partially-packed suitcase from under the bed. Martha closed the bedroom door, but not quite all the way. She noticed Wally sitting in the line of sight to her bedroom door. So, she changed from her nightgown into her traveling attire very slowly, knowing full well that Wally could see her naked body through the cracked-open door.

Once fully dressed, Martha smiled her way back to the kitchen table, where Helen placed breakfast before her. Neither spoke. Wally sat silently, staring at his food, his emotions a jumbled mess. Finally, Wally tried to advance his goal. "Mom, if I go with Aunt Martha now, I'll be back in two or three weeks. Why couldn't I start working at the foundry then?"

Martha, smashing Wally's dream, jumped in before Helen could reply. "Wally, you have your answer. Don't press your mother any longer. Your father won't be home until dinner time and I'm leaving now. Your mother can't make this decision alone so just forget about it."

Disappointed and dejected, Wally departed for the living room, plopping onto the sofa. Back in the kitchen, Martha said to Helen, "Let me talk to the boy. I understand him and he trusts me. I'm sorry I brought up the whole idea of Wally going to Indiana. It's all my fault he's upset. I'll talk to him."

Martha walked in, and Wally stood up out of respect. As she approached him, she softly said, "We will have our time together soon." Martha produced a small matchbook from her pocket and tore off its cover. "Wally, this phone number is where you can reach me in Indiana. Do not give it to anyone else. And never call me on the weekend. Do you get it?" He nodded in agreement but Martha pressed, "Do you understand?"

Wally, realizing the importance of her question, offered his verbal answer like an oath: "Yes, I understand; I will not share it with anyone or call you on the weekend. Promise."

"Listen to your mother, for now," she concluded. Then Aunt Martha took his right hand and held it, staring into his eyes. Wally had never quite noticed how mesmerizingly green were her eyes. "I have the number for the phone booth at Lincolnway Pharmacy." She continued. "Now we know how to speak privately when necessary. When you need me, go there and call me in the morning at 8:00 a.m. If my roommate answers, tell her 'It's Wally calling for Martha, no message' then hang up. Say nothing else. Wait near the pharmacy's phone until 8:30 a.m. If I don't call you back, just call me again the next day." With that she drew him to her and hugged him firmly with her whole body, kissing his left cheek, then his right cheek. All he could think of was her perfect nude body he had seen minutes before. She brushed her mouth and nose with gentle breath against his ear driving the boy crazy, then suddenly pushed him away as if he had done something wrong.

Walking back into the kitchen, Martha gleefully told Helen, "Wally will be happy to stay and to work at the foundry. He was just a bit confused about the difference between a working vacation with me and a real job. I'll be off in a few minutes but will plan on visiting again real soon. And don't worry about Wally—I think I've got him thinking correctly."

CHAPTER 22

As Helen and her children stood at the open front door waving goodbye, the unusual aunt from Indiana raced off, heading north on Southport, turning east on Fullerton. Intending to check on the handsome pharmacist, Martha parked the Oldsmobile directly in front of Lincolnway. Entering boldly, exuding sex appeal wearing her most flattering dress, she immediately discovered the store empty except for Alvin. Lois was at nursing school.

"Good morning, miss," his excited voice rang out. "What may I help you with today? Oh, it's you, Wally's aunt. How's the boy doing?"

With her warmest smile she approached Alvin. "He is doing very well, thank you. There must have been something special in that salve you prescribed. The wound on his cheek from that monster is healing quite nicely." Martha helped herself to the stool nearest the proprietor. "I think your store is even more beautiful inside than I remember," Martha fawned. "Do you mind if I sit here for a few moments before I head back to Indiana? I have such a headache."

"Miss, I'm sorry but I'm not sure I can recall your name. I know I heard Wally say it, but I am not sure I have it right. Is it Martha?"

Crossing her legs, she let her skirt rise well above her knees, revealing perfectly toned legs as she offered, "Yes, what a fine memory. Please call me Martha." The man just stared—and she knew it.

"Okay, Martha. I will make you a customized mixture that will take care of your headache." Alvin placed a precise amount of salicylic acid granules and cocaine with an ample measure of Coke syrup and added carbonated water from his fountain, all poured over a bit of crushed ice and cherry juice. Placing a straw in it, he handed it to his lovely customer.

Martha sipped, then cooed, "I love the taste. It's sweet like you."

Glancing again at her legs, Alvin chuckled, "You don't have to butter me up. Let's see if it helps your headache. Anyway, for someone as special as you, the first one is on the house. Afterward, even you pay retail!" They laughed in unison.

While they were flirting with each other, the door of the pharmacy opened and Wally burst in. "Aunt Martha!" he exclaimed as he raced to her.

"Hey, Wally. Be careful. At least let me get on my own two feet before you maul me. Why are you here?" she demanded.

"I wanted to check on our phone booth, make sure it works. That's all. I had no idea you would be here," her nephew replied. Alvin stepped closer, taking a look at Wally's cheek. "That cut looks fine, Wally. Looks fine. Don't worry about the phone booth, it's public. It works. It's not going anywhere." He then turned to Martha, "Please feel free to sit here as long as you like. You too, Wally. I have several customers waiting for their prescriptions, so please excuse me while I go back to my work. Let me know if you need something else."

Sitting next to his aunt, Wally began to probe. "I guess I can't go with you today, huh? Do you really think you will be back in two weeks? How long will you stay? What if I want to go with you then?"

Now Martha lowered her voice—attempting, but failing—to prevent Alvin from overhearing. "Wally my love, we have been over this. You will have another chance. Even if you take that stupid job at the foundry, you can quit and come live with me later. Now do what I tell you. This is not the time."

The mortar and pestle in his hands, Alvin shook his head in disbelief.

Just then a customer came in, interrupting their private conversation. Martha recognized him as one of the men who visited the hermit upstairs. He approached while slowly looking over Wally and his aunt. "Good morning, Alvin. Is the medication ready for Mr. Feherty, please?"

Looking up, Alvin replied: "Yes, it almost is, Mr. Green. Please give me just a moment to complete the formulation I am blending now. I will have the order bagged up for you in just a minute or two. Sit down, if you like." Removing his fedora, the suit-wearing stranger sat down next to Wally. "Good morning, young man. Good morning, miss. Don't you both live in the building with Mr. Feherty?"

"Yes, I do. My name is Wally. This is my Aunt Martha. She's just visiting us from Indiana," Wally offered innocently while Martha turned away.

"Nice to meet you Wally and Aunt Martha. Hey, Aunt Martha, do you have a last name? I would not wish to be disrespectful or presumptuous, Miss...?"

Martha just ignored him. She did not like young, eager men wearing suits asking questions unless she initiated the conversation. He seemed a bit too nosey and forward with his way of asking her name. As the final word left his mouth, the little spring-loaded bell on the front door jingled, breaking the tension and saving Martha from responding to the young man's question. As an older couple entered, they greeted Alvin and immediately asked for Lois.

With that, the upstairs visitor, Mr. Green stood up and smiled at the elderly woman, nodding his head in respect, he offered a warm, "Good morning, folks, here take my seat. I think my order is ready, please excuse me."

Alvin was just coming from behind his counter with the prescription for Mr. Feherty. "Here you go, Mr. Green. Tell Mr. Feherty, I hope he feels better soon."

From their adjoining seats at the counter, the elderly couple tried to engage Martha in the polite, perfunctory conversation of strangers while Wally sat there, despondent. Alvin, never missing anything, easily saw the desperation on the youngster's face. So, the pharmacist came around his work counter to the fountain without saying a word, smiling broadly, and quickly prepared beverages for Wally and the two new arrivals. Setting a chocolate phosphate in front of Wally he asked, "Wally, you were so helpful to me in the past; I remain grateful. Here is your favorite chocolate soda. You know that I am here all the time, and I hope you'll come by and enjoy something from the fountain more often. We can talk about your heroic actions to save those dogs, or anything else. How does that sound?" The boy did not answer; he just stared at the countertop.

Martha extended her hand to Alvin, grasping it gently. "I look forward to seeing you the next time I'm in town in a couple of weeks." She was slow to let go. "You are marvelous—my headache is gone." Turning to her nephew, she touched his shoulder advising him not to rise. "And you, my love, call me anytime you need me, just like we discussed. Okay?" Moving gracefully, she sashayed down the aisle and out the door, leaving the devastated boy both deflated for the moment but hopeful for what would take place in two weeks.

Looking more closely at Wally, the elderly man asked, "Hey, aren't you the guy that beat up the drunken dog-hater on Southport? Did he give you that cheek or did that brute Sergeant Fitzgerald do it?" Ignoring his questioner, Wally sat staring at the heartless door that enabled his beloved aunt's exit. As the elderly man repeated his questions, the boy stood up and rudely walked out without reply. Then the man turned to Alvin instead. "Isn't that the tough Polish kid who saved those two shepherd dogs?"

CHAPTER 23

As Wally headed back from the pharmacy, he saw Ziggy walking up Southport on the way to Bobby's house and dashed after him. Arriving simultaneously, Wally punched Ziggy in the shoulder. "Ha, I got here first!"

"Holy shit! What happened to your face? Where the hell have you been, Wally?" Ziggy demanded, then pushed him with both hands, as the two began to spar.

"Let's go, Bobby," impatiently echoed in the gangway as Wally modified the calling protocol in between the jabs, hooks, and crosses. All done with open hands, the quicker Wally frustrated Ziggy who took a few slaps while Wally remained untouched. Then Ziggy bull-rushed his boxing partner and bear hugged him to stop the slaps to his face. At the sound of their friend bounding down the stairs, they stepped to opposite sides of the back door, ready to ambush.

Bobby exited. They pummeled their friend with jabs to his arms, chest, and stomach.

With a voice not quite angry, but somehow a little sinister, Bobby demanded: "Okay, knock it off. You both are just afraid to take me on solo—my fists break bones!" As quickly as they started, the boys stopped their assault, and Bobby led the way out of the gangway to the street. "Wait until you guys see what I have! Come on! Let's head up to Weber's Billiards Hall. I've got something to show you."

It was early in the day, and some of the local Poles had gathered to shoot pool. Of the two rows of six tables each, only three tables were occupied, so the proprietor didn't mind the teens hanging out. Bobby led his friends through the cloud of tobacco smoke to the rear of the hall to the worst table—the one least used by the regulars because the stench of cigarette butts and spittoons was most offensive there—but it was the most private. Bobby sat on one of the high stools against the wall, reached into his pocket, and produced a small metal ring holding two keys. "You know what these are?" He scanned his friends' faces. "They are keys to the door of a business around here. And I'm not telling you which...at least not yet." Staring gleefully at Wally, Bobby changed the subject. "I heard you got clocked by your old man. One of the guys at the foundry heard about it and told my old man when they were getting drunk at Greenwood Inn. But I didn't tell anyone what I heard. Is that what happened to your face?"

"You ask me about my cheek again and I'll punch your lights out, understand? Now, what are those keys for?"

"Violence begets violence, huh Wally? Give it some more thought, boy. I don't care how strong you are or how fast. You try to knock me out and I'll break your jaw."

Interceding, Ziggy stepped between them, facing Bobby. "Hey, don't worry about it. Wally didn't really mean it. He is just messed up a little right now. He had to spend six days with his aunt, and his old man beat him. You'd be all messed up too. Okay?"

The angry boy just stared back at Ziggy. "You better not mess with me either, got it?" Quickly regaining his composure, he added, "Okay, Wally. Okay, Ziggy. Let's just forget about it. I won't kill either of you. I need you for a special job anyway." Bobby took out a half-empty pack of cigarettes and lit one, surprised when Wally asked for one too. "Nice—you finally learned how to smoke, tough guy?" Bobby asked, handing his friend a Camel.

"Thanks. I've learned a lot more than just how to smoke." Wally said. "Now what's this job?"

Bobby looked each boy in the eyes, as he whispered. "We're going to rob the liquor store. Do you know how much money he keeps in the cash register? A lot. Especially after payday at the foundry. And if we each carry two cases of whiskey on our way out, we can sell them for a lot more money. And we don't have to break in, we just let ourselves in."

Thinking his friend was insincere, Wally chuckled, "Yah, just act like we own the place! If we had a car, we could take a lot more than just two cases each. Too bad Aunt Martha left, or we could borrow her car. Now, how did you get the keys?"

Incredulous, Bobby replied, "If we had a car, one of us would have to know how to drive, you idiot. Anyway, I saw the keys just left in the back door a couple of nights ago so I took them. That dipshit must have been drunk when he left for the night. I came back the next morning and laughed my ass off as I watched him try to get into his own store. It was great! Then he had to call a locksmith to get in. I couldn't stop laughing."

Wally glared confidently at his friends. "I learned to drive. My aunt taught me. She spent hours teaching me. I learned how to power through a turn—how to fight understeer and oversteer. I learned how to downshift to gain power when it's needed. You two are just losers!"

Ziggy chimed in, "You really learned to drive?"

"Ya, Ziggy. I did." Wally realized Bobby was in earnest so he continued. "First, Bobby, how do you know the locks were not rekeyed? The locksmith might have changed out the lock cylinders so your keys won't work. You think this is simple?"

Growing annoyed, Bobby glared at his friend. "You think you're so smart. I don't need you to pull this off."

Wally shot back before Bobby got the last syllable of his reply out of his mouth. "Okay, maybe not, but maybe you do and don't realize it. You need to go there and try those keys, both the front and the back doors. Do it really late. Have Ziggy stand watch from about fifty feet away. Best if he is across the street. He should be able to see the alley, you, and the storefront from the southwest corner. Ziggy, you'll start screaming if someone is coming toward the store. Drop to the curb and yell that you twisted your ankle. Keep screaming how much it hurts; they will lock their eyes on you and that will give Bobby the sign to move away from the door. Otherwise, just hang in the shadows."

"Okay, okay, me and Ziggy can do that. Then what?" asked the boy with the keys.

Taking a deep breath, now wanting to be part of the contemplated crime, Wally offered, "We can't assume anything, Bobby. Until we know the keys work, we do nothing. But if we're lucky and can get in, we have to watch the place carefully for several days. We must know what days Thompson goes to the bank. And the schedule for every liquor delivery, and even the coal delivery for the building. Maybe his boiler is kept running all year for hot water." The two other boys were now hanging on Wally's every word.

"There is so much more! We have to know when the other nearby tenants come and go. We must know what cops are on the beat each day and know their schedules too. Then we have to know if the owner has more money right before payday for cashing checks, or if he has more money after his sales rush on the weekend after payday. We are only going to do it once, so we have to be smart about it. And where are we going to get a car?"

Mouths agape, the two other boys listened intently. "I can drive, but stealing a car would really complicate our plan. The cops would be on the hunt for the stolen car probably by the time we left the liquor store with the booze. I've got to think about how we swing that part."

Bobby objected. "But everybody likes booze, Wally. We'll be there. We have to take some."

Condescendingly, Wally snapped back. "Then there is the matter of reselling the booze, you dope. Where are we going to keep it? Moreover, Bobby, ask yourself who is going to buy a bunch of stolen whiskey from three Polack punks? Most tough guys would take it from us and then anonymously call the cops, informing them we stole everything. The cops would find us with the cash and whatever booze you kept for yourself. Then you'd go to jail."

Ziggy mumbled his concerns. "I don't want to go to jail. Maybe this is not a good idea. I don't want to get caught."

Now embarrassed at the simplicity of his thinking, the key thief sided with Ziggy. "Maybe this isn't gonna be as easy as I thought. I don't want to go to jail either."

Wally smirked. "Not easy doesn't mean impossible, Bobby. It just means we will also need alibis. All three of us, independent from one another. The minute we claim we were together—to be each other's alibis—the cops would split us up, and question us until one of us made a mistake. THEN we'd ALL go to jail. We each need our own white lie. Something every parent would believe and confirm for each of us when the cops questioned them. Got it? Now, who's the idiot?"

Bobby looked at his friend, with a smile saying: "I'm glad I didn't kill you. You're so smart. You're going to be a big deal one day, boy. Like usual, it will be best if you run the show." Standing up and offering his handshake to the others, with the intent to create the irrevocable bond of criminal youth, Bobby suggested, "Were doing it! Let's go get a Coca-Cola from Lincolnway. We can keep planning our special project there."

Wally objected. "I was there earlier today; I don't want to go back. You guys go without me. And don't do anything— nothing. And don't talk about our project in public. Not even if Lincolnway is empty. That creep Alvin can hear everything that's said in his place, even when its whispered. He's got the ears of an alley cat."

Wally waited at the corner to catch the streetcar. Bobby punched Ziggy in the stomach as they shuffled off, jostling and jabbing at each other all the way to Lincolnway.

CHAPTER 24

The teens had sat there for almost an hour planning how to spend their riches and drinking Coke while thumbing mindlessly through newspapers left on the counter by others. The two would-be thieves got up to leave as Lois returned from school. She skipped in joyfully while Ziggy held the door for her. Greeting the lone customer seated near the pharmacy, Lois placed her hand on Alvin's back, kissing his cheek without distracting him from his work. "Good afternoon, Mr. Green," she called out, sweetly. "How is Mr. Feherty feeling?"

He smiled at the beautiful Frenchwoman. "Mr. Feherty says he is feeling better, but I'm not so sure. I was here this morning to pick up his doctor's prescription, but when I met with him, he seemed slightly delirious. I took his temperature, and his fever was high. His cough is worse. The doctor sent another prescription to Alvin. That's why I'm here again. But after I deliver it, I've got to get back to my office before it gets too late."

Lois began to question Mr. Green about the symptoms. He politely complied, then chuckled, "Sounds to me like you're going to be a doctor one day yourself, Lois. Goodness Alvin, how did you get so lucky, finding a woman so brilliant, charming, and beautiful?"

Having the new medicine bottled and bagged, Alvin handed it to Green, quipping, "The French still owed us for all that help we gave them in the war. Since that big statue in New York they gave us way back when wasn't enough, they shipped over some of the finest people in their country."

Green grinned. "Actually," Alvin continued, "we met at a baseball game. I accidentally bumped into Lois and her uncle, François, while reaching for a foul ball. I caught it, but almost knocked her to the ground. I apologized and handed the baseball to her. I don't know if it was love at first sight, or the bribe of the round souvenir. But anyway, it worked out, didn't it?"

Mr. Green's smile remained as he strolled toward the door. Alvin continued calling out instructions. "Please give our best wishes for a speedy recovery to Mr. Feherty. Tell him if he should begin feeling worse, he should call me at the phone number there on the label. It doesn't matter what time he needs us; the pharmacy phone rings in our apartment too."

As the door shut behind Green, the newlywed couple finally had the place to themselves for just a moment. They embraced and shared a long, loving kiss. In each other's embrace, they found the temporary escape of love's perfect bliss. It blotted out the existence of anything but their two love-filled hearts—a profound, joyful peace that made them impervious to anything the world might dump on them. It was the magic that filled the pharmacy with invisible, but palpable, peace. Gazing into her husband's eyes, Lois whispered. "I am certain of it. We are going to have a baby, Alvin!"

The sound of the back door opening snapped them back to reality. Gently releasing Lois from his hug, Alvin offered a joint pledge, "This shall be our secret for just a short time more, okay?" Smiling, Lois nodded yes.

Apologizing for her delay, Lois rushed to Joe, hugging him gently. Alvin was right behind to shake his hand. "Joe, it's so great to see you again. We are on for Tuesday dinner, right?"

Embarrassed at his interruption of the couple's private moment of affection, Joe cracked his form of broken smile. "I'm sorry, I didn't mean to intrude. I'll be on my way."

"Nonsense, Joe. You're not interrupting anything but a simple greeting. Now, are we on for Tuesday?" Alvin repeated.

"Yes, I am looking forward to it. What may I bring?"

"Now you just bring yourself and a big appetite," Lois replied warmly. "We are so excited to have you as a guest for dinner. We hope you will be able to spend some time visiting with us after dinner, too." His embarrassment at interrupting their private moment, along with the couple's kindness and generosity, were almost too much for Joe's scarred heart to bear. After all, for sixteen years he lived without friends. Moving toward the back door, Lois pursued him, gently taking his hand. "Joe, please stay for a little while. I'll make you something from the fountain. Now, please come with me and sit down."

Joe reluctantly obeyed his hostess, taking the seat nearest the phone booth and back door. "Excuse me a moment. I need to call John Schmidt. It will only take a moment." Gliding the phone booth door open, Joe entered, dropped the required coins into the device and slid the bifold door shut. Lois and Alvin were a bit too far away to hear anything but muffled, unintelligible words as Joe carefully cupped the receiver with his hand.

As Joe popped back out after only a minute as promised, Alvin inquired, "Joe, did you notice anything unusual or unique about the phone itself or the booth? Or is it just like every other one you've used?"

Surprised by the odd question, Joe just stared back. "Unusual? No. Why? Was I supposed to see something unusual?"

"Not really, Joe. I guess I let my imagination get away from me, that's all. That boy Wally just said something odd. Forget about it." Alvin instantly changed the topic. "Joe, did I ever tell you how Lois and I met?" Sipping his fizzy cup of pleasure Lois had just placed on the counter as he exited the phone booth, Joe shook his head no. Just then the front door's bell tinkled. Joe rose immediately.

Lois grabbed his hand. "Joe, you don't want to hurt Alvin's feelings—once he starts telling that story of how we met, he won't stop. Just let him run through it, and then ask him to also tell you when I met his aunt and uncle the first time. That will teach him a lesson." She broke away to help the lone customer who was in and out in just a few moments, picking up a couple of sundries from the quartersawn oak shelves nearest the front door. Pressing the cash register drawer closed after the transaction, she raced back to Joe and Alvin.

Joe was laughing, a lot more than she had ever heard him do before. "Alvin told me something different, that's for sure. He told me how his Aunt Ruth kept calling you François instead of Lois. She didn't know the difference between François and Francoise! And then she kept calling your uncle Louis." He looked at Lois, saying: *"Respectez le nom ansi que la personne."*

Lois, smiling from ear to ear, said "Yes, respect the name and so too the person." I did not know you speak French."

"I rarely have a chance to use it. I am so glad I can with you," Joe replied.

"Oh, my goodness, Joe, what other surprises do you have for us? Or do we have to wait for dinner?"

With his crooked, broken smile Joe said, *"Rispetta il nome e così anche la persona."* Wide-eyed, Lois stared at him with amazement, asking, "Italian also?"

Slurping up the last of his phosphate, Joe allowed the sound to echo out of the glass with the amusement of a child. He laughed again. "My Italian is not as good as my French." Putting two nickels on the counter for the five-cent drink, he thanked them as he headed to the back hallway. Alvin realized he had never seen Joe that happy before. "Can't wait for Tuesday, *mon ami!*" Lois chirped loudly as the back door swung shut behind the odd man.

CHAPTER 25

While his friends planned and schemed at Lincolnway, Wally waited on the street corner to catch the electric trolley—one of those red streetcars running under the maze of crackling overhead power lines as sparks showered to the ground. Wally noticed the air held that odd smell of high voltage running through uninsulated wires. It was a hot, metallic odor similar to that which sometimes permeated his father's clothes after work. The driver rang the trolley's bell frantically as it approached the corner on which Wally stood, waiting, as he saw a delivery wagon blocking the way. Finally responding to the bell's clanging, the wagoner and horse cleared the intersection before disaster occurred. Relieved, Wally was almost as fond of horses as he was dogs.

Wally would travel east, then south to the Loop where he could double-transfer his way to 11th & State, the location of the new police headquarters. He had no idea where the dogs were being kept or who could help him find them. But he figured he would act like he always did—like he owned the place. He would go right to the top, to the new headquarters building and ask to see the guy in charge of the police dogs.

Confidently, Wally walked through the front door and approached the elevated, broad desk that blocked his path. "I saved two Alsatians about a week ago. I've come to check on them. I'd like to see the person in charge of your police dogs, please."

The three officers sitting behind the desk chuckled, looking at each other. "Young man, do you see any dogs around here?" quipped one. The other two snickered. He continued, "We'll keep an eye open for your dogs. What were they, ghost hounds or insane spaniels?" Now they all laughed loudly until the spokesman got serious. "Take this missing property form and fill it out. Try to give a good description—most dogs look a lot alike."

Wally objected, controlling his anger. "Sir, I am not looking for missing dogs. They are two Alsatians that were going to be destroyed. I heard that once it was discovered they had some training, both would be turned over to a police lieutenant who trained dogs in the army. A week ago, two officers in a paddy wagon took them away from my backyard on Southport Avenue."

"Son, there are no police dogs or kennels here. This is police headquarters. There is a multi-purpose police warehouse near the Central Manufacturing District. Do you know 47th Street and Ashland? It's not too far away. Maybe the dogs are there."

"Yes, sir. Is there a streetcar that runs on 47th or on Ashland?" Wally asked, feeling like he might be making progress.

The cop snapped, "Alright, get lost kid. Figure out the trolley lines for yourself. What do I look like, a transit map? Get your ass out of here before I show you what the inside of a cell looks like." Holding a long, angry gaze he eventually turned his back on Wally and walked from the counter to a doorway and disappeared.

Wally knew he would make no progress with the other two cops who looked more annoyed with him than the first, so he walked out the way he came in, took out a cigarette from the first pack he had ever bought and lit it. Leaning against the wall, a few feet from the entrance he pondered his situation. He knew he could not make the trip to the Central Manufacturing District without more time, accurate information, and more money for trolley fares—he only had enough change in his pocket to get back home. And if he did figure out exactly where the police warehouse was, there was no guarantee his dogs would be there. So, he finished his smoke and used his remaining change to get back to his own neighborhood.

The mental turmoil of his world continued to increase. Wally's failed search for Potato and Carrot only made things worse. Anxious and feeling abandoned, he needed Aunt Martha more than ever.

Not knowing what to do, Wally's heart plummeted. He jumped back on the trolley line to head home, where he did not want to be. Staring out the window as each unique streetscape passed, he saw nothing—the stream of buildings, pedestrians, wagons, horses, and motorized vehicles at every bustling intersection all became invisible. He recalled how Aunt Martha talked of living large one day, and he knew the first step would be getting money—lots of money. Would Bobby and Ziggy be reliable, he wondered?

Once home, Wally did not engage in conversation with his mother. He waited on the back porch, sitting on the top step to the first-floor landing, his mind working on his problem until his thoughts were interrupted by his father's entrance. Today he stunk mostly from sweat.

"Hello, son," Peter greeted pleasantly. "Move over and let me sit next to you. I left the foundry a little early today so you and I could speak before dinner. I have some good news for you. You will report to Millicent, the office manager at Schmidt Foundry tomorrow morning. They need a porter to clean around the office and do some filing. It's a great opportunity for you to earn a little money and get some experience. You will need to fill out an application and speak to both Millicent and Mr. Schmidt. Nothing is guaranteed, but you will have a good shot."

Staring at the steps beneath him, Wally replied, "Yeah, I know. Mom told me after you went to work. I suppose I have to go, huh? Because I'm your son, huh? Fine."

Peter considered what he had just heard from Mr. Schmidt about his commanding officer. The father tried to listen more closely to his son than he had ever done before. "Were you surprised when your mother told you, Wally?" He asked.

"I guess. I wish you would have asked me first," Wally replied curtly.

Peter, trying to respect his son's expectation for prior notice of such planning of his life, continued, "Son, you must work this summer. If you do well, you will have opportunities to work part time after you go back to school in the fall. I hoped you would be excited. Why aren't you more enthusiastic? I would like to understand you better."

"Why do you think I would want to work in that foundry? Why would I want to work where you work, anyway?"

Peter changed course, realizing Wally was not yet thinking correctly. "Wally, there is still the matter of your running away instead of completing your punishment. You have not yet washed the walls and floors of this house, and since Martha brought you back home, you did not remain grounded as ordered." Growing angrier with each second, Peter demanded, "Why is it so difficult for you to make the right choices? Why are you so unwilling to obey and respect your parents?"

"I don't know—okay?" Wally snapped back. "What time do I need to show up tomorrow?"

While the fury of a disrespected father grew, somehow Peter kept his composure. "Show up at 8:15 a.m. Millicent starts at 8:00 a.m. She wants you to arrive after she has organized her plans for the day. But before anything else, you will complete your punishment. You will start cleaning after you come home from your interview and clean straight through until done."

"Fine," Wally sulked. He got up and walked down the stairs to the backyard. There he lit a cigarette—he knew it would piss off his father. Soon he would speak with Aunt Martha, to discuss the dogs, the job opportunity, and the keys Bobby found. She would know what to do about all these things. Tomorrow morning could not come too quickly.

CHAPTER 26

Friday morning found Wally waiting at the entrance of Lincolnway Pharmacy just before its opening at 8:00 a.m. As Alvin unlocked the door, the boy walked by the pharmacist without greeting him, pushed his way through the bifold door, then slammed it shut. He dropped in the coins and dialed. A stranger answered—he had to leave a message. Wally then made his way to the stool nearest the phone booth to wait for a call back. Aunt Martha's instructions were for him to wait until 8:30 for a return call. His wait until 8:40 a.m. proved futile.

Walking out silently, just as he had entered, the boy made the ten-minute walk to the foundry. Finding his way through the guest entrance to the office, he arrived at 8:55 a.m. "Good morning, ma'am. I am here to see Millicent. Can you help me? Where is she, please?" He thought the diminutive, gray-haired old woman couldn't be anyone important.

Millicent, amused and annoyed, stared at the boy long enough to make him uncomfortable. She began to toy with him. "Tell me, why do you want to see Millicent, young man?" Although she appeared elderly and tiny, her voice was powerful.

"I have an appointment to speak with her about working here. Can you help me, please?" Wally replied. "Will you let her know I'm here?"

"What time is your appointment and what is your name?" she teased.

"I am Peter's son, Wally. I was told to not come here before 8:15 so Millicent could prepare for her day. I thought I should give her plenty of time, so here I am now. I figured forty-five minutes to an hour would be courteous." Wally answered smoothly, almost convincingly enough that Millicent might have thought he believed what he was saying.

"See the desk over in the corner, Wally?" Millicent said, pointing to the rear wall of the general office. "Fill out this application and place it back on my desk when you have completed it fully. Then, you will have a chance to speak to Millicent." She watched Wally scramble to find a pencil—he did not bring his own. After letting him search the area with his eyes, she called out, "You may take a pencil from this desk. Just return it when done."

Finishing quickly with legible cursive belying his age and powerful build, he placed the application on the desk as instructed. "May I speak with Millicent now, please?" Wally requested.

"Sit down here and tell me about yourself," she instructed.

"Yes, ma'am, but will I then see Millicent?"

With a wry smile, the woman replied, "Wally, I am she." Pausing long enough to see the redness of embarrassment to flush fully on the boy's face, she continued. "Your father would have told you your appointment was 8:15 a.m. He is completely reliable. Now, I want to know why you were forty minutes late. Why, Wally?"

Unwilling to admit his failure, he explained: "Yes, ma'am, my father is very reliable. He told me you start at 8:00 a.m. but needed at least fifteen minutes to organize your day. He was not clear that my appointment was at a specific time. If he had been, I would have been here at that time. I was truly trying to be courteous, ma'am." Barely taking a breath, he continued laying it on thick. "I was up early this morning 'cause I couldn't sleep over the excitement of this opportunity. I could easily have been here at seven o'clock, if so instructed. I would never want to be late for an important meeting like this. Perhaps I misunderstood my father; he and I talked about so many things. To the extent I misunderstood and inconvenienced you, I sincerely apologize, ma'am."

Millicent was impressed with his polite ways, and his explanation seemed reasonable, but she knew Peter too well.

He would have been clear. After all, Peter had asked for this opportunity.

Long skilled at handing every kind of excuse spewed by steelworkers, she then pushed the boy. "Wally, do you realize that mistakes, like not clearly understanding instructions, can be very serious in a foundry? Even for a porter or entry-level clerk." Too aggressively impatient for his reply, she continued, "Failure to follow instructions can have serious consequences. For example, Mr. Schmidt no longer has time to meet with you today." She let the news hang in the air as she watched the mental gears turning through Wally's eyes. Millicent, now tightened the screws on him just a bit more. "Wally, many employees' sons want this job, as do the countless unemployed adult men. Why would I recommend you to Mr. Schmidt if you can't even be on time for your first interview? I tell you what, Wally. I know Mr. Schmidt is already at his 9:00 a.m. appointment with Fritz and his apprentice." Seeing the subtle twitch on the boy's face, she knew her choice of words was not lost on him. She continued, "I'll catch him later and tell him my recommendation—to interview the other boys and then send to him the one I think is our best candidate."

Having been emotionally drawn and quartered by a shrewd business woman, Wally humbly replied, "Thank you for your time, ma'am. I am truly sorry I misunderstood my appointment time. When should I call you to learn of your selection? I am very interested in the job."

Millicent could not resist one last verbal jab. "Wally, if we want you to come back, I'll tell your father. And don't worry, later today when I see him, I'll tell him about our time together. Now I have much to do. Please go out the way you came in."

Doing his best to think on his feet, Wally got in the last word. "Yes, ma'am. And thank you very much for the opportunity. I am very sorry if I inconvenienced you or Mr. Schmidt."

Having fed on disappointment at 8:00 a.m. and humiliation at 9:00 a.m., Wally's emotional devastation was complete. He wandered out of the office and north to Bobby's house. His overdue punishment was the furthest thing from his mind. "Yo, Bob-by," Wally shouted. He lit a Camel; the igniting sulfur of the match head illuminated his face just as Bobby came out.

"Hey, what's up, boy?" Bobby asked. "Let me have a smoke? You know what I did last night? I checked the keys—they work! Both doors. Know what, Wally? I'm ready to go. You want to grab Zig?"

"No, leave him out of this. You and I need to talk first," Wally replied. "Who do you think will crack if the coppers lean on each of us? We both know they'll cross him up with lots of questions and a few smacks with a rubber hose. We have to plan this and only tell Ziggy what he needs to know. If he doesn't know anything else, it will be harder for him to screw things up. Got it?" Bobby nodded. "You never should have included him when you told me about the keys. You should have come to me first. I think we need to string him out with delays and finally make him think there is no way we would ever rob the store. Now, how are we going to do that and still pull it off? I'll tell you how; I've got to make him think someone else did it."

Bobby just beamed at his friend. "You're amazing! You got it figured out already, I'll bet!"

Wally's focus intensified. "No, I don't, but I will. Did Ziggy go with you last night to check the locks?"

"No. Look, there was a full moon. I couldn't sleep," Bobby explained as he flipped the two keys between his fingers. "It was so hot inside, even with all the fans running, I just went outside and started to walk. It was dead. I mean nobody was around, so I just slipped into the shadows. I leaned against each door and took in everything with my eyes and ears—for a long time. When I was sure no one was around, I slipped the key in, turned it, and bang! I knew what we needed to know. I didn't hardly push either door open—just a crack to be sure."

Wally snapped at his friend. "Okay, Bobby. So, you didn't even follow my first instructions. Now I'm supposed to trust you to follow the rest? No way, man, I'm done with this crap." He turned and began to walk away.

His rage building, Bobby called out as he started after his friend. "Wait, don't you dare walk away from me! Wally, you stop and face me like a man!" Secretly, Bobby pulled out a roll of nickels from his pocket and tightly gripped it in his right hand. As Wally turned around, Bobby swung at him with his weighted fist, clipping Wally's chin but not making full contact as Wally instinctively pulled his head back. What happened next, Bobby would not remember for several minutes. He woke up, finding himself face down on the sidewalk. A passing neighborhood lady stood over him, repeatedly asking if he was okay. As he staggered to his feet, he reached in his pocket. The keys were gone! His secret roll of nickels, also missing. "He's dead," Bobby mumbled as he brushed himself off. Then he snarled, "Hey, get away from me, lady!"

Bobby walked into Lincolnway, his mouth and nose pouring blood, his eyes blackened, and his shirt torn to shreds, unable to hide the bruises on his ribs from Wally's kicks.

Alvin started to walk around his work area, heading toward the boy who was apparently in dire need, but Bobby rebuked him. "Don't worry, I'm fine. I almost got run over by the damn trolley. It hit me kinda sideways and knocked me onto the sidewalk. I gotta use your bathroom."

"Sure, you remember where it is, right?" Alvin replied as he watched the boy carefully. "I have plenty of crushed ice. You wash up. I'll get a rag full of ice for your face." As the boy came out of the bathroom, Alvin gave him the ice pack. Then he brought him a chair from the pharmacy area. "Here, I want you to sit in this chair and lean back a little. Put the pack across the bridge of your nose. It's big enough so it will flop under both eyes." Putting the chair in between a wall and one of the cabinets, he knew Bobby could safely lean back without risk of falling. "Bobby, I have to ask you some important questions. First, how is your vision? Is it blurry or clear? And then I also need to know if you have a headache. What day is this? Okay, can you tell me these things now?"

Bobby answered calmly. "Sure, my vision is okay, but my face and jaw hurt. I don't really have a headache. And it's Friday, moron. Why are you asking me this stupid shit?"

Ignoring the insolence but pleased the boy seemed okay, Alvin replied, "That's great! You probably don't have a concussion. Now, keep the pack on your face; it will keep the swelling down and relieve some of the pain. It will help your fat lip, too. Don't talk too much right now. I'll be right behind the counter keeping an eye on you. Try to leave the ice on your face for as long as you can tolerate the cold. Then take it off for a few minutes, but after your skin warms up a bit, put it right back on. Alternate like this, two or three times. I'll mix you up something from the soda fountain."

Walking to the coat rack hidden deep in the recesses of his pharmaceutical storage shelves, Alvin grabbed a clean short-sleeve, white pharmacist's shirt, tossing it on Bobby's lap. "Put this on. Cover yourself up a little, you look terrible." He checked his watch. "Okay now, that's about long enough for the ice. Take it off for a couple of minutes then I'll get you a fresh pack. The trolleys are pretty loud! How did this happen?"

Bobby complied. "I was being chased by somebody. I ran between a couple of cars to get away from him. He had a knife. When he saw me knocked up and over the curb and onto the sidewalk by the trolley, I guess he thought I was dead, so he left. The trolley driver must not have even known he hit me 'cause he didn't stop. I don't think he stopped, anyway."

Shocked, Alvin demanded, "Did you know the man with the knife? Who was he? I need to call the police. Who was it? Do you know?"

"It was Wally," Bobby answered. "You know, the guy who beat the hell out of his neighbor. He has a crazy temper. I thought he was my friend."

Alvin picked up the phone and dialed. Minutes later a beat cop walked into the pharmacy—the same one who interrogated Wally days before. "Okay, what's going on here that I need to know about? Oh shit! Who gave you that face, kid?"

Bobby pulled open his borrowed shirt to reveal large bruised areas on both sides of his ribs. "You know Wally? He chased me with a knife. I ran between two cars to try to get away from him, and I got clipped by a trolley on Fullerton. Half a step further into the street, I'd be dead."

The officer had heard all he needed to know. "Thanks for the explanation. I'll need to take down some facts including your full name and address." He said, as he pulled out a notepad from his shirt pocket. "Tell me about the knife. Describe its size, shape, the color of the handle, anything you can. Exactly where did this happen? Why did Wally threaten you with it?"

Bobby laid it on thick. "Wally told me to stop talking to this girl he likes, but she doesn't even know he's alive. I told him she liked somebody else but he wouldn't listen. Today, when I told him she was going out with this older German kid, he went crazy. I guess he blamed me, I don't know. When I yelled at him that he was stupid for liking a girl who didn't like him, he pulled out a knife and started waving it in my face, so I ran." When asked for a description of the knife, Bobby described a fixed-blade hunting knife with a jigged-bone handle he had once seen in the hardware store.

CHAPTER 27

In the time it took Bobby to recover from the sidewalk beating, Wally made it home. He silently snuck up the rear stairs, went to his room, and changed out of his bloody clothes. The walk had cooled off his temper just enough for him to start thinking about his most immediate situation. Entering through the back door into the kitchen after changing, hiding his hands in his pockets, Wally called to his mom: "It's me—I'm home. I did not get the job yet. I won't know anything more about it until next week. I have to start washing the walls now. What soap do I use and where do you want me to start?" Instructions received, Wally ignored his mother's questions about the interview and just kept working. "Okay, Ma. I'll tell you everything when dad gets home. Just let me get some work done. I want him to see that I have accomplished a lot today."

Having nearly finished washing the front room, Wally answered the unexpected knock at the door. It was the same cop who had interrogated him about the dogs and the neighbor. Wally looked at his name badge above his shield, Sgt. G. Fitzgerald, no first name. Sweat soaking through his cotton t-shirt, he politely greeted him. "Yes, Officer Fitzgerald, what can I do for you?"

"It's *Sergeant* Fitzgerald, got it? Now, is your father or mother home?" he demanded.

Wally answered with smooth cooperation. "Yes, my mom is home. My father will be home around four o'clock. Please come in. Take a seat if you like. May I ask what you want of them?"

Wally politely beckoned Sergeant Fitzgerald to enter while calling to his mother, who quickly raced to the front room. "Hi, Helen. I just need to ask your son a couple of questions." "Wally, did you fight with another boy earlier today?"

Wally deceptively replied. "Yes, sir I did. I had a job interview at the foundry, but was embarrassed about my face, so I went to Lincolnway to get something to cover it up. On the way out I ran into Bobby. We got into an argument. He tried to punch me with a roll of nickels gripped in his fist—he wanted to break my jaw. So, I taught him a lesson. Then, I ran home to change out of my bloody clothes and went to the interview. It was a few minutes before nine when I arrived at the foundry. The cop took in all the information, studying the young man's face intently—the dishonesty was invisible. "Do you own a knife?"

"No."

"Show me your fists."

Wally held out both his hands. The knuckles were swollen, and the skin was broken in several places, the redness exacerbated by the constant contact with the wall-washing water.

"Why do you ask about a knife, sir"

The cop ignored the question. "Shut up, Wally, I'll ask the questions. Helen, does Wally own a knife?"

Helen responded. "No, I'm sure he doesn't. We only have five kitchen knives from Chicago Cutlery in our kitchen. They are all in their wooden block. Do you want to see them?"

Nodding in the negative, Fitzgerald turned his attention back to Wally. "Where did this take place?"

Wally cooperated freely, looking intently at the cop without blinking. "We fought about a half-block south of Fullerton, on the east side of Southport. There was a lady walking toward Bobby, and I think she stopped to see if he was okay. She is that *starsza pani* (Polish for old lady) who lives with her oddball kid in one of the apartments above Lincolnway. I recognized her. I'm sure she recognized me too. Oh, and here is the roll of nickels he held in his fist when he tried to punch me. I had no intention of stealing it, just had to take it away from him."

Standing up, Sergeant Fitzgerald demanded, "Helen, I need to search Wally's room for the knife—take me there."

"Of course, Sergeant. Follow me up the rear stairs. Wally's room is in the attic." Helen willingly led the way.

Once in the spartan space without closets or furniture except for a bed and one small bachelor's chest, Fitzgerald easily completed his fruitless search, first complaining, "Shit, it's hot up here, kid." Then he continued, "Okay, Wally. Helen, I am sorry if my visit upset you but there is nothing more for me to discuss with you now. I'll follow up with the witness. But I'll be back if Wally's story is not corroborated."

Back to washing and ignoring his mother, Wally pushed himself like a world-class long-distance runner, setting a pace near full speed and never breaking stride. The front room was done. Soon the dining room. Then the kitchen—finally the pantry and bathroom. At 4:00 p.m., as the front door opened, Wally was just sitting down on the rear porch steps, recovering. Only two of their three bedrooms and the porch remained. He completed over one half of the square footage in less than six hours—and did it well.

As Peter entered, he smelled the slight scent of Fels Naphtha Soap and observed the now glistening walls and floors. Good, he thought, as he strode over to greet the love of his life. Calmed and refreshed by the hug that reunited them after every separation, they felt ready to call the younger kids in from the yard. Helen yelled out the back door, "Kids, your father's home!" Seconds later, the little ones swarmed Peter. The six of them gathered around the table, eager to share reports of each other's happenings. Though Wally hadn't joined the happy family, Peter made no effort to look for him, and the other children didn't ask his whereabouts. All understood the oldest boy was now, at a minimum, a temporary outsider.

When Wally finally entered the room, all heads turned in silent acknowledgment as Peter addressed his son, "Wally, I had an unexpected conversation with Millicent today. She told me you showed up quite late. We can discuss that issue later. However, Millicent also said she was very impressed with you."

Dumbfounded, Wally replied, "I made her very angry. She hated me. Why would she say something like that?"

"Millicent deals with the owners of the foundry, its customers, suppliers, and the employees. She knows the nuances of how to deal with these different constituencies. She is one of the shrewdest and toughest people I've ever met. Anyway, she told me she raked you over the coals, and you handled it with courtesy and aplomb. Millicent said it troubled her a bit to give you such a hard time, but she thought it was the only way to salvage the opportunity for you. If you could stand up to her onslaught, you might be a good employee. She was also impressed that you said you would call her to follow up. So, you will report to Mr. Schmidt tomorrow morning at 7:30 a.m. This means you are to arrive at the office door at *7:15 a.m.* Got it? Afterward, you'll come home and finish your cleaning."

Wally plopped down in a kitchen chair, smiling in relief and surprise. "Come on—this is too crazy. She hated me!"

"Really, Wally? In the adult world, every introduction to a new person is a form of interview, whether you know it or not. You are just lucky that Millicent was caring and clever enough to examine you so discreetly with the intent of helping. Now, tell me why you were so late."

White lie time! This is getting easy, Wally thought.

By now, deceptions slipped effortlessly from his lips. Repeating the lie delivered to his mother and Fitzgerald was effortless. "I was so embarrassed about my face, I waited at Lincolnway to see if Alvin might have something to make me look better. I got there before he opened at 8:00 a.m. I figured I had enough time to get something to hide my scar and then run to the foundry. That's when I ran into Bobby—you know, the car thief? He wanted me to do some bad things with him. I told him no. But then he started to argue with me and threaten me. Finally, he tried to punch me. So, I beat him up pretty badly. You can ask mom. Sergeant Fitzgerald was here earlier because Bobby told him some lies about me. But I told the cop the truth, and he said everything would be okay, and that I was not in trouble. Dad, I had blood on me, so I snuck into the house for some clean clothes, then ran to the foundry. I talked my way around being late by saying I misunderstood you." The second white lie repeated, it almost seemed truthful in the young liar's mind.

Helen, having listened closely to her son, came to his defense. "Peter, there was a witness. Wally is telling the truth. When he got home, he worked so hard to please you. Look at how clean everything is."

Peter nodded in agreement. "Son, let's have our meal and a quiet evening together. Tomorrow you will meet with Mr. Schmidt. Go straight there and afterward, come home directly to finish your punishment. Soon we will put the last week behind us."

CHAPTER 28

As the screech of the factory's whistle rudely destroyed the Saturday morning quiet, Wally reached the foundry's office door precisely at 7:00 a.m. All night he had reflected on his problems and began building freedom's plan. Wally realized the use of white lies could be helpful again. He understood vicious compliance need not appear as such, rather living white lies would be just as useful as telling them. He would play along as if he wanted to work at the foundry until he could escape with Aunt Martha.

As the office door opened, Wally was greeted by a man with a long, prominent scar on his face. The boy found this strangely comforting. Wally had to suppress a laugh, however, as he took in the enormous bug eyes peering out at him from the man's spectacles.

Immediately extending his hand, Wally spoke first. "Good morning, Mr. Schmidt. Thank you for seeing me. I hope this is still a convenient time for you."

John Schmidt immediately understood Millicent's description of the boy's polite charm. "Wally, come in. Would you like some coffee? The pot is just to your left. Cups, cream, and sugar are there on the counter."

"Thank you, sir. I don't care for any, but may I get you a cup?"

Schmidt smiled. "I have mine already. Come sit down in my office. We will talk about life and business."

Wally entered, respectfully allowing Schmidt to walk before him. Looking around in disbelief at the fine architectural millwork and furniture, his mouth fell open in wonder. Two walls of polished six-panel mahogany paneling—their pattern repeated over the twenty-four-foot depth of the office—served as the backdrop on one side of the office to an ornate desk with curved legs terminating in claw-and-ball feet under a leather top and brass hardware on the drawers. Further into the room, two matching chocolate leather Chesterfield sofas with deep-buttoned leather upholstery and brass nailhead trim sat opposite one another. A Farahan Sarouk rug—perhaps of the finest workmanship ever made—elegantly adorned the floor between them. A few framed photographs containing images of soldiers in various groups—some looking well-worn from battle, others formally dressed for inspection—provided the finishing touch above the desk. Wally zeroed in on one particular photo of three soldiers.

"Go ahead, take a closer look. That is me with my commanding officer and General JJ Pershing," Schmidt offered.

"Are you the one with all the medals and ribbons, or is that your commander?"

"No, Wally, I am the lieutenant; the other fellow with all the decorations is my captain. No greater soldier has ever served his country. The third man is General Pershing, the leader of our forces in the Great War."

Now, turning his observations back to the office, Wally gaped at the wall furthest from the office's entrance with its matching mahogany floor-to-ceiling bookcase filled with countless leather bindings offering the wisdom of the ages. The boy felt as if he had entered another world. How could such a glorious room be hidden within the sprawling, metal-walled, rusting foundry? Nothing this beautiful could exist anywhere near the ugliness of the main buildings, belching smoke, searing heat, outdoor storage, muddy barge landing, and railroad spurs.

Schmidt gestured where the boy should sit. "Wally, this office, the likes of which I am sure you have never seen, is one of the results of forty years of endless working and striving by my father and family. I had the honor of taking over our family's business once my father and uncles had grown too old to work hard. You may think I am lucky to have this office as you see it now—but it was not luck; it was earned. It is now my obligation to leave an even better foundation for the next generation. A key part of that rock-hard foundation is our commitment to honesty, fairness, and open communication that my father preached every day of his life. I have added 'accuracy, accountability, and action' to our guiding principles.

"Yes, Mr. Schmidt, I understand," Wally mouthed as he stared at the wall of photos.

The CEO abruptly stopped talking, smiled, then added, "My office door is open to every employee. That is all I have to say. Now you shall tell me about your current situation and your future aspirations."

"Thank you for allowing me to see your office, sir," Wally started. "Your family must be very smart and hard working. I had no idea places like this existed anywhere around here. It's like a room in some castle." The boy was buying time with compliments. He had no idea how to answer such a serious and open-ended question.

"Tell me about yourself," Schmidt demanded.

"I guess I like cars." Then silence. Schmidt simply waited. "And I went to a baseball game once. I liked it, but somebody took me—I can't afford to go there on my own."

Schmidt decided to get down to business. "Wally, let me see your hands." Wally complied. "You fight, don't you? And I have heard about your neighbor and his two dogs—and what you did to him. How do you explain your behavior?"

"Sir, it was not fair for him to abuse those innocent animals. I had seen him be cruel before but the last time—the time I beat him up, it was the worst ever. Those dogs are nice dogs. They are not mean to everyone. They are just protective of their property. I guess I could not stand by and watch him kill one or both of them. I didn't know how else to stop him. I had to before it was too late!"

"So, you're a man of action, are you?" Schmidt inquired. "Why didn't anyone else do anything about it? There were neighbors all around, weren't there?"

"I don't know if there were neighbors around to help. I didn't think about that—it never occurred to me. I just had to stop the beating. I couldn't wait for anyone else to intervene. What if no one did?" His natural resolve was evident.

John Schmidt took his time in replying, staring at his now empty coffee cup. "Wally, would you please get me another cup. Black please. When you get back, I am going to give you a couple of riddles and you'll try to answer them." Schmidt intentionally watched how the boy handled the coffee cup, pleased that Wally exercised care to not grasp the cup by its brim, but by the bottom and its handle. Wally set the refilled cup down gently next to where his host sat, instead of trying to hand it to him—good.

"Thank you, Wally. Now remember, there is no rush. You take your time, but try your best to answer these riddles. Most people can't solve them, so don't feel bad if you don't. You may ask me questions about the puzzles if you like." Picking up an empty, clear glass bottle from a shelf behind his desk, he counted out five dimes as he dropped them down its neck, shaking it loudly. Then, inserting a cork loosely into the top of the bottle he handed it to Wally. Schmidt asked, "Can you remove the coins without breaking the bottle and without removing the cork from the bottle?"

"Okay, Mr. Schmidt." Wally stared, his mind racing. Holding the bottle high above his head, he stared at the bottom. "You say I can't take the cork out of the bottle, or break it, right?" Not looking up or waiting for a reply to his rhetorical question, Wally took his index finger and forced the cork down into the bottle, turned it over, and shook out the dimes.

Laughing with delight at the speed of the boy's solution, he told Wally to pocket the dimes as a reward for finding the solution, then introduced the second riddle. "Clearly, you like dogs. Let's say your dog runs into the woods. How far does he have to run into the woods before he can run out?"

Wally asked, "How big are the woods?"

"Any size you like. Big or small, it makes no difference," Schmidt replied.

Wally stood up, mumbling "Any size, huh...makes no difference, huh?" Looking at his feet he took a couple of steps forward. Then he turned, still staring down, and stepped back in the other direction. Standing in silence, he turned and this time took four steps forward, pivoted, and took two steps back. As a big smile came to his face, he looked up at Schmidt and blurted out, "My dog can run halfway in, 'cause once past the halfway point, he'll be on his way out."

Again, laughing with delight, Schmidt continued: "Wally, you have a very quick and sharp mind. I've never had someone figure out those two brainteasers so quickly. Now let us talk about your values. Can you name the Ten Commandments, and in order?"

"Yes, sir." He proceeded to rattle them off effortlessly. "I am the Lord your God; you shall have no strange gods before Me. You shall not use the name of the Lord your God in vain. Keep Holy the Lord's Day. Honor your father and mother. Thou shall not murder. Thou shall not commit adultery. Thou shall not steal. Thou shall not bear false witness. Thou shall not covet your neighbor's spouse. Thou shall not covet thy neighbor's property."

Schmidt, clearly pleased, stood up and approached the brilliant young man. "You will start work with Millicent on Monday. She will be your boss. And since you are Peter's son, I will expect perfection from you. So, if you do not understand exactly what you are to do with any assigned task, you ask her questions until you are certain you can perform your duties perfectly. Understand?" Wally nodded in the affirmative. "Good," Schmidt continued, "Millicent will speak to you about your schedule. Come here Monday at 2:00 p.m. She will spend an hour or so with you to show you around and explain your responsibilities before your regular schedule begins Tuesday morning. If you need anything, go to her. Do not interrupt me when my office door is closed or if I am speaking to someone else—except if you are aware of an imminent, dangerous situation that poses an immediate threat to any person or to this foundry. Just like with your dogs, waiting could cost a life. Otherwise, everything can wait when my door is closed. Understand?"

Nodding his head yes, Wally replied, "I understand, and thank you, Mr. Schmidt. I shall be here Monday at 2:00 p.m. sharp!" Schmidt shook Wally's hand and showed him to the door. It was 7:55 a.m.

CHAPTER 29

Running from the foundry to Lincolnway, Wally burst through the door at 8:05 a.m. and headed straight toward the phone booth. Alvin stood preparing prescriptions while Joe Metal Harpy and Lois occupied the two middle stools, quietly talking. The adults greeted an oblivious Wally as their salutations went ignored.

The eager young man dialed Martha's number desperately. Five rings, then eight, then ten. Damn ringing, endless damn ringing! After more than a dozen rings, the operator came on the line. "It does not appear anyone is answering. Please hang up. I will return your coins. Please try again later." The coins clanged mockingly into the return slot.

Immediately, Wally reinserted the coins and called again. This time a woman answered. Remembering his instructions, Wally replied to her, "This is Wally for Martha. No message." He impatiently slammed the phone down into its bracket.

Taking the seat furthest from Joe and Lois and nearest the booth, Wally waited in a pool of panic. He just had to tell Aunt Martha about everything that was going on—everything he planned to do. He needed his mentor to approve his intricate plans for Bobby, Ziggy, and the liquor store.

Just then, brrrring! brrrring! beckoned from the phone booth. The sound exploded like fireworks in the boy's mind. He could hardly believe it! He jumped for the receiver. Pushing the bifold door closed behind him, Wally frantically launched into detail to the only person who understood him, the only person he could truly trust.

The three adults looked at each other with knowing amusement—all grinned at the youthful exuberance on display. Alvin continued his work as Lois got up and walked behind the counter. Out of curiosity or suspicion, Joe relocated to the stool nearest the booth—prime eavesdropping real estate.

Though whispered, Joe managed to hear most of the boy's words. He sat astonished at the plot unfolding from the glass, steel, and wood cube. Joe squirmed in his seat, his ears burning with the squalid details, his concentration now unbreakable.

The instant he heard the receiver bang into the holder, Joe spun himself around on the stool. With a guttural voice that made the boy's soul tremble, he demanded: "May I use the phone now, son?" Wally looked at him, truly noticing his grotesque face and his penetrating eyes for the first time. Fully aware that staring is impolite, the young man could not help himself—he stared, not wanting to blink. Suddenly, he felt as if the man behind this hideous face could see through his eyes, read his mind, and peer into his very soul. Wally's blood ran cold as he looked away in fear of being exposed. At the same moment Joe also looked away, seeing his own reflection in the boy's eyes.

Now gripped with panic, Wally sputtered, "Yes, sir. I am done. Thank you for asking." Then he bolted for the door.

As if flipping a switch, Joe's voice instantly turned calm and gentle, deceptively musing to Lois, *"L'enthousiasme de notre jeunesse est fidèlement au service de nos rêves, quelle que soit leur valeur."*

Lois, bubbling over with delight, called out loudly, "This wise man is also a poet, Alvin!" She translated for him. "The enthusiasm of our youth faithfully serves the dreams we hold, regardless of their worth." Lois grabbed the deformed but intelligent man's hand. Pulling him up from his seat and hugging him, she said, "Who are you really, Joe?"

Joe Metal Harpy, now noticeably embarrassed, slowly, gently moved away from her grasp. "For a man such as I, there is only honor, observation, and thought, except for the hard work I must do to supply my needs. The dreams of my youth are forever gone, never to return. That is who I am, Lois. Nothing more."

Lois, ashamed of the emotional harm caused by her own carelessness and insensitivity, pleaded with Joe: "My dear friend, I did not mean to pry. Forgive me. It is only my fondness for you that makes me try too hard. I apologize for being so thoughtless."

Joe tentatively flashed his fractured smile. "I know, Lois, your heart is one of kindness and pure charity to all. Please don't trouble yourself. I know you meant no harm or disrespect. I am just grateful that I have a dear friend like you and with whom I may speak *Français*. I look forward to Tuesday evening."

Joe exited out the back, leaving behind his distraught friend. Lois just stood motionless, her mouth open in impotent silence.

CHAPTER 30

Monday morning, Wally awoke early as he contemplated his orientation day. Knowing that Millicent was both clever and shrewd, he had used the mindless time of his weekend's remaining punishment to strategize. He theorized that false charm will be as obvious as the scar on his face and quiet hostility would be like bad breath—invisible but unpleasant and apparent nonetheless. He concluded, I can be polite, obedient, and diligent, but I won't be broken. And I won't be owned—by her—or anyone. Perhaps humor will disarm her.

Monday afternoon Wally arrived at the foundry fifteen minutes early. Millicent pointed to the chairs in the waiting area nearest the entrance of the office. He took her cue. "Thank you, ma'am. Please don't let me disturb you. I'll sit here until you are ready for me." Wally sank into a seat and picked up the day's *Chicago Herald-Examiner*. The leading Hearst newspaper in Chicago, it vied with the *Tribune* as leader of the city's morning circulation in 1934. All the same stuff he sighed. Some politician had been caught taking a bribe. Lou Gehrig hit for the cycle in the Yankees victory over the White Sox 11-2. People in Europe were never happy and were fighting again, and some famous gangster just robbed another bank and killed somebody. Wally glanced at the stories, reading the first paragraph of each, unable to endure much more. He flipped the pages until he reached the local news. A photo of Potato and Carrot donning badges, lay positioned under the headline "Chicago Police to Create K-9 Unit." He read on.

"The Chicago Police Department announced Friday it will be adding a police dog unit to the force. Lieutenant B. Vander Hooten, who led allied dog training in Ghent, Belgium during WWI, will lead the new unit, which will start with two Alsatian dogs, (a.k.a. German Shepherd Dogs)."

"That's it? That's all to the story? Shit!" Wally mumbled.

Millicent glanced up. "Excuse me, did you say something?"

"No, ma'am," he replied pleasantly. "I just was reacting to a news story I read about some friends of mine. Sorry to disturb you."

Millicent put down her notebook. "Okay, Wally, come over here and sit next to my desk. I'm ready for you now. First, we are going to have a talk about Friday. I want us to begin on the right foot."

The trainee did as instructed, settling into the cushionless oak chair beside her desk. "I know that your father explained to you why I treated you the way I did," she began. "Now it is *my* turn to explain it to you. Primarily, I wanted to punish you for being late. This would, at a minimum, help you for the rest of your life. Timeliness is a trait you must embrace. Being late is disrespectful to others. No one likes to be disrespected, do they?"

"No, ma'am."

"Giving you that lesson was required by the values I hold, but it also provided an opportunity to check your intellect and maturity. Frankly, I expected you to walk out of here with your tail between your legs. But you did not. You asked how to follow up with me later to determine whether I selected you, always remaining courteous. That took some brains and some courage. Your flexibility with the truth, however, has placed you on probation. If I ever catch you telling anything but God's honest truth, you'll be out on your ear faster than you can say goodbye, Miss Brownley."

Wally nodded his acknowledgment. "Thank you, ma'am. You are generous and patient. I'll try not to let you down."

Aggravated, Millicent raised her voice a bit. "Let *me* down? No, that's not it at all. You must understand, the Schmidt family has been running this place like a finely-tuned Swiss watch for decades, now with over one hundred employees. Even after forty years, there has been only one fatal accident, although this can be very dangerous work. Do you understand?"

Wally nodded yes as his mind calculated how many people must have worked there over forty-plus years. "That must be a record or something."

Millicent continued. "One person was one too many to the Schmidt family, especially Mr. John Schmidt, the founder's son and our leader. Everyone here knows that Mr. Schmidt was a hero in the war. Because he is a brave and powerful man, fluent in German, he volunteered to attempt to infiltrate enemy lines as a spy. He risked his life to acquire information about the enemy's activities. He nearly lost his life in the process but he got the critical information. If not for his commanding officer though, the battle might have been lost and he would not be alive today.

"Oh my," Wally remarked. "I did not know he was a war hero!"

Mr. Schmidt is a unique man; he refuses to display his Distinguished Service Cross he was awarded for his heroic actions. But more than his humility, he is especially deserving of loyalty and respect because of how he now leads us. He inspires his employees to do their best. For example, after the stock market crashed, he kept everyone employed, cutting his own salary first. Wally, do you understand that millions of people watched as their investments sank twenty-eight percent in two days? Since then, the equities market has sunk eighty percent in these last five years? While the financial world was in turmoil, he took money from the company's coffers to help keep this place running. When the banks were making trouble for us, and our sales were down, he did not think of himself. He pulled vast sums of money from his family's resources, mortgaging everything he had, risking personal bankruptcy. He discounted prices to only cover costs so he could win customers—just to keep the place running, not just for his family, but for all of us."

"But everyone in the neighborhood talks about how rich the family is," Wally objected.

Millicent continued. "Yes Wally, led by Mr. John Schmidt, the family survived its financial trials and is profitable again. No one here will ever forget all he did for us. Let me give you another example. Years before, when Mr. Harpy was injured and could not work for months, Mr. Schmidt continued to pay him while he recuperated, then gave him his job back. There are still so many of our neighbors struggling—did you know the Schmidt family funds a nearby soup kitchen at Belmont and Racine?"

Wally, now questioning the worth of his anticipated manipulation with humor, locked on to her every word. "Okay, ma'am, they're a really nice family. I didn't know any of this."

Millicent continued. "Now everyone wants to work here. We get calls, letters, and applications every day. Why do you think I had to treat you in such a way? It was to see what you were made of—to see if you deserved to join us. Now you had your solitary chance with tardiness and lying. Another misstep will be your last at Schmidt Foundry."

His face staring downward, a bit chastened and embarrassed, Wally just nodded yes. "I really am sorry that I was late and lied about it."

Softening her voice, Millicent continued. "That's better. Confession is good for the soul. Now listen, your father is a highly-respected man here, and I am sure you do not want to dishonor him. We shall put this behind us and never speak of it again. I believe you can, and will, become a member of this family—don't let us down."

This newsflash left Wally shocked. His father had never mentioned any of these important things about the Schmidt family. Impressed and a little humbled, he now knew for certain humor was the wrong strategy. But regardless of these fine people, moving to Indiana with Aunt Martha remained in the back of his mind. "Thanks for explaining these things to me, ma'am."

"You're welcome, Wally. Now, here is a list of your responsibilities, broken down between daily and weekly tasks. They are also listed by order of priority. Where you see items marked with "QT" after them, you will only complete these tasks when no one will be disturbed by your presence. Now, let's walk through the list. I will read it to you, explaining each task. Then you will take the list and explain each back to me, so I can make sure you've understood. Afterward, I will ask you to tell me about each task without the benefit of the list. This will tell me how closely I must watch you at first."

To Wally it all seemed too simple, work beneath his keen intellect, but he pretended to be interested. Subjected to Miss Brownley's training process, the new employee made sure to ask her a battery of questions. When asked to repeat the task processes without looking at the list, he rattled them off effortlessly while he added suggestions for reorganizing the tasks to increase efficiency. Amazed, Millicent started to take notes on what the boy said about improving things.

At about 3:30 p.m., with his training complete, the trainer dismissed her pupil. "I'll expect you tomorrow at 8:00 a.m."

Gently he pleaded for relief. "If I skip my thirty-minute lunch, and stay a half hour later, may I begin at 9:00 a.m., please? I would be so grateful if we could adjust my schedule this tiny bit."

Millicent studied his face. "Wally, I am sure you realize that employees do not set their schedules—management does. It is perplexing that you would be so bold. This must be something very important to you." She recalled his tardiness for his first interview.

"Yes, I know it is inappropriate of me. I just hope that you might consider my proposal, since I am only a part-time employee. Perhaps you might just try out my request for one week. If you are satisfied with my work and the adjusted schedule, we could make it permanent. If it does not work the way you wish, I will make arrangements to start at 8:00 a.m."

Miss Brownley, amazed by his negotiation skills and audacity, sighed deeply. "You may start at 9:00 a.m. only one day this week—you pick. Now, pick your day, and we shall discuss this no more. Just be aware that Mr. Schmidt can overrule this privilege at any time, so don't assume things will go your way. Understand?"

"Thank you, Miss Brownley," Wally replied as he headed to the door. He stopped and turned, "I will come in tomorrow, Tuesday, at 9:00 a.m. instead of 8:00 a.m."

Aunt Martha and Wally spoke on the phone for thirty minutes on Tuesday morning. Only one piece of the plan remained unresolved. Aunt Martha's temper flared. "Figure it out yourself, and in time. You are not going to back out or delay. Understand?" With that, she slammed down the receiver.

Wally wiped his sweaty palms on his pants, his heart beating wildly. Leaving the phone booth, he thought, how can I complete the plan without reviewing the details of the missing piece with Aunt Martha one more time? Desperate, he obsessed over the problem as he walked to work.

Sergeant Fitzgerald was out walking his beat on the same side of the street as the boy. "Wally, you'll want to know I did speak with your neighbor lady. She saw the fight and confirmed your story. That friend of yours, Bobby, has a new understanding of the consequences of filing a false police report." Fitzgerald, laughing, added, "Just because you beat his ass so good, I only gave him half of the usual lesson. Oh, I kept his roll of nickels too—ha!"

"Thank you, sir." The distracted boy replied.

"You should consider becoming a cop, Wally," Fitzgerald continued. "You think like one, and you act like one. Hell, maybe one day you could work for Vander Hooten with those dogs you saved."

"Maybe," Wally offered to appease the man. He knew full well he'd never consider the idea.

"Well, see you around. Keep your nose clean kid, you hear?"

"Yes, sir." And with that, Fitzgerald swaggered away, twirling his billy club by its leather strap.

Suddenly, the final piece became clear—Wally's plan coalesced to perfection—nickels. All that remained was the waiting.

The first week at the foundry went by quickly, with Wally's performance beyond exemplary. He completed his cleaning tasks flawlessly, and even Mr. Schmidt noticed the difference. Every day Wally would make notes and before going home, ask questions of Miss Brownley. Often after leaving, he would add to his notes for exploration the next morning. At first annoyed by the constant questions, with each passing day, Miss Brownley willingly offered detailed answers to the boy's queries. Soon, she was flabbergasted when he began to offer advice on how things should be done. Listening with an open mind, Miss Brownley embraced his ideas.

Late Friday afternoon, Millicent called Wally to her desk, informing him, "Mr. Schmidt and I wish to reward you with a 9:00 a.m. start time for two days next week. Keep it up, young man."

Wally picked Monday and Tuesday for his late start. Speaking to Aunt Martha as soon as possible was critical. The second day was a contingency should he not reach her Monday.

Wally had successfully improved office supply storage and organization. Next, he conceived of a way to cross-reference files that allowed production and sales to interact better and faster, with less risk of errors. By Friday of the second week, Millicent came to expect great things from her assistant.

That evening, Helen greeted her son at the door. "Your father and I are going to make a special dinner on Saturday evening to celebrate our good fortune. We have much to be grateful for—your father's promotion, the success of my seamstress work, and now your new job. You know, Wally, there are many families struggling. So, we will celebrate our blessings, but we must also look for a way to use our good fortune to help others. That's why we are increasing our weekly donation to St. Joseph's, for a start. The original idea for this feast was your father's. He wants to recognize how well you are doing at your new job. Millicent told your dad about your irresistible urge to improve how things were organized. She said you had brilliant insight into creating clever solutions."

How perfect, he thought to himself. A celebration tomorrow, and I'm still being seen as a neighborhood hero because of the Alsatians. Saturday night should be a breeze, and no one will ever suspect me.

After Friday's dinner, Wally spent the evening playing with his little brothers and sisters in the backyard. Once again, he glimpsed the hermit upstairs peeking out of the rear window. Peter and Helen allowed their children to be excused without cleanup chores to reward them for good behavior. They enjoyed the time alone in the kitchen, cleaning up while discussing the craziness of the last two weeks and its resolutions.

When they finished, Peter joined Wally outside. Together they sat down on the backyard bench. "How did you ever learn about cross-referencing files? Did you learn about it in school?"

"No, dad," Wally replied. "After Miss Brownley explained to me how all the files were organized so I could do some filing, I asked a few questions—like who used them, how often, and why they needed them. She also let me briefly flip through the papers to study them. Soon, my ideas just seemed obvious. I thought to myself, what if I were a salesman? How would I want things? And then the same thoughts if I were your boss, running production. And it all started to come together as I took papers from her To-Be-Filed bin to the filing cabinets.

When I explained it to her, she made me explain it to her three more times. She asked a bunch of questions and then told me to write it all down. So, I did. She studied what I wrote and then, right when I was leaving Friday, she told me it would work, and I could begin to set it up on Monday."

"I'm so proud of you son," Peter admitted. Then he couldn't resist hugging him, adding, "I love you, son."

Wally smiled, "I know, dad. Me too."

After a moment, Peter excused himself and returned with two cold bottles of Coke. They drank their bottles dry, enjoying their beverages in silence.

CHAPTER 32

Saturday afternoon, the blaring sound of a car horn reverberated off the house on Southport Avenue. It was Martha, of course. They all knew the signal. Everyone raced to the front door and out into the yard except Helen, who was tethered to her cooking. The little ones had long ago forgotten the unpleasant words spoken by their aunt during her last visit. They mauled her with little hugs and kisses. Helen basked in thoughts of their good fortune—Wally was back on the right track, and now her sister had shown up for the family feast by happy coincidence. How fortunate that she could join the celebration!

The children enthusiastically escorted their aunt into the kitchen.

"Oh, my goodness. How wonderful you can be here with us," Helen chirped. "Wally had two great weeks at his new job. He is already improving things there and being such a good son again. Thank you so much! I'm sure your guidance really helped him see things more clearly. It is fitting that you, of all people, should be here for our celebration."

Martha grabbed her sister by the shoulders and gently hugged her.

"I was so concerned about surprising you," the older sister replied. "You know, just showing up without warning. But I just had to see how my Wally was doing after his first couple of weeks on the job. Sounds like it was terrific. I knew he would do well." Martha took a look around the kitchen strewn with crockery, the pots simmering on the stove, the vegetables half sliced, and then actually offered to help prepare the celebration dinner. Deliciously complex smells filled the stifling hot kitchen as the window fan attempted to exhaust the summer heat.

Wally's favorite dinner of stuffed cabbage rolls began that evening with appetizers—something the family usually only did for Christmas and Easter dinners. Two types of herring were served, one in cream sauce and one in white wine, both with onions. The next course was leek soup, based on a recipe Helen took from The House of Prussia and carried across the Atlantic when she was fifteen. The smell of fresh-baked bread still lingered in the house since its early morning baking.

After everyone had their fill of the grand meal's main course, Helen served a homemade apple strudel. Getting up from the table Martha announced, "Come on, Wally. Let's walk to Lincolnway. Maybe I'll buy you a chocolate phosphate." This was their excuse to get out of the house.

"Martha, keep being such a good influence on Wally and he'll be running that office one day," Helen called as the pair headed to the door.

As the duo made their way north on the sidewalk, Wally pulled out his pack of Camels and offered one to his aunt. "Light it for me—just like I did in the car for you when I taught you to drive," she said.

Wally complied, lighting it in his own mouth, then placed it between Aunt Martha's lips. His heart raced a bit as this definitely felt dirty. The thought of the cigarette touching his lips and then Martha's made him feel sexually excited. It was almost like a kiss. This was not what he wanted to happen, but it was happening, and he liked it. Placing the cigarette between her lips felt intimate—her lips were luscious. He felt this feeling before, when she put her hand upon his thigh, when she hugged him the last time, and the time when she undressed in the girls' bedroom. He tried to put it out of his mind but the image of her perfect naked body would not be exorcised as Martha reached for his hand, taking it gently in hers

Martha's radar detected the sexual tension, knowing she remained in control over him she redirected the conversation toward tonight's mission. "We need to focus on your special project, Wally. Walk me through your steps again, especially the alibi."

Wally, shaking off his arousal and pulling his hand away from hers, explained. "No car, no bottles, no flashlight. Store keys, gloves, jacket, and hat. The screwdriver and pry bar I took from the foundry last weekend. Your trunk key. Bib overalls with loose straps. One canvas bag—do not overfill it; it must zip closed and fit in my overalls in case I have to run. Take one roll of nickels but no other rolled coins, only paper money. I know the beat cop's routine. He will not be anywhere near at 2:00 a.m."

"Good, Wally. Now keep going. I want to hear every detail."

"The nearby baker arrives around 3:45 a.m.—the asshole. A couple of months ago I saw him through the open back door of the bakery. He was pissing into a huge vat of dough he was mixing, laughing out loud at himself. The pig! I should find a way to fix his clock, too."

Annoyed, Martha snapped at him. "Forget about the baker. Don't break your concentration when we are talking business."

"I'm sorry," Wally replied, then continued. "Anyway, start with the biggest bills first. Fill the sack neatly to maximize how much cash will fit, and zip it shut. Stuff it in the front of my overalls, cinch the straps, exit the rear door; stay in the shadows for five to ten seconds looking and listening to verify no one is nearby. Take the perpendicular alley south. Throw one role of nickels in Bobby's back yard. Quietly put the tools in the trash, two doors south. Drop the store's keys in the sewer the next block south. Do not leave the gloves. If someone is in sight, just keep walking. One or two more lots to the south will be okay. Exit the alley at the end of the block. When I put the sack and gloves in your trunk, I must lean into the trunk like I am digging for something so no one can see me taking the sack out of my overalls. Take the small shopping bag you have left there for me, so it looks like I went into the trunk to retrieve something. Lock the trunk. Your car will be parked where we planned, three houses south of our house. Sneak in the back way—don't worry, I've gotten in and out many times without anyone knowing it. Then, I go to bed."

Martha beamed at her nephew. "Okay, keep in mind what I told you before. Speed, silence, and confidence. Once you are out, don't look around, just walk like you're minding your own business—like you own the place. Keep the hat on and your collar up. If anyone is around, change direction so they can't get a good look at you. Do not run unless you must. If you are chased, do not get caught. Run until you die, if you have to. Now tell me again, what are the routes and where are the hiding places if you must run? Tell me each of the hiding places you'll use if you are running and must dump the bag. Then tell me about the alibis."

Wally walked her through the escape routes north, south, east, and west noting the hiding places he had identified along the way. Then he addressed her other question—the alibis. "My first alibi, if I have to run and get caught after dumping the bag, I just say I was peeping in a girl's bedroom window. That's why I ran. But don't worry, no one will be able to catch me."

Martha coldly replied, "You better not, or you'll be on your own. Now give me the second alibi."

Confidently, Wally continued. "The family had a wonderful dinner. You and I took a walk afterward. Then everyone sat in the backyard together. I went to bed around ten. You are my alibi. At 2:00 a.m. I got up to take a leak. I saw you in the yard having a smoke. I joined you, and we sat outside and talked. I went back to bed at 2:30 a.m. The bedroom you are using faces the back porch. I never could have left the house without you hearing and seeing me. Close enough?"

The brilliant boy had thought of everything, thanks in part to Sgt. Fitzgerald. His enemy, Bobby, would be set up to take the fall. Ziggy would eventually crack under questioning and confirm Bobby had the keys and talked of robbing the liquor store. It was brilliant.

CHAPTER 33

Wally's plan came off perfectly in only fifteen minutes. He stuffed the bag full of cash and placed it in the trunk, locking it after grabbing the decoy sack. Entering the backyard, he found Aunt Martha perched on the bench. "Give me the car keys and sack. Go change your clothes and come back down here with me."

On Wally's return to Martha, Mr. Feherty cracked open his back door, a single eye spying curiously.

Martha held a bottle of vodka. "Take a belt of this. Have you had vodka before? If not, take small sips until you get used to it. Your nerves are going to say thank you." She paused to observe Wally. "You're shaking inside now, aren't you?"

Wally took a small sip, then a larger one. He liked it. "Yeah. But I'm kinda excited too. I feel powerful."

He lit a cigarette and placed it between Martha's lips. "How many people did you see? Anyone in the alley, backyards, or on the street?" she asked.

Placing his hand on Aunt Martha's thigh, Wally felt beyond elated. He figured it out and executed it, now eager for 10:00 a.m. "Yeah, I guess I only saw that *jot* in the alley behind Lincolnway. I don't think he noticed me. Anyway, all I saw was his back as he was heading east, away from me. I didn't see anyone else. It was so easy for me to crouch among the trash cans and quietly slip in the evidence. The cans could not have been arranged better for my cover. It was great!"

They drained the vodka bottle slowly until empty. Martha put it in her purse. As she leaned over to do so, she let her nightgown fall open to tease the boy again with her bare breasts. "Go try to get some sleep, the vodka should help. We have one more step tomorrow." She stood up, hugged him with her full body, and kissed his ear with her lips and breath, driving the boy crazy with lust. Slowly she broke away.

Wally climbed the stairs again, this time without Feherty opening the door. Lying in bed with his eyes wide open until daybreak, he was suffering a near overdose of adrenaline and testosterone. Wally's mind spun into intense fantasies about sex, wealth, and revenge as he stared at the rotating blades of the attic's window fan.

At first light, everyone got up early, still basking in the glow of the celebration dinner. Wally came down to join them, and soon each was taking their turn using the bathroom. Sunday Mass was at 8:00 a.m. For the first time in his life, Wally considered not going, but knew the battle with his parents would not be worth the fight—at least not this time. Besides, he didn't want anyone to be suspicious now that they saw him as the family hero. So, he dressed properly and joined everyone on the walk to church. Lagging a few yards behind, with the morning breeze in his face, he could smoke without being seen or smelled by his parents. Martha and Wally discussed in whispers, the 10:00 a.m. final step. Occasionally, she subtly brushed her hand across the boy's ass.

An hour later, after Mass the morning sun seemed satisfyingly warm, and the air smelled of the foundry as the family exited the church. Wally felt as if he had never seen a more glorious azure-blue sky. A cool breeze blew gently off Lake Michigan, providing some relief in an otherwise hot and dirty city. Eagerly, they all proceeded home to enjoy hard-boiled eggs, pastries, coffee, milk, juice, cheese, and fresh fruit. After breakfast, Martha offered, "Let's all walk up to Lincolnway. I will buy cashews, licorice twists, and gumdrops for everyone."

Accepting their aunt's offer, they walked to the pharmacy, stopping just outside. A small crowd blocked their way. It was a little past 10:00 a.m. Many people had gathered and various police wandered in and out of Town Liquors. Ignoring the unusual activity, Aunt Martha reached in her pocket and produced two fifty-cent pieces. Giving them to Wally she instructed, "Take your brothers and sisters inside and help them pick out lots of candies. Don't come back out with more than two-bits change or I'll send you in to buy more." The four little ones snaked through the crowd as they raced in, leaning against the cabinets, and pawing at jumbo glass jars of goodies as Wally dutifully watched over them.

Outside, Sergeant Fitzgerald approached the adults. "Good morning, Peter, Helen. It's a fine morning, isn't it? Who is this lovely lady with you?"

"Sergeant, this is my sister, Martha. She is visiting us from Indiana for the weekend."

As they exchanged pleasantries, more policemen arrived. Fitzgerald stepped aside to join his comrades. "The tools were found right where you thought we might find them, but no keys yet," one officer explained loudly enough for the adults of the family to hear. "That punk who filed the false report with you has been taken to the precinct for interrogation. Good news—he turned seventeen five months ago. The boys will send his parents home after a while. Then the real interrogation can begin. A couple of the guys are talking to that ox, Ziggy. You know, the big moose? He's singing like a bird."

Fitzgerald turned back toward Peter. "Is your boy, Wally, inside? We need to talk to him about his friend Bobby and something that happened last night."

"What do you want with Wally?" Helen cut in, agitated. "We were all together yesterday evening having a celebration.

He slept in his bed all night. We were all home sleeping, like you would expect. What's going on?"

Just then, the kids shuffled out with their confectionary treasures. Wally walked right up to Fitzgerald. "Good morning, Sergeant Fitzgerald." Helen shooed the little ones away from the cop. "Kids, go look in the window of the lamp store a couple of doors down. Look for a new lamp for our front room. It's time we get a new one." The kids raced to the storefront, feeling they had a very important job to do.

Fitzgerald started questioning Wally. "You used to hang around with Bobby. Where were you last night from midnight to sunrise?"

Wally coaxed his face into a countenance of childlike innocence. "Sleeping. Why do you ask, sir?"

"I'll ask the questions here—you answer. Got it? Now, what do you know about any keys your friend Bobby might have had that didn't belong to him? You follow me, boy?"

"I don't know much," Wally replied innocently. "He had some keys to some store he was bragging about, but I never knew if he was just talking big, or if he was up to something. That's what we were fighting about. I told him no. I wouldn't help him rob any store and he got really mad. Anyway, he and I haven't been hanging around together anymore since before he tried to hit me with that fistful of nickels. You know, I told you all about it. Remember, I gave you that roll of coins after I took it from him? You should talk to Ziggy. He's still hanging out with Bobby."

Peter stepped in, a little annoyed that his son was being interrogated in public. "Sergeant Fitzgerald, please explain to me what's going on. I don't think it's appropriate to question Wally like this on the sidewalk. Please explain what's going on and how it applies to my son."

"Of course, Peter. I would not question Wally in the open like this if he was suspected of a crime; I'm just looking for information. We already have a suspect in custody, plenty of evidence, and another boy who confirms the keys to the liquor store were in Bobby's possession and that he said he wanted to rob it. You see, last night someone robbed the liquor store of all its cash—right after their busiest weekend of the month. Funny thing, all the rolled coins were left, except the nickels. We already found the burglary tools near the home of the boy who is suspected of having the store's keys. There was one roll of nickels found dropped in the grass of his backyard, near the back porch stairs. And now your son helps corroborate Ziggy's statement about the keys and the suspect's intent. We only need to find the cash. I'm sure the boys at the precinct lockup will get a confession out of that punk soon."

Defensively, Martha jumped in. "My nephew, Wally, would never have anything to do with other kids who are robbers. You heard him—he doesn't hang out with Bobby—they had a big fight. Anyway, the bedroom I'm using while visiting is at the base of the stairs in my sister's house. It's been so hot; I hardly slept a wink last night. So, if the boy would have tried to leave the house, I would have heard him. Nobody could use those creaky old stairs without me knowing it. Anyway, around two in the morning, I went into the backyard to have a smoke. Wally came down in his PJs and sat with me for a while. He said he couldn't sleep either—you know all the excitement about the dogs he rescued becoming police dogs, plus the family had a celebration for him last night, and the heat in the attic must be unbearable even with both fans running on high. You know, Wally is a big hit at the foundry office, too. We are all so proud of him."

Fitzgerald pulled out his notepad, jotting down some notes. "Thank you, folks. Enjoy the rest of this beautiful Sunday." Then he joined the other cops who were searching the liquor store for evidence. Martha and Wally executed the last step, establishing Wally's alibi, just as planned. It was perfect.

Frustrated, the evidence technicians poured over the crime scene, but found nothing. Next, they unsuccessfully focused on fingerprints. The police department had recently expanded its resources of The Henry Classification System, used for collecting and comparing fingerprints as evidence. First adopted by law enforcement in New York, big cities all over the country were struggling to use this new, but difficult to use, forensic tool.

But since the new science of manually matching finger-prints was time-consuming and often failed to provide reliable results, some cops turned to the ancient and repulsive skill of coercing confessions out of suspects, whether guilty or not. Bobby served as the latest victim of this barbaric practice; the whole time objecting while being beaten. "I did nothing wrong. How could I return what I don't have? You should search Wally. He must have done it. He always talked about easy ways to make money." Bobby never varied from his statement that Wally had taken the keys from him on the Friday morning when they fought.

The interrogating officers relayed everything to Sergeant Fitzgerald upon his return to the precinct. Luckily for Wally, he had his parents and aunt as alibis, and Bobby had none. There was his two friends' claim that Bobby had the keys. Then there was the roll of nickels found in his backyard as evidence. Plus, he had previously filed a false police report. To Fitzgerald, it was cut-and-dried.

As the family leisurely returned to their home, Martha took Helen's hand, slowing her down so they could speak privately for a moment. "Helen, it was so wonderful to be part of the celebration with you yesterday. I hope to come back soon—maybe in a week or two. But I am a little worried that I may make myself an unwanted guest by visiting too frequently. So, before I make plans, I need to know how you feel about me coming back for a night or two sometime soon. Do you mind?"

Helen beamed with joy as she hugged her sister, and replied, "We all love having you visit us. You are welcome anytime. If you can let me know ahead of time, we'll fix a special feast in *your* honor. After all, you are a big part of the reason my boy is doing so well now. And I am so happy you and I are reunited. My life is so much better with you back in it." Martha flashed a satisfied smile.

Once home, the family gathered in the yard to enjoy the day of rest. Around noon, Martha prepared to return to Indiana, giving Wally a silent call with her eyes to join her inside. They found privacy in the dining room.

Martha reached into her purse, produced a thick fold of bills, and handed it to him. "Wally, I will keep *the package* for a couple of weeks as we discussed. You need to make sure no one finds any of it around here. We don't want to mess up your next project, but I want you to have a couple of bucks now."

Wally studied it, peeling back the corners, counting. "Five, ten, twenty .... The wad of cash was huge, and there was more in the trunk. Okay, Aunt Martha, I don't need much." He kept only three fins—fifteen dollars—and handed the rest of the bills back to her.

Pleased, Martha shoved the cash into her purse and quickly redirected the boy toward the future. "Just like we discussed, the next time will be a bit harder and more dangerous. You need to study everything. We can't execute our new plan in less than two weeks—understand? Most importantly, you must confirm the couriers' schedules."

Eagerly, Wally replied. "Yes, I know everything I need to prepare. You can count on me. I'd do anything for you."

"Good. You call me Thursday morning each week and report on your progress. I will hold onto the first take, and when the second project is complete, liquidate the merchandise in Indiana. At that point, you'll have enough to move in with me, and Jack will help you get set up. You'll have a business of your own, making more cash in a month than your father earns in a year—probably double! You are quickly becoming a man with all the brains, skills, and looks to get very rich." Martha hugged him, this time pressing her entire body firmly against his, and holding on longer than before. They kissed each other on the lips longer this time. Then Martha briefly inserted her tongue in his mouth, driving him crazy with lust. Wally, holding her lower back, pulled her tightly to him. He didn't want to let go, frustrated with the waiting.

The sound of the back door opening interrupted their perverse moment. Martha pushed him away whispering in his right ear, as the others came inside, "Two weeks my love, only two weeks."

As the rest were coming into the kitchen, Martha raced to the back bedroom before anyone saw her and Wally embrace. She grabbed her overnight bag, and took it to the front door. The family followed, and one by one hugged her good-bye—except for Wally—who just stared at everyone in this, his torturous scene. As she slid into the Oldsmobile, Martha called out. "Helen, I'll try to come back in two weeks."

CHAPTER 34

The excitement in front of Town Liquors lasted all Sunday afternoon. Between the gawkers and busybodies wishing to view the crime scene, peering at it from the outside, countless people strolled the sidewalks. The pharmacy remained packed, as old friends visited and newcomers discovered Lincolnway.

After an exceptionally busy day, Alvin and Lois prepared to close the store for the night as Joe Metal Harpy burst through the back door. "Good evening, Lois, Alvin. All that excitement was just a little too close to home, don't you think?"

"What do you mean, Joe?" Lois asked.

"From what I have heard, it was a pretty slick job. The robbers knew which day they would find the most cash on hand. They knew what hours would be the most isolated. Strangely, the owner said no booze was taken. No, this crime was focused on speed, stealth, and escape. They left no evidence. No fingerprints, no sign of forced entry, nothing. Somebody with brains thought through this caper. And the kid who was arrested, he won't break, even with a bunch of evidence piling up against him and some roughing up. He's either innocent or tougher than nails."

Intrigued, Alvin replied, "Joe, how do you know so much about this?"

"I ran into a cop in the alley. Then we just got talking."

Lois was becoming a bit worried now. "Joe," she asked, "Why did you say it was too close to home for us? What did you mean?"

"Well, I guess it was too slick, too professional." He looked at his friends earnestly. "Having somebody around the neighborhood who can pull that off so cleanly makes all the businesses vulnerable. Not even a forced-open door or broken window—nothing. Just the cash register was busted along with the strongbox in the cabinet underneath it, but both of the store's doors were locked. My real concern is now for you. Ever since the Harrison Narcotic Act of 1914, criminals look for certain drugs that used to be easily available. I worry that a knowledgeable thief will focus on your store. In addition to your cash, he would find significant value in some of the drugs you dispense. These are much smaller than booze, and therefore easier to steal. Let's take a look at your doors and locks sometime soon. What you have now may not be adequate. If need be, I can help fortify your security. There is a safe company a bit further south down Clybourn.

You might want to look at that option, but you would need a couple of very large safes, I'm sure. That would be something to seriously consider." Joe excused himself and headed out the back door for the evening. Lois began to worry.

The next evening, Joe showed up with a collection of iron bolts and locks of various kinds. Alvin and Lois, totally surprised, challenged their concerned friend as the parts clanged onto the counter. "Joe, what is all this stuff? What do you intend to do with it?" Alvin asked.

"You aren't suggesting we put bars across our storefront, are you?" demanded Lois.

"If you will allow me, this material is some of what is needed for your rear door and windows. Most of it is staged outside. I can have it installed this evening. The alley is the most vulnerable place because it's dark and screened from view. We should start there. Tomorrow evening over dinner, we can discuss your options for securing the front of your store. That is, if you wish to discuss it then. Otherwise, we can talk about it at another time to your liking. Please accept my offer of help in the way it is intended—protecting one's friends when you can. This, to me, seems to be an obligation of true friendship. It is part of my code of honor." Joe explained.

Lois ran to him and threw her arms around him, sweet tears sticky on her cheeks. "We are lucky to have you as a friend!"

Alvin put his hand on Joe's shoulder. "Yes, Joe. I think improving the security of our store is needed. I would never contemplate turning down such generous help, and I would be a fool to not recognize your wisdom."

Lois followed Joe out the back door. The foundry had sent over a truck loaded with more iron and hardware, a ladder, and unrecognizable wood assemblies. As the man went to work, she stood in the doorway amazed. It was as if Joe had prepared blueprints and specifications just for them. He assembled a complex platform from the wooden pieces to create a scaffolding system. On it he placed large pullies with heavy ropes. He then began climbing across the rear facade like a drunken squirrel on a giant tree.

Alvin turned off the neon sign and locked the front door. He hung the Closed sign in the window. Stepping alongside Lois in the back doorway, he too was amazed. Watching as Joe grappled with the large pieces of iron, Alvin couldn't imagine how one man possessed so much strength. Soon Joe's assembled platform supported the largest and heaviest parts, placed in perfect alignment and skillfully connected to the building.

Sweat glistened on his exposed skin and pooled on scaffolding. Joe worked as if possessed—scaling the scaffold, descending, adding, and connecting this to that. In astonishment, Alvin called out, "Joe, I would like to help you, but don't know what you need. Is there anything I can do?"

Without turning from his work or stopping, Joe replied, "Yes, very good timing. Go inside and open the two rear windows, the one in your storage area, and the one in the bathroom. Slide the bottom sash up a little and the top one down a little. Stay inside near the pharmacy window. In just a few moments I will need your help to hold the window cages firmly against the wall from inside." Alvin did as instructed and was soon bracing the newly-assembled grates. He held each against the outside wall, one hand on top, and one on the bottom, while Joe completed the installation of the masonry anchor bolts. They next moved to the bathroom window and repeated the installation. Within another fifteen minutes, the final touches of the rear door grate were completed and the steel hasp was tested.

Joe handed Alvin a rather large padlock with three keys. "One key is for you; one is for Lois. The third one is for the police or firemen, or anyone else you wish to have emergency access. The rear windows to the store and to the basement are now protected. This lock is for the back door gate. Even the coal chute is now padlocked—the same key opens both. You can plan on being present for deliveries or remove the lock from the chute, your choice. But now it's secure."

An amazed Alvin insisted, "Joe, this must be very expensive material. Let us know the cost and then double it in payment for your labor."

Joe scoffed. "The price of true friendship cannot be measured in dollars. And anyway, I bartered with John Schmidt to get all the materials for free. So, your cost for my labor is simply our dinner tomorrow." Laughing, with a broad grin on his face, Joe added, "Object and I'll take it all back down."

Alvin's faced blushed in embarrassment of such generosity as he forced a laugh at Joe's quip. Lois dashed into the store as Joe disassembled his scaffolding and loaded it onto the truck. She grabbed a towel soaked in cool water and a bottle of Coke, handing him the refreshing combo just before he hopped in the cab of the company's truck.

"J'attends mes amis avec impatience, demain soir." Joe exclaimed after guzzling the soda and handing the empty bottle back to Lois.

She called back to him as he drove off, "We cannot wait for tomorrow evening either, dear friend."

Later that evening they heard Joe walking up the creaking stairs to his apartment after returning the truck to the foundry. Compelled to offer more expressions of their gratitude to him, Lois moved toward their apartment's door, but Alvin intercepted her gently. "We can show our love and appreciation over time, when natural opportunities occur. Let us not force ourselves upon him, lest we embarrass him." Lois, relented, bowing to her husband's obvious wisdom in the matter at hand.

Unknown to them, from the bay window of his apartment Joe spent the night keeping watch on the front of Lincolnway Pharmacy. It was not yet secure.

CHAPTER 35

After Tuesday's shift at the foundry, Joe walked home, detouring south along the Chicago River away from the direction of his apartment. He knew where wildflowers grew along the river's banks—sturdy plants that could thrive in the shadow of industry. From the river's edge, he collected black-eyed Susan, crested iris, and three of the long-shafted flowers of the prairie blazing star. Once satisfied with his selection, he gathered them into a pillowcase which he soaked with water. Racing home, he pulled out the only glass vase he owned, a masterpiece of colored glass by René-Jules Lalique. Filling it with water, Joe trimmed the flowers to length, arranging the natural beauty to honor their perfection.

While the thirsty flowers soaked up the water in their vase, Joe bathed and dressed in the finest lightweight Italian wool, black dress slacks, perfectly polished black Italian leather shoes, and a crisp white dress shirt. All his clothes looked new, fit perfectly, and were brought to sartorial splendor as he pulled on a classic gray double-vented herringbone sport coat made of an exquisite tropical weight blend of silk and wool. Absent his disfigurement, anyone might think him a statesman or actor, ready for presentation to an adoring public. It would be the first time Joe socialized since the foundry accident. His heart was filled with a mix of fear and excitement.

Downstairs, Alvin closed up the pharmacy. Upstairs, Lois had spent the afternoon preparing their meal. At precisely 6:30 p.m., the time of his invitation, Joe knocked on the door of the rear apartment. With a beaming smile that lit up the hallway, Lois beckoned Joe entry.

Holding the bouquet behind his back, he brought the arrangement around into Lois's view before entering. "Please tell me where you would like me to place this vase. I picked these for you this afternoon." Joe's lovely arrangement with its perfectly complementary French vase made a big impression.

"Why, thank you, Joe. They're absolutely beautiful!"

Joe set the flowers where Lois directed. She inspected the glass more closely. "Lalique?" she asked, stunned, as Joe nodded yes.

Reaching for his hand, Lois continued. "Joe, your taste in flowers is exquisite. And the vase is magnificent. Although I wish them to last forever, I will return the vase to you once the flowers fade."

"Lois, this vase had not held flowers for many years. Why don't you keep it here so I may bring you flowers more often?"

"Joe, that is not right. You should bring flowers to brighten your own apartment. This vase is something you should enjoy. After all, it is yours and it is beautiful." Lois' reply received a subtle sigh from their guest as Alvin came out of the kitchen.

As Alvin greeted Joe, the dinner guest next produced a small package from his jacket pocket. He handed it to his friend, who unwrapped it. Inside he discovered a miniature plaque bearing the image of a round and healthy tree, with *Etz Chaim* (Hebrew for Tree of Life) written below. One dozen small gems—possibly emeralds, sapphires, and rubies—set like fruit upon the branches, glistened brightly. Intricate silver scrolls highlighted the golden tree. Free of tarnish, Alvin wondered if the fine lines were platinum. Admiring his friend's elegant taste, Alvin turned the piece over. The signature on the back read, House of Vever. He noted the item's heft. Mostly gold, he wondered? The workmanship was outstanding. "Joe, this is beautiful! Exceptional! Who is the jeweler?"

Joe replied softly, almost as if to honor the plaque's meaning. "It is something my father picked up decades ago in France. Now it is mine. Vever is known as one of the finest jewelers in all of France. I believe Proverbs 3:18 refers to the Torah when it says, 'She is a tree of life to those who grasp her.' Is this not the case?"

Alvin, enthusiastically shook Joe's hand and replied, "Yes, I believe you are correct. Thank you, but this is very expensive. I fear it is of extraordinary worth. We cannot accept something this valuable."

Joe did not release Alvin's right hand, but gently took hold of Lois's hand with his left to complete the connection between them all. "It is fitting that you two keep it. You shall leave it to your children, as a remembrance of your heritage and Lois' childhood home. I have no one to whom I can leave such treasures. In as much as it is mine—and therefore may do with it what I want—my wish is that you accept this token of my friendship. Please say yes. If not for me, then for your first born."

Alvin realized it would be rude and destructive to refuse Joe's gift. "We shall cherish this forever." Eagerly, Lois added a hug and a kiss to express her joy and gratitude. At that moment, Lois resolved in her mind that Joe would be the first to hear of their recently discovered secret. Even though at the same time, she could not shake an eerie, mystical feeling that somehow, he might already know she was pregnant—but that was impossible.

"You are most welcome. Thank you for accepting it." Joe replied.

Leading their friend to the dining room table, they lingered over a scrumptious dinner and delightful conversation. Joe noticed his friend had not exaggerated about the quality of Lois's cooking. The French cuisine was exceptional. A kind and caring hostess, after the meal, Lois started to clear the table as Alvin led Joe to a comfortable seat in the living room. But the guest had something else on his mind. As Lois raced through clean up, Alvin waited politely for Joe to sit before taking his own seat.

Moments later, Joe grabbed the armrests and flung himself to standing. "I need to retrieve something from my apartment. I'll be back in a flash!"

Joe returned with a bottle of an unknown liquid. Holding up the dusty, greenish bottle with a yellowing and tattered label, he handed it to Alvin as Lois entered the room from the kitchen. "My love, Joe just brought this bottle in moments ago. He ran out of here like a man possessed. Look! The label is dominated by the letter N contained within a circular wreath and above it a crown. It is dated 1811, the label reads: *Grande Fine Champagne, Imperial.*"

Lois jumped forward toward her husband and gently, carefully reached for the bottle with both hands as if reaching for a holy relic. She studied the label, then burst out, "Alvin! Joe! *'C'est la comète,'* this is 1811 cognac, the year of the comet! The very cognac of Napoleon himself! My goodness, Joe, however did you find such a thing?"

From a padded box, they did not even notice he had carried in, Joe produced three balloon glasses. "I shall tell you the story of this bottle as we enjoy our opportunity to taste the only true perfection of the vine."

The mysterious but endearing man poured a bit for each, handing the glasses to his friends. "First, please wait to drink. Hold your glass this way." He showed them how to warm the brandy with their hands. "Now, you must understand, 1811 is regarded as the greatest vintage of the nineteenth century throughout the vineyards of Western Europe—perhaps the entire world—and quite possibly of all time. A long, hot summer and warm, dry autumn provided an abundant harvest of perfectly ripe grapes. At the same time, there was an extraordinary astronomical event. A comet appeared, brilliant enough to be seen by the naked eye. Astronomers tracked it for seventeen months. At harvest, they say it appeared even wider than the full moon. This is why 1811 is known as 'The Comet Vintage' and cherished around the world over all other cognacs. No other vintage compares, and perhaps none ever shall."

Alvin and Lois exchanged surprised glances. Who was this man—poet, philosopher, builder, collector of fine things, and master of languages, but sadly trapped in a repulsive physical package. If only people could get beyond his frightening exterior to reach the awe-inspiring interior! "Tell us how you came to possess such a thing, Joe," Alvin insisted.

"Let us first savor this glorious fruit of the vine for it has been touched by heaven itself!" With the warming complete, he raised his glass and offered a toast. *"Que cette maison ne connaisse que la paix et la prospérité et que ses occupants vivent en bonne sante.*" Lois translated for her husband: "May this house know only peace and prosperity and may its occupants live in good health."

Before the combination of warmth and flavor crossed their lips, each followed Joe's example by sampling its aromatic properties captured by the snifter. Then they slowly sipped the warm liquid velvet. Its bouquet and taste were captivating—like nothing they had experienced before. Singular in its qualities, the cognac was bold and powerful, but smooth and satisfying.

"Exquisite!" exclaimed Alvin. "It seems to have the aroma of citrus, perhaps tobacco. I've never known something this wonderful. It tastes sweet but somehow also slightly bitter, but not in an unpleasant way. It warms like nothing I have ever tasted."

"And I detect hints of vanilla, and perhaps caramel, too." Lois added.

While they savored the experience of drinking the world's finest cognac, Joe addressed Alvin's question. "Alvin, now that you have tasted perfection, I will answer your question of how this magnificent liquid came into my possession. The family of a French colonel gave it to me as a gift after the war. They were very generous."

Alvin objected. "Wait a minute, Joe. That's not the whole story, is it? This rare item would not simply be a gift without something far greater to the story. Now please, tell us."

"Okay. I shared the cognac so I guess I opened the door to the story." With that he settled into his seat, seemingly staring at nothing, a blank look upon his face as he began in a suddenly monotone voice. "Many of us were called to duty in the American Expeditionary Force to serve in France and Belgium during the Great War. Some of us saw battle. Some saw many battles. I had the honor to serve and the misfortune to see many die. Perhaps it was fate, or perhaps it was luck, but in The Battle of St. Miheil, I was able to help a grievously injured soldier. Thankfully, he recovered."

Joe paused to gather control of his thoughts and emotions, the expression in his voice returning. "Well, some of the French generals seemed to think what I did was a big deal. I can't say if it was, or if it was not. I simply did what needed to be done at the time. Anyway, in helping my comrade, I started a string of events culminating in the rescue of a French colonel and one of his companies, including every one of its one hundred men. They were outflanked and about to be destroyed. Anyway, his family owned a successful vineyard for many generations, and they showed their appreciation with a case of six bottles. I had a heck of a time getting them back to the States, but things just worked out." His heart dropped, realizing he had just disclosed certain aspects of his past life—something he swore he would never do.

"Joe, you honor us by sharing. Please tell us more. We can only imagine what other extraordinary things you might know or have seen."

"Certainly, Alvin," Joe obliged, no longer staring at nothing. "Now, where to start?" He paused for a moment, his hand on his chin. Then he continued. "My father studied chemistry, french, and commercial law at Marquette College in Milwaukee. I was born the year he graduated, in 1895. Immediately after, he pursued and received his law degree from Harvard. Afterward, the DuPont Corporation hired him. When I was four years old he needed to spend as many as nine months a year in Europe, so, we acquired a home in Paris. Because of my father's travel around Europe, I was most often privately tutored there. When I came of age, I followed my father's footsteps, matriculating at Marquette. There, I studied mathematics. I excelled, so I guess that's why the army wanted me as an officer. Unfortunately, my parents retired back to Wisconsin but succumbed to the Spanish Flu while I was fighting in Europe." Now the man's face plainly registered his pain.

Sheepishly Alvin offered comfort. "Joe, it is enough that you have shared these things with us. I shall ask no more. Your friendship is more than good fortune for us." Alvin and Lois stared down at their glasses, not knowing what else to say. The amazing complexity of Joe Metal Harpy just kept growing, both in awe-inspiring ways, but also in profound sadness.

As Joe broke free of his discomfort, he swirled his cognac, tears forming in his eyes. He set down his glass, pulled a linen handkerchief from his pocket and dabbed his eyes. "Forgive my tendency toward melancholy's irresistible distraction. Sometimes I need to be stronger. I don't want my story to ruin the pleasure of this evening together, and this heavenly elixir we share. Let's talk of happier topics. So, Lois, tell us about your childhood in France."

The young woman, a bit shy in speaking of herself, demurred. Joe had no idea of the implications of his request. But Alvin lovingly encouraged her until Lois was ready to open up, too. After hearing Joe's story, she lovingly hoped the parallels of loss in her exceptional childhood might, in an odd way, be comforting to Joe, so she decided to speak freely.

"Although in danger and persecuted, my parents worked on the Jewish rights movement with others in Warsaw. As hostility to all Jewish people worsened, fearing for their lives, they escaped to France when I was very young. Still activists for the cause when the Great War broke out, they worked as best they could from Paris. When I was only eight years old, they were both found hanged in the *Foret Domaniale De Fontainebleau*. My father's younger brother, Uncle François, took me in. He too was hunted but managed to avoid capture for years. One day, he announced, 'we are leaving.' We escaped to Spain, but still a marked man he brought me to America. He is the only family I know." Now weeping gently, Lois set down her glass, only a small disk of amber liquid at its bottom.

"My dearest Lois. I shall never forgive myself for such prompting. But while you have lost much, you have found God's favor in your freedom and your marriage. You honor me by sharing your family's story. Somehow, I know your children and your children's children will be a blessing for generations. Let us speak no more of our pasts this evening."

From tenant, to friend, Joe was now becoming part of their family, even though their first dinner together had been more emotionally raw than any of them could have foreseen. Joe and Lois now shared a special bond—one only they could understand. Each experienced the maturity of heart which comes from bearing one's own suffering and profound loss but then replacing it with gratitude for all that is, in spite of the pain. After attempting and failing with a few perfunctory topics, the evening's visit drew to a close.

The next couple of weeks at work for Wally went as planned. He developed and implemented the sales and production cross-reference system and presented other ideas to Miss Brownley for improving the personnel files. He hoped that would get him closer to the payroll process. It would be his crowning glory to figure out the perfect payroll heist before he moved to Indiana. Martha would be so proud!

During the two weeks before Aunt Martha's return, Wally spent a lot of evenings watching the block containing Lincolnway from across the street, partially hidden in doorways of the multistory office and industrial colossus on the north side of Fullerton Avenue. He invented excuses to enter the other storefront businesses on the pharmacy's side of the block as well, looking for opportunities. Exactly what, he did not know, but he stored all the data in his mind's nearly infinite capacity. He often walked the alley behind Lincolnway, considering all of the rear entrances. Meanwhile, Bobby still languished in jail. Although Ziggy was regularly spotted wandering the streets searching for Wally, the young thief successfully avoided him.

Wally's first Thursday call to Martha took forty minutes. Alvin could not help speculating on what might be going on with Wally as he heard the boy keep dropping coins into the pay phone intermittently. Love? Girl trouble? Something else? Perplexed, he shook his head at the boy's odd behavior.

The prior evening, Alvin stayed late assisting Joe with installing an alarm system. If tripped, a horn would blare loudly in the store along with a strobe light. And a buzzer would sound in the rear apartment. As Alvin closed up the pharmacy that night, Joe started work on the alarm. A few minutes later, Mr. Green stuck his head through the front doorway, asking, "May I trouble you for more cough syrup and aspirin, please? I know you are already closed, but Mr. Feherty is still struggling a bit. It looks like he is improving, but I don't want to take any chances. He and I had to work long on one of our projects and I lost track of the time. I'm sorry I caught you after closing time."

Simultaneously, Green watched the alarm installation, his interest growing while Alvin prepared his order. Green spoke to Joe. "Sir, that is a very clever design you are implementing—hidden doorframe switches, and invisible pressure sensors around the window and entry—all low voltage. How did you come up with it?" Green asked Joe.

Alvin looked on bewildered as he noticed Joe did not try to hide his face from Mr. Green. Instead, standing up, he replied directly with some technical terms about types of switches, wires, and transformers. "That's brilliant!" Green exclaimed. "It appears to be a modification of systems New York City banks often use on their vault perimeters. And your pressure sensors are almost impossible to notice. Again, how did you come up with it?"

"It's nothing," Joe replied. "I just picked up some ideas from army telegraph and telephone engineers trying to improve headquarters' security and communications during and after the war. It's similar to what you say, but without a central station. The low voltage makes it easy for even an amateur like me. How do you, a guy in an expensive suit, know about such things?"

The man extended his hand to introduce himself, while staring intently at the tattoos on both of Joe's forearms. "I'm Daniel Joseph Green, Special Agent with the Federal Bureau of Investigation. I came to Chicago from New York, by way of DC to train at the Scientific Crime Detection Library at Northwestern University's Law School. The director told me to stay—with all the mobsters, this is a very busy field office. I guess they needed an investigative scientist like me."

Delighted, Joe gave Green a hearty handshake. I'm Joseph Harpy, steelworker, and a part time handyman, I guess. It is a pleasure to meet you, Mr. Green."

"Mr. Harpy, please call me DJ, that's what my friends call me. Why does your name sound familiar? Did you grow up in New York?"

Noticing Mr. Green's focus, Joe casually rolled his shirt-sleeves back down to his wrists, and with his broken smile replied, "No, my father was a lawyer with DuPont Corporation. I was born in the States, but grew up mostly in France. Once I came back to the States, I came to Chicago for a job and ended up staying because of people like Alvin, Lois, and the Schmidt family. I doubt we know each other unless you spent much of your childhood in Europe, like me. Now, if you'll excuse me, I've got quite a bit left to do."

"Well, maybe I didn't know you before, but I'm glad to have met you now." Extending his hand again, he repeated his interest in a possible friendship. "Delighted to meet you, Mr. Harpy, and I didn't mean to delay you. I apologize."

Relieved, he replied. "Please, just call me Joe."

"Okay Joe, I hope we can talk again soon. I want to know more about your alarm system." Alvin handed the bag of medicines to Mr. Green. Walking out he called to Alvin, "Thank you for the medicines for Mr. Feherty."

An hour later, as Alvin and Joe completed the installation, Lois came down from their apartment to check on their progress. "Joe, I have taken the liberty of setting you a place at our table for dinner. I hope you'll join us."

"Thank you, Lois, I would enjoy that very much. But you won't get me to bring more cognac unless I have time to dress properly."

She and Alvin chuckled at his reply, happy that he could now truly be himself with them. Alarm installed, switched on, and a delicious dinner consumed, Joe returned to his apartment, again spending hours sitting on the bay window studying the shapes and shadows of everyone on the street. Ever since the war, he found it difficult to sleep, and now his protective instincts were on high alert. Many nights he would wander the streets and alleys, but tonight, regardless of the new alarm, he kept watch.

CHAPTER 37

A couple of days before her arrival, Martha and Wally held the second week's Thursday call and confirmed their plan was ready to proceed. Alvin, distracted from his work, had observed the boy's call as somewhat boisterous, both by the increased volume of Wally's voice and his gesticulations inside the booth. Straining to hear what was being said with his face staring down at his mortar and pestle, Alvin didn't even notice Joe striding across the back threshold and onto the best eavesdropping stool.

Meanwhile, Wally grew evermore consumed with his phone call. Martha spoke excitedly to her nephew. "I can't wait to see you Saturday, and guess what? On Sunday, you will get to meet Jack! We will all stay at the house where you and I bivouacked. I have to stop there and drop off some things Jack needs, but don't worry, my love, I'll be at your house Saturday afternoon." In excitement, Wally could scarcely keep from jumping up and down and repeating her words. Martha continued, "Wally, you will not be going to work at the foundry next week. This is your chance at freedom and our chance to be together. Our plan is still set for Saturday night. Tell me again, you're sure about the couriers?"

"Yes, I am certain." Wally replied.

"Good!" Martha exclaimed. "That means Lincolnway is supplying the hospital now. You'll need the largest zippered bag with your overalls again. We might get north of five grand on the street if there is as much in the pharmacy as I estimate—plus the cash on hand. Have you memorized the list of drugs?"

"Yes, and I can even spell the full chemical names," the young thief assured his accomplice. "I know exactly what to take. I also know a couple of derivations for each. Don't worry, I won't miss a thing. I've studied all about the narcotics we're after." He repeated all the instructions to confirm his complete grasp of every detail.

With that, Wally said goodbye, pushed open the phone booth door, and intended to set off for the foundry. But turning to exit, he was startled to see Joe Metal Harpy, standing inches away, blocking his path. The terrifying man stared the boy down.

"What are you looking at, freak? Aren't you supposed to be at the foundry? Go to work! And quit staring at people!" Wally tried to push his way past Joe to the exit.

Joe grabbed the boy's arm. "Who were you talking to? Your Aunt Martha again? When is she coming back to visit?"

Now furious at being accosted, Wally reared back with his free arm to punch Joe, but the older man effortlessly blocked it. Joe slid his grip from the boy's biceps, down to his wrist, and maneuvered the boy's arm, twisting it behind the teenager's back. Applying more pressure, the boy cried out in pain but still resisted.

"Let me go you, freak!" Wally screamed. But Joe increased the pressure as he slammed the boy into the phone booth door. The tempered glass panel fractured, resembling a spider's web.

"Tell me when she is coming back and I'll let you go." Joe Metal Harpy increased the pressure even more to convince the boy there was no escape. "Keep resisting me, and I'll dislocate your shoulder."

"Okay, okay. She's coming Saturday afternoon. She loves me. She wants to see me again. What's the big deal, you monster?" Joe released the boy's arm.

Alvin watched, dumbfounded at the fury unleashed by his mysterious friend. Wally sped to the door and outside like a shot. "Joe, what was that about? Why did you want to know about his Aunt Martha?"

Joe, looking down at the floor like someone truly embarrassed at his own aggression, or perhaps concealing a lie, replied, "I'm sorry to have acted that way, Alvin. I just think she might be a bad influence on him. That's all. If she's around,

I may need to talk to her. I'll take care of the broken glass. Don't worry, I'll repair it after work this afternoon. Alvin, I am so sorry. My behavior was detestable—please forgive me."

Alvin remained stunned. His friend, the poet, philosopher, and linguist suddenly became a force of intense physical violence, effortlessly subduing a powerful young man. He wondered what horrors his friend must have lived through during the war. Not sure what to say about it or Joe's concerns about the relationship between Wally and Martha, he offered something he hoped might help. "Joe, it's alright. I understand that you did what you thought best. You are such a wise and insightful soul. I am certain you knew what you were doing, and I won't give it another thought."

Neither man said another word, nor did they look at one another. Joe turned and exited through the rear door. It was then that Alvin realized Joe should have been at the foundry.

CHAPTER 38

Finished with his third and fourth weeks at the foundry, Wally received his pay Friday afternoon. Miss Brownley handed him twenty-one dollars, and with it, two silver dollars. Referring to the latter, she said, "These are a gift from Mr. Schmidt. He has been in and out of the files with his auditors the last couple of days. Everyone was very impressed with your cross-reference system. They can't wait to see your next system completed. Keep it up, Wally. You might have a real bright future here after you graduate high school."

Smiling, Wally snatched the paper bills and coins from her, and moved to the door. His plans forefront in his mind, he nevertheless appeared gracious. "Thank you, ma'am. And thank Mr. Schmidt for me, just in case I don't see him soon. You are all very generous." Planning to be headed to Indiana by the end of the weekend, he couldn't resist dropping the subtle hint about not being able to thank Schmidt himself. Wally liked everything in his life to be neat and tidy— especially using his newly-mastered skill of the white lie.

Once home, he handed over all the cash as dictated by his father. Peter counted the bills upon the kitchen table, then let Wally pocket one-third of his pay, the undisclosed coins notwithstanding. Grumbling to himself, Wally murmured under his breath, "He has no business telling me what to do with my pay. I'm making him look good with the improvements I'm making to the office."

Despite no longer having friends to hang with, Wally walked to Lincolnway. After verifying Ziggy was not there, he went inside to have a Coke and look over things one last time. The security on the rear of the pharmacy was formidable. Wally had watched the alarm being installed on the front of the store while hiding in the shadows across the street. He knew he couldn't avoid the sensors around the inside of the entrance or storefront. Standing up, he subtly, quietly spit on the marble floor when sure no one was looking, and laughed to himself, the fools never thought to study security from every angle. Few things could ever escape Wally's powers of observation. He reasoned no one would ever figure out how he did it—his second perfect crime.

CHAPTER 39

Saturday morning, the day of Aunt Martha's highly anticipated third visit, Wally arrived at Lincolnway around 8:15 a.m. He bought a chocolate phosphate, then took a seat on the rearmost stool—the one nearest the phone booth and the only stool he preferred. Just like the evening before, the boy sat slowly sipping his phosphate, waiting. Occasionally he looked around the pharmacy. Although glancing at a newspaper, he didn't read it; he didn't make conversation with anyone; he just sat. When Lois tried to engage him in small talk, clearly annoyed, he gave one-word answers. She gave up. Thirty minutes after the boy took his favorite seat, DJ Green came through the front door and took the vacant seat next to Wally who immediately jumped up and made a beeline for the back door.

With the pharmacy momentarily empty of other customers, DJ called out, "Alvin, Lois, come see this. I must talk to you." He opened a portfolio exposing newspaper articles and photos containing images of soldiers, important people, parades, and military medals. "I thought I recognized the words on those tattoos!" DJ exclaimed.

Lois leaned over to see why Green seemed so excited. "What are you talking about? What tattoos? What are you doing with all of this stuff Mr. Green? I'll need my counter back for my customers, please."

DJ Green's excitement was out of control. "I knew the tattooed phrase on Joe Harpy's arms sounded familiar. I knew it—I knew it—I knew it! That was the clue. It was his company's motto—the motto of the most famous company in the army. I checked the names of all the soldiers in it—there was no one named Harpy. The only name close was that of its famous captain—Joseph Harper. He couldn't hide behind a name change. He is a bona fide hero. No way did I ever think I would meet him. The man is a legend!"

Spreading out the content of his portfolio across the fountain's counter from end to end, Green went on. "Your friend, Joe, is one of the most decorated American soldiers in the Great War, Captain Joseph Harper. Look, this is a photo of him receiving the Distinguished Service Cross, the second-highest United States Army military award given for extreme gallantry and risk of life in actual combat—he's receiving it from General JJ Pershing himself. Alvin, Lois, he earned it four times! He received multiple Silver Star Medals which is awarded for singular acts of valor or heroism. And there is more, much more. Look here," Green expounded, pointing to one of the photos. The French *Croix de Guerre* with a silver palm! Alvin, that means he was awarded it by the French Army five times for acts of heroic valor! The silver palm is almost impossible to attain."

Joe's two friends stood in stunned silence.

"This is unbelievable." The words tumbled from Alvin's lips, propelled by shock and concern. Then he focused on one photo taken under the Arch de' Triumph. "What is this one?"

"That is the French President Raymond Poincaré and French Prime Minister Georges Clemenceau who personally awarded him the Légion d'Honneur. Here are several articles from US and French newspapers describing the ceremony. It was quite an event."

Lois began to gasp, reaching for Alvin's arm for support. "Oh my, Joe, what happened to you? Look at him Alvin, he was so handsome. My dear, sweet Joe!"

Green continued to gush. "There were rumors that President Wilson might award him the Congressional Medal of Honor, but the man just disappeared. Not even the Army or the White House staff could find him. Do you know how he ended up here? Why did he change his name? Although I can't think why someone would choose the name of mythical female demons from Dante's Inferno. What happened to him—why did he want to hide?"

Husband and wife stared at each other in disbelief. "Mr. Green," Alvin spoke up, "thank you for sharing this information, but I almost wish you had not. Joe is a very private person who does not speak much of his past. I think it best that you keep this information to yourself, and never speak of it to anyone, especially Joe."

Green's face blushed apple-red. "I did not think about it that way. I'm an investigative scientist, so that's just how my brain works. I see a mystery and I try to solve it. Once I had a clue that he might be Captain Harper, I could not resist looking into it." He slapped his forehead with his hand, then began to quickly gather all of the historic material back into his portfolio as the bell on the front door tinkled, announcing more customers. Green then shook his head in disbelief at his own folly. "Yes, of course. It shall remain our secret. I am so sorry to have intruded on a hero's privacy and to have made you uncomfortable. You can count on me to not divulge anything about him or his past—I promise." Portfolio zipped shut, DJ Green exited, his excitement turned to embarrassment and regret.

CHAPTER 40

Saturday, Martha arrived right on time. Helen greeted her at the door, smothering her with affection. "Martha, Wally's last two weeks at work were even better than the first two. He might even get a raise if his next filing system is as good as Mr. Schmidt hopes it will be. And everything has been much better between him and his father. You have been such a good influence on him. You're the best big sister I could ever hope for."

Martha laughed wickedly. "Glad to hear Peter didn't hurt him again. Wally's a special boy and becoming such a man so quickly. I love him like he was my own. I'm going to keep an eye on Peter to make sure he doesn't do something stupid again."

Helen just stood dumbfounded, not sure what to make of her sister's comment. "Martha, I am so happy we are reunited, but please don't be so hard on Peter—he's a wonderful man." The younger sister paused, but Martha did not react, so Helen continued. "Maybe you could open up a little and tell me at least part of what you've been up to for all these years. I so want to share in your life again. And maybe it would help me understand why you say some of the things you do."

"You're right to be curious," Martha admitted. "I'm sorry that I've been so private. How about Monday morning, after Peter and Wally have gone to the foundry, you and I can just sit and talk over some coffee? All morning if we like. I think I owe you that and more—you've been such a wonderful sister again." With that Martha grabbed an apron and suggested Helen relax for a little—Martha would help take care of things in the kitchen.

The criticism of Peter forgotten, the sisters prepared dinner while Wally watched the little ones in the backyard. Peter had another Saturday meeting with Fritz and Mr. Schmidt at the foundry office that would hopefully end in time for the family's meal together.

Right on time, but looking a little exhausted, Peter returned home. It was the first time Helen had wondered if all the work and study was taking a toll on her husband. Concerned, she served dinner with just an extra bit of love as its secret ingredient. Cooking was one of her favorite, tangible expressions of affection for Peter and her entire family.

After their bountiful feast, the exceptionally warm weather drew the family toward the shade of the front porch. Across the street, the fading rays of the evening sun illuminated the front of St. Joseph's Church, making the gothic architecture look more like art than reality. It beckoned everyone's imagination as they listened to Peter recite the melting points of various metals and alloys. Preparing himself for a major exam at metallurgy class Monday night, he explained how alloys are made by combining different elements in precise proportions and temperatures, himself never noticing the church's facade.

Martha interrupted Peter. "Excuse me, but my back is stiff from the car ride. Come on Wally, take a walk with me. That should help my back. If not, we'll go to Lincolnway and ask Alvin for something." The two stepped off the porch together and out the wrought iron gate leading from their front yard onto the city sidewalk. They headed north toward Fullerton Avenue. Alternatively passing from the heat of the early evening sun, to the cooler shade of trees and buildings, they walked on until, Martha, certain they were not visible to the family, stopped and said, "Light me a cigarette, my love. Put it on my lips, my love." He obeyed. It drove him wild.

"Tonight, when I am done, let's go alone in the garage. I need to be with you, hold you, touch your body. I am going crazy thinking about your body. Maybe we can both sneak up to the attic or go somewhere in your car," Wally pleaded pitifully.

Martha took his hand in hers. "Wally, Sunday night we will have a bivouac party. It will be late and there will be plenty of food and vodka. There will be other women Jack knows there.

After the party winds down, you and I will have to share a bedroom. You know what that means don't you? I can't wait for you either, my love. But we must wait until we have privacy for the entire night, not hiding in your parent's garage. Just you and me in bed for hours, Wally."

The boy grabbed her shoulders, pulling her to him, hugging her, desperately kissing her on the lips as her cigarette fell to the ground. Martha shoved him away. "Control yourself!" Everybody knows you around here, and some know me too. Let's not get people talking before tonight's job is done. We can't call attention to ourselves. You can wait one more night." Wally obeyed, not contemplating that Martha would want to spend the next night with Jack.

After her scolding, she worked to change the boy's focus. "I told Jack all about you. He definitely wants you to work for him as his new driver. Did you hear me? You're going to drive for Jack! Oh, Wally, you are going to have money, fame, and me. But tonight, I need you to concentrate only on the job." They walked around the block and back to the house, saying little as nightfall brought Wally's second job for Aunt Martha ever closer.

At a quarter-after-two, her head near the bedroom window, Martha heard Wally exit by the rear porch stairs. Good! He was on schedule silently ran through her head.

Carrying two metal bars, one flat and one round, the teen robber silently approached the back door of the tailor shop next to Lincolnway. Using the stiff round bar, he spread the doorframe just enough to allow the doorknob's shallow bolt to loosen contact with its corresponding slot in the jamb. It opened easily. There was no deadbolt. He entered quietly, shutting the door behind him. The inside part of the knob did not have a key but a thumb latch. He verified it was locked behind him.

Switching on his Eveready Soldier Boy D-Cell Flashlight, Wally moved down the stairs, into the basement. He had changed out the clear lens to a red one, reducing the chance anyone might see its light while on the first floor. At the front portion of the tailor shop's basement, he opened the metal door leading to the vaulted sidewalk. Its unexpected loud creaking startled the boy as the cool air from inside washed over him filling his nostrils with the vulgar, damp stench of the city's secret underground.

Wally spit, then laughed to himself for reassurance—the idiots did not think of security from every angle. It would be the perfect entry point for the brilliant young thief.

His heart pounding, the coolness of the man-made cavern offered Wally some temporary relief on the hottest weekend of the year. After ten steps, he reached the metal door that led into Lincolnway's basement. It was locked from inside, as expected. The day the five boys, led by Wally, helped Alvin unload, he took note of every aspect of the store, even the latch mechanism on the basement door to the vaulted sidewalk.

Struggling to force open the metal basement door even a quarter of an inch, he pried again and again with the pointed tip of the ridged round bar until he finally could insert the second, flat one made from a soft alloy. In spite of his trembling hands, he carefully bent it at the precise angles needed for its purpose. Now sweating profusely, after multiple unsuccessful tries he was finally able to force up the door-width bolts hinged together and mounted on the interior face of the door. The frame and door edge only slightly dented, the bolts lifted as the flat bar performed as expected. At last, he was in! His excitement growing, he walked up the pharmacy's basement stairs, being careful to not make any noise.

Once on the main floor, Wally briefly switched off his flashlight—enough light poured in from streetlights for him to reach the pharmacy's locked shelves without it. Now in the rows of cabinets of glass, framed by narrow rails and stiles of oak, he saw countless small trays each containing specific drugs. Alvin had everything placed in alphabetical order by their pharmaceutical names. It could not have been easier and faster for Wally. He switched on the flashlight. The red lens provided just enough light to read the labels and locate the targeted drugs without being visible from outside. The thin wooden frames of the cabinets failed to secure their contents as Wally pried them open with the iron rod, shattering the glass as the frames flexed and gave way. His heart raced, fearing someone might hear the breaking glass. None did—the noise of the building's air conditioning attenuated the sound. Completing the entire burglary from entry to exit, in ten minutes, he decided he had time to quickly grab two packs of Camels. Why not a couple of packs? He chuckled as he stuffed the front slash pockets of the overalls. With great care, he exited the way he came.

The small dents in the vault door were virtually unnoticeable from the inside of the pharmacy's basement, and the three horizontal steel bolts hinged and pivoting together on the door's face still functioned properly. Once back in the vault, he carefully closed the door behind him, first placing the flat steel bar with its perfect angles, between the door and its frame. He pulled the door shut firmly against the flat bar, first positioning it to hold the bolts above their latches. He struggled to pull the flat bar back as the pressure of the closed door held it tightly. Without warning as he strained with all his might, the flexible flat bar scraped free, straightened by the pressure of door against frame—Wally fell backward. The married latches fell into place. The door to the vaulted sidewalk was now locked from inside just as he had found it. The flexible alloy bar worked as planned.

The city of Chicago created these mysterious spaces when they elevated most roadways to combat frequent street flooding. Trying to save money when they passed the first spending ordinance in 1855, the city engineers chose to only raise with fill, the street portion of the public right of way. The adjacent sidewalks were treated differently. Steel frames were installed at the new roadway elevation and new concrete sidewalks were poured in place, leaving the area under them hollow. First-floor doors of buildings became basement doors into the newly-created vaults.

Exiting the rear door of the tailor shop, the only clue left by the thief was a bit of splintering to the rear door's frame. This time there was no evidence to plant and no *jot* in the alley.

CHAPTER 41

Wally spotted Martha's car exactly where it should be. After setting the two bars in the trunk, he pulled the zippered sack from his overalls and dropped the gloves on top of it. Taking out the decoy bag, he noticed his bag of cash from the liquor store robbery was still there. Reassured, he hurriedly shut and locked the trunk.

When Wally reached the backyard, he found Martha sitting on the bench. She nodded, proudly and approvingly as he handed her the car keys and bag. Sneaking up the stairs, he changed out of his sweat-soaked clothes, and returned to the yard, just like before. She winked and pulled a bottle of vodka from her purse and handed it to Wally. After a few celebratory belts of liquid courage, the young Romeo stretched his arm around Martha and kissed her on the lips. She held his arm with one hand and placed the other on his thigh. As their lips separated, he drew closer and kissed her again, this time longer and more intensely. But Martha pulled away. "Wally, this is not the time or place for you to have me. Tonight, at the house in the woods, you and I will make love all night until sunrise."

But her nephew wasn't listening. He kissed her again and placed his hand on her breast. "Stop it!" she commanded. "You will never have me if you don't obey. You must wait until we are alone at Jack's place."

Wally continued trying to kiss and fondle her with mounting aggression, until finally Martha slapped his face. She jumped up from the bench. Stepping back a couple of paces from him, she suddenly brandished her dagger—the one she always carried since her mother gave it to her in Poland. Martha shot the lad a cold, steely-eyed glare. "If you ever try to force yourself on me again, I'll stick this in your heart, you monster! Understand? I have NO qualms about cutting your heart out of your chest and stomping on it!" Wally sat speechless, now believing that his aunt might be capable of anything, even murder. Humiliated, he raced to the back door and up the stairs to safety, his mind and hormones out of control.

Unable to sleep in the sweltering heat, Wally ventured downstairs to the kitchen around 4:00 a.m. thinking maybe some cold milk and a snack would help him sleep. He carefully snapped on the light, hoping not to wake anyone. He was stunned. Was it Martha? Yes, Martha!

She sat alone at the table, whispering to someone who wasn't there. "Aunt Martha, I'm sorry," he whispered. But the woman didn't reply, continuing her mysterious conversation with no one. "Aunt Martha, who are you talking to?"

Looking up with a blank stare, slowly she replied, "This little girl, here. Don't you see her?" Martha's voice began to tremble. "She's only thirteen. A very bad man just hurt her so I've given her milk and cookies to make her feel better." Still staring at her imaginary friend, she continued, "Don't worry, I'll protect you. He won't do it again. You feel better now, don't you? Aren't momma's cookies good? Everything will be fine. I'll give you a knife."

Wally, temporarily frozen in place, heard the door to his parent's bedroom open. Breaking free from his horror, he retreated onto the porch and back to his attic room before anyone else saw him. Scenes of the last few weeks kept playing in his head, how she had teased him, threatened him with a knife just an hour ago, and now this psychotic conversation. Crazy Aunt Martha had thousands of dollars of his procuring, and she was now in control of his life. Again and again, he relived these scenes, doubting completely whether he should go through with his plan to leave home to join her and Jack in Indiana. But if he stayed at home and angered her, he certainly risked arrest.

Whomever came out of the parent's bedroom, mother or father, Wally hoped they did not see and hear Martha's mental breakdown, or it would get in the way of recovering his share of the money. Suddenly, he realized that irrespective of his aunt's mental illness, he had to go to Indiana. At a minimum, he had to first ride with her to the house in the woods. Maybe he could get all the cash and leave the drugs with her as an equitable split. Wally shuddered as he realized the dawn was breaking and tonight, they would go to Jack's house. Her insanity quelled the flames of his lust. Now, his only idea was to go into the girls' bedroom and take the car keys from her; then drive off in the Oldsmobile. But she would not comply, even probably try to stick her knife in his chest as threatened. Certainly, his father would hear the commotion and intervene if he tried, then everything would come out. He had to wait.

Sunday Mass seemed impossible to imagine for Wally, but he forced himself to wash and dress in preparation. By the time he joined the family in the kitchen, Aunt Martha was interacting with his parents as if she was normal. She, too, was ready to attend church—Helen and Peter detected nothing amiss. Wally alone had seen Martha's psycho show.

The thought of walking with her or speaking to her seemed inconceivable. But he knew he had to muster the strength. He had no choice but to meet Jack and spend the night at the isolated country house. Wally knew little about the relationship between Jack and Aunt Martha, just that she called him a *friend*. Suddenly, he became even more gripped in terror, realizing he knew little about Jack or why Martha said he liked her more than the other girls.

Hopefully, he could escape late in the night with her car and some of the spoils of his crimes. But he knew she could turn him in at any time—Martha had him trapped. With things spiraling out of control, Wally couldn't even focus on where he'd go and what he'd do if he escaped with the car. Consumed by his dilemma, his usual problem-solving brilliance was now useless.

CHAPTER 42

Sunday morning, while Wally's family prayed in church, Alvin disabled the alarm and entered his store, flipping the sign to Open. He started his day as he always did, heading first to the pharmacy storage area, unlocking all the cabinets and double-checking all the items were facing forward so labels were easy to read. In moments, he felt the broken glass crunching under his feet as he stared into the cabinets in utter disbelief.

Racing to the front door, he relocked it. Alvin turned the sign from Open to Closed and switched off the neon sign. He then called the police. Within minutes, sirens wailed and police cars surrounded the entire block around Lincolnway.

Officers cordoned off the sidewalk and alley as Sergeant Fitzgerald waited at the front door. Alvin rushed over to him. "Sergeant, I think we have a real big problem here. I keep a large quantity of narcotics on-site for the hospital's use. It's all gone! All of it. It will be worth a small fortune on the street. The thief must have known when I receive shipments—but how could he? The couriers come in civilian dress. The packages they carry are always nondescript, and the transfer process is discreet."

"Step out here," Fitzgerald tilted his head toward the outside. "Until the evidence technicians arrive, I don't want anyone inside. Tell me exactly what happened—didn't your alarm sound?"

Perplexed, Alvin answered, "No sir, the alarm was on, but not triggered. It was still functional when I opened the door this morning."

Projecting a wry expression, Fitzgerald parroted back, "The door was locked, the alarm was on, and I suppose the iron gate on the back door was locked too? But still someone got in? What do you take me for, an idiot?"

"No," Alvin replied. "I do not take you for anything but one of Chicago's finest doing a difficult job. I don't understand how anyone got in here. The alarm was set and operational. The back door is still secure."

The cop replied sardonically, "Okay, that's your story. We'll just have to see how it checks out. When Captain Murphy gets here, he'll take charge."

Fitzgerald's caustic attitude didn't faze Alvin. "I will cooperate in any way—and every way—possible. This was a significant quantity of high-grade pharmaceuticals. I hate to think of all the patients suffering in pain if the hospitals run short. And if it falls in the hands of addicts, there will be death on our streets as well."

"Who installed that metal grating on the back door and windows and who did your alarm system on the front?" Fitzgerald demanded.

"My tenant, Joe Harpy. Do you want me to call him down or do you want to go up to his apartment? I'm sure he won't mind," Alvin offered. Just then, Joe stepped out of the apartment lobby.

"Good morning, Alvin, Sergeant Fitzgerald." Joe began.

Fitzgerald interrupted the man. "Look Mr. Harpy, I want you to stay in your apartment and do not leave until one of our detectives or I tell you it is okay. Understand? You stay put! You're a suspect!"

Startled, Joe demanded, "Suspect? For what? What's going on?"

By then, Lois had heard the commotion and appeared behind Joe in the entryway.

"Hi, Lois. You go to your apartment, too. We will be up to see you in a few minutes."

Lois pushed past Joe and ran to Alvin. Opening his arms as she came near, he embraced her. "We've been robbed, darling. All the narcotics—and the cash in the register, but that's it. The store will be fine. The thief did little damage. Please, go upstairs and wait. Sergeant Fitzgerald says we will be interviewed once the detectives arrive and the evidence technicians get started."

Lois wouldn't have any of it. "What do you mean, we've been robbed? How could anyone break in with the iron bars on the back and the alarm on the front? What's going on?"

Alvin hugged her more firmly now. "I know, my love. It makes no sense. We will have to cooperate with the police and hope they find the thief. Joe, please wait upstairs. Lois, you too. I'll be up in just a moment."

Confounded by the improbable circumstances, Fitzgerald had to consider all possibilities. "You know what, Alvin? This doesn't smell right to me—not at all. You go to your apartment now! I don't want any of you around here. For all I know, the three of you pulled this off. Alvin, give me your keys for the front and back. Now, get out of here. And don't try to escape out the back stairs. I already have men posted there."

As the three suspects headed up to their apartments, Joe offered Alvin and Lois to wait with him in his apartment. Entering Joe's sanctuary, Lois scanned the scene. "Joe, this must be the cleanest bachelor apartment in Chicago!"

"Thank you," he grinned. "I am delighted that you two are the first to see it. Please, sit down. I shall bring us all some tea." This man who had faced death a thousand times was unfazed by the suspicions of Sergeant Fitzgerald.

Lois stared at the wall-to-wall bookcase at the opposite side of the room. There must be three hundred books upon its shelves, she thought to herself.

Before Joe even put water in the kettle, the door sounded. Bam, bam, bam! A thick Irish brogue boomed through the door, "Open up! Joseph Jeffrey, it's Michael Martin, you old son of a bitch!"

Joe threw the door open and a husky man with a big, round face towered in the doorway. The giant creature grabbed Joe, wrapping him in a bear hug. "Sergeant Murphy reporting for duty, captain!" The two men hugged as if their lives depended on it. It was as if both had been utterly deprived of joy their entire lives until that moment. The onlookers' faces registered their surprise to see the emotion dripping down two burly military men's faces.

Eventually, the man with the big, round, and now somewhat red face noticed Joe's guests and released him. "Excuse me, lads—I did not expect anyone to be here." Chuckling, he turned toward the couple. "Michael Murphy..." he announced, extending his hand to Joe's friends, "...Captain of Detectives."

Standing up, Alvin shook his hand. "Nice to meet you, Captain Murphy, though I wish it was not under such dire circumstances. I'm Alvin and this is my wife, Lois."

"How do you do?" Lois smiled warmly.

Then, turning to Joe, the detective demanded, "Joseph, bring us some of that special herbal tea you always talked about. Unless you still have a bit of that cognac. If you do, I could use just a wee nip."

Murphy led the pair in small talk while Joe prepared the kettle, tea, and honey—no milk. "So, I understand you own this building and Joseph is one of your tenants."

"Yes, and he has become a dear friend as well, captain. What a remarkable man—he and I speak French together. And he even told us how he came to possess that rare cognac," Lois replied.

Joe returned with an intricate bamboo tray carrying the hot refreshment in china cups on matching saucers, each gently rimmed in black and gold with a unique floral pattern. "Michael, there shall be no cognac on Sunday, even for you. But another day and I might just find a wee bit, as you say."

"Is there no justice in this city for a thirsty man, forced to work on the day of rest?" Murphy replied. They all laughed at his clever pleading, highlighted by his thick accent. "To find my friend in the midst of such tribulation cuts me to the quick. Shall I ever suspect you of any crime other than playing love's fool? No, never! Joseph, 'twas that woman who was the devil's daughter herself. What, that a man like you should be deserving of a traitor to love. No, I say! For no soldier could have done what you did with a true and loyal maiden in wait. This is the true crime which the Good Lord's ultimate mercy and justice must resolve."

All the color left Joe's face. He slammed his cup to the table, breaking it and the saucer beneath, sending shards of china flying onto the laps of his guests. "Speak of her no more, Michael. And do not speak of the war again!" As the volume of his voice increased, so did the tension in the room. After so many years, Murphy never expected to get such a violent reaction.

Lois began to speak, Alvin failing to stop her. "Joseph, it's okay—we heard him call you captain. We know the legend of Captain Joseph Harper. We loved you before we knew it, and our love and respect for you has continued to grow. We know you are a private man. We would never wish to intrude upon your past."

He stood and growled orders as if he were back in the war. "My name is Joe Harpy, *not* Joseph Harper!" Lois looked away, mortified as Joe continued. "Captain of Detectives, I will be waiting here for my turn at your interrogation. But expect no more hospitality. Now get out!"

The big man jumped to attention. "Yes sir, captain," Murphy replied as he shuttled Alvin and Lois out of Joe's apartment and into their own. Murphy straddled the threshold of Joe's apartment, blocking the door's closure. "No matter my faults, which are many, I know the man who saved his lieutenant, and then the entire French company without a casualty. I know the man who organized the special training camp in Belgium. Aye, he was the one who broke through enemy lines when outgunned, saving many while repelling the enemy's first counterattack, making victory at Cantigny possible. And then, miraculously led our company against the diabolical, fifth counterattack to seal our victory. Whose actions at Belleau Wood are legendary. This man will remain my hero. And I pray in the memory of my sainted mother, he allows me to remain his friend as well." With that Murphy grabbed the doorknob, pulling the door from Joe's grip, and slammed it firmly.

The traumatized war hero fell onto his sofa, weeping bitterly, inconsolably—the man had seen too much death and suffered too much misfortune for a dozen lifetimes. As the liquid of heartbreak poured from his eyes, he slid off the sofa and onto his knees. He chanted a desperate prayer—the only practice that had prevented him from taking his own life countless times before.

CHAPTER 43

Captain of Detectives, Michael Murphy rose to his position in part because of his highly-logical mind, his disarming personality, and his understanding of human nature. But mostly it was his inexplicable ability to smell a lie that made him unique. After interrogating witnesses and suspects, sometimes immediately and other times over protracted sessions, the combination of these skills resulted in an unparalleled ratio of arrest-to-indictment-to-conviction. Criminals across the Midwest knew of his name and feared his reputation. Among the riff raff, he was simply known as The Irish Giant.

After exiting Joe's apartment, Murphy stood silently in the hallway, his hands folded in prayer. "Lord God Almighty, have mercy on Joseph. Strengthen him and bring him peace." Taking a deep breath, he raised his fist and knocked. Alvin opened the door to the couple's apartment. With a calm voice, the Captain of Detectives instructed, "Let the three of us sit down and have a chat. No need for you two to speak with me separately. You lads are not suspects." Alvin led him to the kitchen where they gathered around the table, leaning forward in intensity.

It took Captain Murphy about half an hour to interrogate the couple. He asked questions about the security system, customers, drug couriers, Joe, and the hospital staff. Eager to cooperate and be helpful, the couple answered everything in detail. The interview yielded a full understanding of their regular customers, other tenants, the neighboring businesses, and the couple's schedules and habits. Murphy admired their uncommon honesty and sincerity. Dozens of pages of his notepad now full, he stood up from his chair. "This has been a fine discussion, me lads. Now, I shall take my leave of you; I have much to do on the scene. Stand firm. My team will chase these villains to the gates of hell, if we must. But find them, we shall." While he reassured Alvin and Lois, he remained unaware that downstairs, the evidence technicians' intense scrutiny of the crime scene was proving futile. Moving to the apartment door, Murphy stopped and turned. "Lois, my dear, fret not. Your words were full of love and respect. You did no wrong in loving a man so worthy. Be patient; few have lived a life full of trials such as he. Give him just a wee bit of time. The terrors of his past sometimes flood his mind. Of this, I am sure—it was not your words that prompted such rage, but mine of that woman. You two continue to love him with all your might. I suspect he shall need you now more than ever. That's an order!"

As Captain Murphy closed the apartment door behind him, he put his face near Joe's door, projecting his voice through the thick hardwood, "Joseph, I shall have use for you when I return from the crime scene. We shall talk soon, my dear brother. Fear not, all will be well, for we are the fierce."

Joe counted each of Murphy's steps as the detective descended the creaking staircase. Hearing the entry door slam behind Murphy, Joe walked to the bay window in the front of his apartment and watched him enjoin Fitzgerald in discussion. By the looks of it, the conversation was growing agitated, especially for Murphy. Then, Joe saw Murphy wave off Fitzgerald, turning his back on the sergeant, as The Irish Giant headed into the crime scene.

Ten minutes later, Captain Murphy exited the store, apparently giving orders to Sergeant Fitzgerald. Joe observed the movements, the body language of his former subordinate, realizing the cops must have discovered something. Joe counted as he heard the steps creak. Someone was headed toward his door. Opening it as Murphy lifted his hand to knock, a wry smile crossed Murphy's face. "Sergeant Fitzgerald will be more reserved next time—calling you and those two fine people suspects before I even arrived on the scene. I told him

I'd tan his backside with my dear grandfather's shillelagh if he was ever so careless again." Joe let out a small laugh.

Lois, standing inside her apartment, ear against the door, silently waved Alvin over to join her. Moments later she flinched as Murphy's voice bellowed, "Hey! You two, standing behind the door eavesdropping! I'd like to speak to you again." The couple shot each other guilty glances. They opened the door.

"Sergeant Fitzgerald and some of his men will be coming by shortly. They have…'guests' with them. We'd like to use both your apartment and Joe's to interview certain people. I know this may seem highly irregular, and I am sure it is much to ask of you, but it is the comfort of your residence and proximity to the crime scene that will be my advantage. Dragging everyone to the precinct will certainly make it harder to find witnesses—and here they just might open up a bit. Worry not, it shan't be long."

Joe spoke from the open doorway of his apartment. "My apologies to you Lois, Alvin, Michael. My behavior was abhorrent. Please forgive me. Come in, everyone. I heard your request, Michael. Of course, you're welcome to use my apartment for as long as you like." As the group made their way back inside Joe's place, they noticed that he had already cleaned up the debris. Joe turned his back on the trio as he went to the bay window, again watching the crowd and the police below.

The Irish Giant suddenly startled, called out: "Joseph, you look like a man who knows something. I can sense it—I smell it. What is it you are hiding? Or is it something you know but assume is useless? It may not be, so tell me what is on your mind."

Without turning from his gaze out the window, Joe rejected Murphy's inquiry. "Nothing. You are imagining things. Why would I keep anything from you? You are foolish to think so, Michael. I am just deeply concerned for my friends."

Staring down to the street below, Joe saw Martha, Peter, Helen, and the children arrive on the sidewalk directly across the street from Lincolnway. He firmly punched his closed fist against the window's casing.

CHAPTER 44

The swarm of police cars and swelling crowd piqued the family's curiosity as rumors spread through the crowd. "What is going on?" Helen asked Peter.

"I have no idea," he replied. Martha looked at Wally, one eyebrow raised. He knew to keep quiet. Unable to get close to the scene, they stood across the street gaping at the commotion. Martha cooly puffed on her cigarette.

Fitzgerald spotted Wally across the street and headed over to the family. "Good morning, Peter, Helen, Martha. Another beautiful day. Unfortunately, someone broke into the pharmacy. Peter, I'd like to speak with Wally. He's friends with Bobby and is always hanging around Lincolnway. I'll also need to talk to any of you who can account for Wally's whereabouts last night. Please don't get too concerned. We must follow every witness and lead we can identify. For starters, we are interviewing everyone who was inside Lincolnway the last couple of days."

"Why Wally? Is he a suspect?" Helen demanded.

With a smile, Fitzgerald replied, "No, ma'am. Like I just said, we are interviewing everyone who visited Lincolnway on Friday or Saturday. Lois says Wally was there both days and he knows Bobby who conveniently just got out of jail—maybe he saw something. But as long as we are talking, Peter, tell me, where were all of you last night?"

"Certainly," Peter replied. "We spent the evening together and all retired around eleven. We went to 8:00 a.m. Mass this morning, then had our breakfast, as usual. Then we decided to come down to Lincolnway for a treat. And now, here we are."

Martha jumped in. "Two weeks ago, you asked the same things, and I told you I sleep in the bedroom right next to the staircase. Last night, just like two weeks ago, I never heard Wally leave. He was home, absolutely. He was home all night."

"Yes, ma'am, I am certain you are correct. Best if you join us as well. I'll want to take down your statement and Captain Murphy will probably want to talk to you, too. As I said, we need to speak with everyone who was in the pharmacy Friday or Saturday, but we will interview others as well—people like you, who might help us, too. It's basic police work. Peter, I don't have any questions for you or Helen."

Peter looked at his son and sister-in-law to reassure them. "You two cooperate with the sergeant. Give your statements and come back home. The rest of us will walk home now. We'll see you both in a little while."

Martha objected. "I don't need to give another statement. I just told you everything, copper. Why do you need me to give a statement if Wally is not a suspect? You can't push us around like this. What are you trying to do, find somebody to hang it on because you're too lazy to figure it out?"

Fitzgerald remained cool and diplomatic. He decided to use the kid glove approach after his recent tongue lashing from Murphy. "Ma'am, you're absolutely entitled to be upset. I am so sorry if I've improperly implied something. It's just that we must get a statement from *everyone* whom the captain demands. If you would be kind enough to give me your formal statement, we'll get you on your way. Now, may I have the pleasure of escorting you inside?" Shooting the man a poisonous dart with her eyes, Martha nevertheless took his extended arm.

Upstairs, Joe remembered the trauma of weeks ago, as he recognized the woman who cringed at his face in the pharmacy. She was coming inside. He grabbed Murphy by the arm saying, "It will be best if I wait inside my bedroom, with the door closed. I shall listen to all that is said, in case I might help."

Murphy barked, "No, Joseph," pushing Joe toward Alvin's apartment. "You wait in the bedroom of the other apartment," Joe barely got down the hall and into Alvin's apartment without being seen.

When the captain had finished with Martha, he interrogated Wally, both from the kitchen of the rear apartment, Joe listening through the bedroom door. After the boy was dismissed, Murphy spoke to the *pani* and her son who lived in the other front apartment—the old lady who saw Wally beat up Bobby. Eventually, several other neighbors who patronized Lincolnway on Friday were identified and brought in front of Murphy. Slowly, methodically, hour after hour, Murphy questioned people, but no meaningful clues emerged and Joe offered no insights into anything he heard from behind the bedroom door. Murphy planned to interview Agent DJ Green and others the next day at the precinct office.

When he finished questioning everyone who was found that evening, Captain Murphy summoned Sergeant Fitzgerald from downstairs back to the front apartment. There he gathered Joe, Alvin, and Lois. "Fitzgerald, walk me through your notes on the liquor store robbery, especially about that boy who insisted he did not do it. Something tells me both crimes were committed by the same man, someone as clever as a Guinness float. We may have a professional on our hands."

"Captain, can we just call it a day?" Fitzgerald whined. "It's dinner time. I'd like to have something to eat and see my kids before they go to bed." Murphy just ignored his subordinate.

Alvin didn't hesitate to offer hospitality in reply to Fitzgerald's bellyaching. "Lois and I will be happy to prepare a meal for the five of us. It will be no problem at all."

Murphy laughed, digging at Fitzgerald, "See sergeant, nobody pulls an inside job and then feeds the constables!"

Fitzgerald had no choice but to comply. He began with his notes on the liquor store robbery. Murphy was particularly interested in Bobby's false police report. Alvin confirmed the time and the extent of the boy's injuries. Murphy put his hand in the air, motioning for Fitzgerald to stop. "Alvin, tell me the time again. When did Bobby enter? And when did you call the department?"

"It was a little bit after 9:00 a.m., I think. Sgt. Fitzgerald mentioned my call time was logged by your department dispatcher as 9:14 a.m. That sounds exactly right to me."

Pleased with Alvin's answer, Captain Murphy then directed Fitzgerald, "Get me the *pani* from the other apartment again. She's the one who saw the fight, correct? Better yet, just go next door and ask her if she can confirm the exact time, then come back here and tell me what she says. Next, I want you to get Wally's mother. And, Fitzgerald, you said something about that kid Wally having a job interview that morning, right?"

Fitzgerald nodded obediently, pissed off that he would probably miss the first servings of food. The apartment was full of enticing smells. "Yes captain, he was at the foundry. He had an interview with Millicent Brownley. I confirmed he had a brief interview that morning, the time of which was just as the boy claimed."

Murphy blasted out one more order: "Better yet, go get Millicent Brownley, and then afterwards, Wally's mom. I want to talk to Helen last." Continuing his assembly of the puzzle's pieces, he asked Alvin, "What time was the lad Wally in the pharmacy the Friday before the liquor store was robbed? By God's good grace might you remember such a triviality?"

"He made a brief phone call at 8:00 a.m.," Alvin explained, "and stayed for about half an hour. He waited by the phone, like someone was going to call him back. That's why I can remember it. But then he just left. He also came by on Saturday, but did not use the phone or say anything. He just sat for a while and then left. Why? How did you know he was there, captain?"

Murphy stared at Joe, as he answered Alvin's question. "It's one way Bobby's story makes sense. That is just one scenario of many I must consider. But, it's the hottest one right now."

"What do you mean?" Alvin asked, but Murphy ignored him just as the door opened.

Fitzgerald had returned with Millicent, but Murphy was surprised to see John Schmidt following right behind. "Michael Martin Murphy! Good to see you again, you old Irish ox! I hope you don't mind, but I was passing by Millie's house when I saw Sergeant Fitzgerald standing at her front door speaking to her. I stopped and offered my help. Now here I am!"

Just then Joe stepped into Schmidt's field of view. "Joe? What are you doing here? Oh, this must be the new apartment you told me about."

Murphy's booming, matchless laugh rang out. "Hell, we might just have the whole company assembled here if anyone else shows up!" Not giving Joe a chance to reply to Schmidt, Murphy continued. "Yes John, your presence is not forbidden. Please sit down and listen. If I have any questions for you, I will ask them in due course. Otherwise, I shall solicit your opinions after I speak with the most stylish Millicent Brownley. Either way, do not speak until I so request." Turning to the woman, he added, "You look elegant as always Millicent. How is the Duchess of Steelmaking this evening?" Schmidt couldn't help but smile at this sergeant from the war who served under him, now masterfully in charge of the situation.

Captain Murphy questioned the office manager about the interview. At one point, Millicent explained, "Wally was about forty minutes late for an 8:15 a.m. appointment. I gave him quite a tongue lashing, but he wasn't too flustered. That impressed me. It's almost like the boy had nerves of steel. Anyway, he left around nine."

Murphy nodded. "Okay, thank you, ma'am." He tilted his head toward Fitzgerald. "Go get the mother. Now!" Then he continued with Millicent. "Tell me about Wally's hands. Did you see them? Did they look all beat up, or did they look normal, you know, uninjured? No split knuckles or anything?"

Millicent smiled. "I remember he had such nice penmanship. I certainly wanted to look at his hands. Such a big young man, writing so perfectly on his application. His hands looked fine."

Abruptly, now his mind moving at a pace the others could not comprehend, Murphy dismissed Miss Brownley and John Schmidt. "Thanks. That's all I need from you two right now. John, if you ever get caught up in barbed wire and shot to pieces again, now at least you know where Joe lives so you can call him for help." John chuckled and gave his old sergeant a hearty slap on the back. Shaking hands, the two men simultaneously repeated their company's motto: *"Only the fierce are fearless!"*

On the way out, John embraced Joe and would not let go. Their devotion to each other was palpable. Joe held on tightly, as if released he might collapse where he stood. "John, for all these years you and Michael have loyally guarded my secret. But now others know. John, others know." Pleading in anguish to his confidant, "My name is Joe Harpy. It's Harpy, damn it!"

Trying to help, Alvin attempted to comfort his friend. "Joe, Lois and I have told no one else. Your secret is safe with us, we promise."

Eventually, releasing John Schmidt's embrace, Joe stumbled toward a chair.

Lois whispered to Alvin. "So, this must be the man that Joe saved. The largest employer in the neighborhood, the owner of Schmidt Foundry, and this man is now his boss. I wonder why Mr. Schmidt didn't give him a more intellectual job?"

Millicent, however, overheard, quickly joining the couple in their hushed conversation. "Joe would not have it. He wanted to toil in anonymity. Believe me, John tried." Changing the subject, Millicent continued, "There is a photo of these two in Mr. Schmidt's office, both in full dress uniform—Joe's chest covered with medals. You have to come by to see it. Joe was the most handsome man in the world. Like a movie star. More importantly, from what John says, he was the finest soldier that ever served this, or any, country. But now look at him." Lois began to weep as she kept repeating through her tears, *"Oh mon très cher frit."* (Oh, my dearest friend.)

As the discussion of Joe's identity was happening in the front apartment, Sergeant Fitzgerald arrived at the house on Southport hoping for cooperation. Peter's family had just finished their dinner and Aunt Martha was organizing her things, planning to leave in about an hour. Helen answered the door, with her sister at her heels. "You bastard!" Martha screeched indignantly into the man's face. "I knew you wanted a fall guy! You're the reason for all the crime in this crappy town! You don't know how to do your job, flat foot!"

Pulling her sister back, Helen continued berating the cop. "You told me my Wally was not a suspect. Why are you here? Now, what do you want—for me to turn in my own son for something he did not do? We have all told you, he was home all night!"

Unphased by the histrionics, Fitzgerald remained professional. "Yes, ma'am, I know what you said. Let's all just calm down. I told you this is not about the pharmacy, it's about when Wally beat up Bobby. I came here to fetch you, Helen, not Wally. Captain Murphy told me to come get you and I'm just doing my job. He thinks you might help fill in a missing detail that might help prove Bobby was the perpetrator of both crimes, like we think he is. You want to help, don't you?" Knowing his technique was calming the two women down a bit, he continued acerbically. "If Murphy thought Wally was involved, he would send me here to get him, wouldn't he? But he didn't. So, now, Helen let's get going. Come with me for just a few minutes, satisfy the big gas bag Murphy, and get him off my back and yours, and we'll put Bobby in jail for a long time."

Helen stepped back, shooting a worried glance at her husband. "Helen, this policeman is simply doing his job and we have nothing to hide, and we know Bobby stole a car, and who knows what else," Peter reassured her. "If we can help solve these terrible crimes, we must. Don't worry sweetheart. Martha, Wally, and I will look after the little ones."

Helen had no choice but to grudgingly consent to Sergeant Fitzgerald's request. At the same time, Helen, Martha, and Fitzgerald stood talking on the front porch, DJ Green returned to Mr. Feherty's. Green's arms laden with grocery bags—he waited patiently on the sidewalk, not wanting to interrupt, but hearing all that was said. When Green reached the hermit's apartment, he couldn't resist sharing what he had just overheard.

Feherty, trained in the law, had worked for the Federal Bureau of Investigation (FBI) and became a top legal analyst. Only a few years after his family's tragic demise, the lawyer-agent could no longer bring himself to leave his apartment. So rather than lose him from the organization, the Bureau allowed him to remain at home, performing a modified workload from there. Feherty was often called on to review agent field reports, juxtaposing them with the applicable federal and state statutes. His photographic memory allowed him to connect seemingly unrelated details to cases that provided field agents with complex avenues to pursue in complicated mob organizations. His apartment lay filled with various boxes of files, articles, and books, organized in a way only the reclusive agent could understand.

FBI agents visited him two or three times a week, bringing new materials and benefiting from his brilliant legal mind. Soon, all the leaders of the Bureau's Chicago office were tutored by him. Conferences sometimes lasted for hours, as he proposed multiple statutes to crimes that no one else would even suspect might apply. He explained many legal nuances to his law enforcement professionals turned students, with a depth of understanding worthy of a Supreme Court Judge.

Soon, all the agents dispatched to make the document transfers learned to bring food to the hermit genius as well. The director in charge of the Chicago office worked out an unofficial payroll adjustment that allowed the agent-messengers to shop the local grocer without dipping into their own pockets. And it was DJ Green, the investigative scientist, who had the least need for Feherty, but who always seemed to bring him food on the weekends ever since the crime lab opened two years ago. They had become friends as well as professional colleagues.

CHAPTER 45

Helen, the pure and innocent heart who survived life under the shadow of the Monster of Warsaw, stepped into the apartment above Lincolnway not knowing what to expect. Fitzgerald politely introduced her to Captain Murphy, while Lois offered both something to eat. "It is so late, and none of these men have had time for a proper dinner, so I've been bringing out a variety of dishes. Perhaps Sergeant Fitzgerald interrupted your dinner. If so, please try to enjoy something, Miss Helen. Look, I've spread things out on the kitchen table." Turning toward the officer, she continued, "Sergeant Fitzgerald, please take time to eat something. You've been running around the neighborhood for hours."

Fitzgerald needed no prompting. He'd been waiting for this moment! Abandoning all forms of etiquette, both forearms planted firmly on the table, he shoveled heaping spoonful after spoonful into his mouth, as wayward crumbs fell around the plate.

"No, thank you," Helen replied to her hostess. "We have already had our dinner, and I am anxious to get through the questions so I may go home. My sister is leaving this evening, and I must say goodbye to her."

Murphy nodded. "Okay, I understand. I'll be brief. Was it 8:00 a.m. on Friday morning when Wally left home for his interview, yes or no?"

Helen responded, "Yes, sir. It was just a few minutes before eight."

The captain continued, "What time did he get home after his interview?"

The mother answered, "It was a little after nine. I'm not exactly sure, it could have been as late as half past nine. He said he ran into Bobby. They had a fight, then he snuck into the house to wash the blood off of himself. Then he went to the interview. That's why he was late."

Captain Murphy dismissed her. "That's all the questions I have for you. Thank you, Helen."

Sergeant Fitzgerald, clearly dismayed, called out, "Captain Murphy, may I speak to you in private for just a moment, please?"

As they stepped into the hallway, shutting the door, Fitzgerald demanded, "We just dragged all these people here, and for what? It's the same story."

Murphy smiled—the kind of grin that can only be formed by the odd combination of wisdom paired with condescension. "Bobby's story should have immediately tipped you off that Wally was lying. Bobby's fabrication about the cause of his injuries should have not been dismissed after you confirmed the location of the fight. No report from the trolley operator should have been your other clue. Bobby's motive to do so should have been obvious to you. He wanted to hurt Wally. Fitzgerald, don't you see? Wally took the liquor store keys! Bobby hoped you would search him looking for the knife and find the keys instead. But you focused on only one witness confirming the location of the fight and so decided to believe Wally. But you did not contemplate the exact time of the fight or why Bobby would lie." Just to rub it in, Murphy repeated, "He wanted the police to find the keys on Wally—get it? And then there is the matter of the boy's hands...Aye, you're as thick as a donkey."

Fitzgerald tried to defend himself. "But I checked with transit dispatch too. Nothing was reported. They said if a trolley clipped someone like the boy claimed, it would have been right at the front door of the bus. The driver would have heard it and so would everyone else. And they told me it would have been impossible for the driver to not see it! That was confirmation Bobby was lying."

Irritated at the shortcomings of his subordinate, Murphy paused, staring at Fitzgerald. "Now we have multiple witnesses answering the most important fact. We can prove Wally lied to you and his mother about the time of the fight! You fool—doesn't the time Bobby stumbled into the pharmacy tell you what you needed to know? Once Helen said it could have been as late as 9:30 when Wally returned home, everything fits. Fitzgerald, you should always assume everyone is lying to you until you can prove they are not. Actually, you should always assume that everyone involved, even the witnesses are most probably mistaken or lying, until the judge's gavel falls its last. Sergeant, now escort Helen home but don't give her any hints about what may be going on! Try to reassure her, we don't want her tipping off Wally."

Helen stood waiting in the apartment, a bit dumbfounded by the questioning. Did the police suspect her precious son Wally had lied? Fitzgerald came back through the door first and asked Helen to allow him to escort her home. "Everything is fine, Miss Helen. Let's get you home so you can see your sister off and forget about this whole thing."

As they were leaving the apartment Murphy asked Fitzgerald, "Who's on the Southport beat tonight?

"The usual boys—Stanley, Bill, and Frank. Oh no, you're not going to bring them into this are you? You're an asshole," the sergeant replied as he headed down the staircase, not caring if Murphy even heard his answer.

As the nervous mother and Fitzgerald turned from Fullerton onto Southport, Murphy raced down to the call box. "All three of you hop in a wagon and get to Peter's house as fast as you can. You'll have to bring in Peter's kid, Wally. Fitzgerald will be there shortly. Even he will understand why I sent you. Use billy clubs and cuffs if you have to. But bring him in *now*!"

Then Captain Murphy bounded back up the stairs to Joe's apartment. "Joseph, do you think the boy had an accomplice? And where do you guess they've stashed the cash and the drugs? Joseph, there is more here than meets the eye, I smell it. And I believe you might be the one to help me find the final pieces." Staring blankly at the wall, Joe said nothing in reply.

As she and Fitzgerald walked, Helen's maternal instincts demanded an explanation. "What are you thinking? Why was Captain Murphy so concerned about Wally's schedule that Friday a month ago? Bobby lied about what happened, where it happened, why wouldn't he lie about when?" Then she tried to make a defense. "Maybe Bobby lay in the street a while. Maybe he tried to shake off his injuries but eventually came for help. Wally's story was confirmed by the *pani!*"

Taking her gently by the arm, Fitzgerald replied. "I already told you, it's time to forget about the whole thing. We're finally done with that big gas bag. Murphy now knows Bobby is guilty. That's what he and I were talked about outside the apartment just now. Everything is fine."

When Fitzgerald and Helen arrived at the house on Southport, they found the paddy wagon parked in the alley behind the Peter and Helen's house. Two cops leaned patiently against its side. The third cop patrolled near the front yard gate. As Helen opened the gate to approach the front door, it opened.

"What is it? What's going on? Why are all of you here?" Peter shouted out to them. Helen fell into her husband's arms.

Fitzgerald did not answer his questions directly. "Peter, Helen is fine. Where is your son, Wally? I need you to bring him to me now. We must to speak with him next." The boy's mother stood frozen with dread realizing, contrary to what they told her, the police were convinced that Wally was involved.

Peter replied innocently, "I'm sorry Sergeant Fitzgerald, but just a few minutes ago Wally and his Aunt Martha took her car to the pharmacy to pick up Helen. You must have passed each other while walking back here. I expect they'll return shortly." With a whistle and a wave, Fitzgerald summoned the cops in the alley. Leaving the wagon, they entered the backyard, one man stayed by the back door guarding it, and the other waited for the signal to enter the house. Fitzgerald addressed Peter, "I believe you, Peter, but we need to search your house for the boy. It just has to be that way. And I need a description of the woman's car. Will you cooperate?"

Trying to calm down Helen who was now despondent, Peter replied, "She is driving a black '33 Olds sedan with copper-colored wheels. And yes, you may search the house. We have nothing to hide. But, please, don't scare the little ones or question them. Okay?"

Trying his best to keep things from escalating, Fitzgerald offered reassurance. "Of course—we will simply walk through each room for visual inspection and leave immediately, but I must verify Wally is not here. I'd like you to wait with me while my partners go inside. And don't worry, they'll just tell your little ones they are trying to find a missing purse."

Their inspection of the first floor and attic bedroom completed, the officers knocked on Feherty's door. Opening it, DJ Green invited them inside and flashed the cops his credentials. They had never seen an FBI badge before. "I am Daniel Green, FBI Special Agent, Forensic Sciences. This is Mr. Timothy Feherty, Senior Legal Adjunct to the FBI." One cop took Green's badge in his hand and gave it a long hard look.

The second cop glanced at it and shrugged. "Sure. Looks good to me."

Briefly explaining their purpose, the cops were granted access immediately. When they finished their sweep through the rooms, Feherty spoke to them. "I'd like to have a talk with the detective in charge. I may have some information pertaining to your investigation. May I join you? Will you allow me this professional courtesy, please?"

Green was shocked to observe his friend, this grandfatherly fellow turned recluse, suddenly wanting to leave his self-imposed prison. "May I join you as well, at least to escort my friend here back home afterward?" he asked.

"We would be grateful to have your assistance," one officer answered. Immediately, the other cop swung the apartment door open, motioning them to hurry along outside. All the law enforcers converged at the front of the house to report to Fitzgerald—the boy and his aunt were really gone, along with Martha's luggage. Fitzgerald cringed when told the two strangers were FBI agents.

Maintaining guard, two cops stayed near the suspect's house although they all realized the boy and his aunt probably would not be returning. The other two cops and their FBI companions took the paddy wagon back to the pharmacy. As they rode, in response to Feherty's non-stop questioning, Fitzgerald reluctantly gave them a more detailed overview of the two crimes. Growing agitated in reaction, claiming to have much more to share, Feherty demanded he give his description of certain events directly to the captain only. The feisty old lawyer would permit no argument against his demand.

Arriving at the pharmacy building, Fitzgerald ordered a lookout bulletin for Martha's car from the police call box on the sidewalk in front of the liquor store as the others started upstairs. "This is Sergeant Fitzgerald. Broadcast an all-points bulletin now! Black Oldsmobile F-33 sedan. One adult female and one teenage male fleeing arrest on suspicion of the robbery of Lincolnway Pharmacy."

Following the group up the stairs, Fitzgerald reported, "Captain Murphy, the boy and his aunt are gone. So is the dame's luggage. I have men staked out at the house in case they return. The all-points for the car is being broadcast now!"

Murphy seemed unfazed by the news the pair was missing. "Thank you, sergeant. I'm not surprised. I just should have figured this out faster. Who are these gentlemen?" he asked.

"May I introduce you to Daniel Green, FBI Special Agent, Forensic Sciences. And this is Mr. Timothy Feherty, Senior Legal Adjunct to the FBI. Gentlemen, meet Captain Michael Murphy, Captain of Detectives, Chicago Police Department." Fitzgerald ignored Joe, Alvin, and Lois with his introductions. If he had his way, all the interviews would have happened in the precinct. He eschewed the presence of civilians when serious police work was being performed.

Captain Murphy shook each man's hand and then politely introduced the others. "Gentlemen, delighted to meet you both. May I introduce you to Alvin and Lois, the owners of the exceptionally-fine Lincolnway Pharmacy, and this is Mr. Joe Harpy, possible witness, tenant, and the man who installed the pharmacy's security system. While I am delighted to meet you both, how is it that I send the sergeant to retrieve a suspect and he brings me two federal agents? I'm glad I didn't send him to bring me a judge—I might have gotten an armed bank robber instead!" Everyone but Fitzgerald burst into laughter.

The hermit Feherty, now growing comfortable being out of his apartment, offered. "We may be of assistance, captain. I have been living on the second floor of Peter and Helen's home for many years. Agent Green has been visiting me often the last few weeks. He and I may have relevant information."

Murphy thanked them. "Yes, I wish to hear what you have to offer." Then turning to Fitzgerald, he commented, "You know, sergeant, while I have applied logic to the divergent stories of the two teenagers, the only non-circumstantial evidence we have implicates Bobby but it is inadequate. Furthermore, I cannot tolerate certain incongruities. He will not fold; he sticks to his story like an innocent man. Unfortunately, we have means, motive, and opportunity and his alleged past possession of keys, but we cannot prove he's linked to the robber's tools. And anyone could have thrown the nickels in the boy's backyard. We have no witnesses and he sticks to his story that Wally must have done it."

Everyone's attention fixed on the captain's logical progression; Fitzgerald objected. "It has to be him. He told his friends he was going to do it and we found the tools in the trash near his home. And Wally was home when Thompson's was robbed. I don't know why you can't accept this, Murphy. Why would you work with the District Attorney to order us to let Bobby out of jail after the first robbery? But you did, and now both robberies are on you!"

Sneering with disdain, Murphy rolled his eyes at his subordinate, "Just give Alvin back his keys, sergeant." Then he addressed the others. "So, let's say we go on a little jaunt in our minds, and together build a circumstantial case against Wally.

This does not uncover evidence, does it? We will find ourselves with a circumstantial case versus another with some physical evidence—but not enough. Gentlemen geniuses of our federal government, our department's technicians found no forced entry, fingerprints, footprints, torn clothing, dropped tools, bodily fluids, or other clues. Nor do we have eyewitnesses for either crime. As improbable as it sounds, both crime scenes were locked up as if normal. One must wonder if a felonious phantom lurks upon our alleys and streets—one who can pass through solid walls."

"Nothing at all?" DJ complained.

Captain Murphy, shook his head in disgust "Not a thing. Except now it appears our alternative suspect is legging it. We can give that a go, but what information or ideas might you two have to offer?"

Feherty spoke first. "So, you're The Irish Giant, scourge of criminals. I am delighted to meet you! Your record for turning arrests into convictions is most admirable. And your unorthodox techniques are legendary." Murphy smiled, pleased that even federal agents knew of his skills. Feherty continued, "But, I shall not digress. The nights of both robberies, Wally made two trips down and back up the rear staircase. I did not observe this pattern any other time in the last few months—only those two nights. On one of these occasions, the boy and the woman consumed alcohol together in the backyard. It was at least 2:30 a.m., probably a bit later. I saw them kissing. I hate to think it was his mother's sister he was trying to grope. That's just wicked!"

Murphy whistled long in reaction to the perversion, while staring at Joe.

Feherty continued. "The aunt drives a 1933 Oldsmobile F Sedan with Indiana plates reading 666DC."

Murphy interrupted. "Fitzgerald, get that plate number on the bulletin now!" The sergeant dashed down to the call box.

DJ Green chimed in. "Captain Murphy, you say there are no physical clues. But there is a great deal of success with canine tracking where our primitive investigative techniques fail to find evidence. I recently read a newspaper article saying your department has two Alsatian dogs. While a canine will not likely succeed in tracking an automobile traveling over urban distances, you might send one through the crime scenes. He might show you the local trail the perpetrator took, and in doing so, find the missing drugs, or cash, or at least the local termination of the criminal's path before departing in a vehicle. But I warn you, from the work we did with canines in New York, you must protect them from spilled drugs and broken glass. While they will naturally try to avoid these things, such debris can prevent the animal from locking on the right trail—and the drugs could be deadly!"

Murphy jumped from his chair calling after Fitzgerald who was lumbering down the stairs to the call box. "Tell Lieutenant

Vander Hooten to bring whichever of his dogs is the best tracker. I want him here in less than fifteen minutes."

Next, he turned to Joe, "We have made your apartment our field office. It was highly presumptuous of me, but necessary. I had no idea we would interview so many people thanks to Lois' fine memory. Joseph, I beg your indulgence for a short time more. Let's see what the canines can tell us. Would you mind if we kept working here until then?"

Without looking up, Joe softly replied, "Yes, Michael, you may even spend the night here if your work demands it. I seldom sleep and never have company, so you may stay as long as necessary." Murphy began to worry the army officer he knew as the bravest of men might be losing his grip. Whether this was justified despondency or the stench of his self-pity, the man's condition now deeply concerned Murphy.

With a guarded "thank you," to his friend, Murphy addressed the federal agents. "Gentlemen geniuses, I can't wait to hear what else you know."

With that, Feherty turned to his associate, "DJ, do you have anything else you wish to share?"

"No sir, I guess I rarely saw either of them, and only briefly spoke to the woman once."

"Of course, why don't you go home to your family, DJ," Feherty replied. "But I will remain. I am quite pleased to be of use in this departure from my hermit ways. Yes, I think I will stay here and listen. I suspect there might be much more here than any of us could have ever imagined."

CHAPTER 46

Soon from the street below, the grinding of gears echoed off the storefronts as the modified paddy wagon, turned canine transport, skidded up to the curb. "Captain Murphy, the dogs are here!" Vander Hooten called from the street.

Murphy bounded down the stairs as they creaked and strained under his weight. Bursting onto the sidewalk he greeted the lieutenant, the Commander of the Canine Unit. "Benjamin, thanks for getting here so quickly! Which of your magnificent beasts did you bring?"

Laughing, Benjamin replied, "For you, I have brought both. Fitzgerald tells me you have potentially two crime scenes. Dagg is the one with the scars. He can track anything that has been around the building in the last three weeks, maybe longer. He's always quickest to pick up a scent. We'll start with him. If he doesn't pick up the trail, the other, Drake, might. Sometimes the scents around a crime scene can stimulate one dog more than the other. Now, walk me through the likely path of the perpetrator, and we'll establish our launch point for tracking. What scent evidence do you have?"

Murphy had been giving this much thought. "I don't have a garment or any physical evidence of the suspect, just the crime scene. The store was locked up tight, and the perimeter alarm was on and functioning properly. It seems very likely the path began at the rear of the tailor shop where the door appears to have been jimmied. The culprit went down the stairs into the shop's basement through the vaulted sidewalk to the pharmacy. This seems to be the only possibility, however unlikely, since the pharmacy's metal door to the vault was locked from inside. The only thing we have to go on is the tailor shop's rear door jamb was gouged, nothing else. The tailor insists it was not splintered like that when he locked up Saturday afternoon. It's our only clue on the entire block. Does that help?"

"Yes, that will be fine. Actually, these are the kind of circumstances where a good tracking dog can offer the department much value." Pausing, excited to show off his skills, he snickered an inside joke to Murphy. "By the way, my dogs only understand Dutch. Don't talk to them or bother them in any way." Benjamin chuckled as he took Dagg out of the wagon. "Not harsh German, like other trainers use. It was to my great benefit to serve at the canine training camp during the war. It was such a bonus that we used Dutch, my family's native tongue."

Opening the carrier for Dagg, the other dog, Drake, became agitated, panting, barking, and then howling. Vander Hooten had never seen Drake act that way. He did not allow Dagg to acquire a scent until they arrived at the tailor's rear door. *"Zoek,"* (track) as he pointed its nose at the doorknob and latch, giving the dog direction to sniff the door's hardware. He then guided the dog to the basement stairs. Dagg strained against his pinch collar toward the vault's door. *"Zoek,"* Benjamin commanded again at the large metal door. The dog took a series of five-in, one-out breaths through his prominent black nose and barked loudly. Once under the vaulted sidewalk, Dagg pulled his handler to the pharmacy's vault door, now left unlocked by Murphy standing on the other side.

Vander Hooten next let the dog lead him to the handle of the basement door—he did not have to command again— he knew Dagg was clear on the target scent. The dog's pace quickened. Dagg excitedly pulled his handler to the rearmost fountain stool, sat, and wagged his tail with great enthusiasm. The detective rewarded the canine with a piece of dried lamb lung and a pat on the head. Dagg next identified the phone booth, then the area behind the pharmacy counter at the base of the pilfered drug cabinets. Turning the dog back to reverse the course, Benjamin directed, *"Reveiren"* (search).

Dagg started moving more quickly now, tracing the prior course perfectly and pulling his handler out the tailor shop door, through the alley with a determination Vander Hooten had never seen before—the dog seemed possessed, as if insanely tracking a bitch in heat. He could hear Drake alternately barking and howling from the vehicle parked in front of the pharmacy.

Stopping at the two trash bins that held the burglary tools from the liquor store robbery, Dagg again sat to indicate scent found. Then he pulled south. Reaching the street perpendicular to the alley, Dagg raced to change direction and dragged Benjamin past the trash cans where the evidence against Bobby was found, leading them to the rear door of the liquor store. *"Reveiren,"* Vander Hooten commanded again as the dog now pulled him south down the alley, all the way to the next street and then west to Southport. Unrelenting, the dog tracked north until he stopped at Peter and Helen's house.

Moments before, Murphy broke off from following Dagg and his handler. He had seen all he needed to confirm his theory. The dog had identified one person's scent at both crime scenes and the trail ended at Peter's house. While the tracking was not evidence adequate to produce a conviction, he now knew upon whom to focus all his efforts. Murphy was certain there was only one suspect worth considering and that Joe was somehow involved. Running to the pharmacy, the big man was puffing harder than a man his age and size should, but he did not slow his sprint. He charged up the stairs to Joe's apartment, finding the door locked. He pounded on the door while calling, "Joseph, open the door! Damn it, Joseph, open the door!" But there was no reply.

Hearing the commotion, Alvin and Lois exited their apartment, Mr. Feherty right behind them. "As soon as you left, Joe threw us out," Alvin cried. "Lois thinks something is very wrong."

With that, Michael Martin Murphy drew a breath, lowered his shoulder, and hurled himself against the apartment door. The jamb held, but began to splinter. Again, with all his might, he charged the door like a bull blinded with rage. Finally, it flexed and gave way. Crashing to the floor, the door now beneath him, he quickly got to his feet. Lois gasped in horror. Joe sat on the couch holding a gun. Murphy hurtled himself at Joe. The men struggled furiously. "Joseph! No! Joseph, it's not worth it!" Alvin jumped upon the two larger men. Somehow, as they wrestled, he pried the Colt .45 caliber Government Model 1911 semi-auto pistol from Joe's grip. But Joe refused to be taken. The Irish Giant managed to pin his old buddy to the ground. Joe's fists swung at him wildly, viciously. Murphy took a blow to his jaw, then another, but he would not release his former captain. Blood gushed freely from his chin. Suddenly, as his valued friend's blood dripped down onto his own face, Joe stopped, snapped out of his frantic state by the color he had grown to hate.

Believing he already knew the answer, Murphy got off of Joe asking, "Why did you want to hide when the boy and his aunt were coming up the stairs? Joseph, answer me. Why did you want to hide?"

Joe struggled to his feet, walked to the dresser in his bedroom, and opened the top drawer. Retrieving a tattered envelope, he extracted the letter inside and began to read, "JJ, it has been only two days since my last letter, but it seems like an eternity. I am haunted by loneliness. Why did you leave me? I don't think I can take it anymore. Every night I dream of a monster. He forces himself upon me. He is too strong! I can't fight him off! I think I am losing my mind."

Through his tears, Joe replied, "Yes, Michael, Wally's Aunt Martha is my wife. I have not heard anything from her since this last letter. It arrived the day we began to assemble forces at Nancy, France. That is until I caught a glimpse of her in the pharmacy weeks ago, but she did not recognize my wretched face. Perhaps the foundry's explosion did me a favor."

Murphy firmly grabbed his friend by the shoulders. "Joseph, you shall not let this evil child of Old Hairy Legs defeat you. You and I have battled much worse than this, and I shall be at your side until the Good Lord comes to take us to our reward."

"From Cantigny, to Belleau Wood, to the Battle of St. Mihiel and then to Argonne when Black Jack beat them into the ground, she never sent word. Not even after Germany signed the Armistice on November 11th—nothing." Joe's voice trailed off as his eyes dropped.

Mr. Feherty, standing by quietly, now came close to the two men. "My son, Brian, died at Cantigny, May 30th, during the last of Germany's six counterattacks. I have never spoken of it until now. I had just lost my wife the month before to the Spanish Flu." The old man crumbled onto the edge of Joe's bed, heaving and trembling with emotion. Choking through his tears, he continued, "How is it that fate has brought us together like this, men whose souls have been permanently scarred by war, just to relive our pain?"

As Joe struggled to regain his composure, Captain Murphy gently held onto Mr. Feherty's shoulders with both his hands. "Tis truly the deserving fate of those committed to duty, honor, and valor to be among others of this highest of callings, and so too, their families. For each family's sacrifice was of the greatest kind—of a kind that must be shared. Sir, I knew your son. He was the finest sergeant in our division, even better than I. Tis my wish this day your memories are freed from silent grief. Sir, they must be, so thy grief shall be changed to pride. It will be our privilege, Joseph and I, to help unlock them from the hidden recesses of your heart. Now stand up, good sir, and meet Joseph Jeffery Harper, the true and only Captain JJ Harper."

Hearing that name, Feherty regained his strength. He stood and addressed the disfigured, but noble man. "My son,

Brian, wrote of you, Captain Harper. I read many stories in the press. Sir, should I live a thousand lifetimes, I shall consider meeting you my greatest privilege. You saved many men from suffering and death. It was you who initially turned the tide at Cantigny. How you saved the French company at St. Mihiel was beyond improbable. Your Légion d'Honneur is well deserved." Pausing and staring at the true man of medals, he summoned from the depth of his soul all his remaining strength, blurting out, "Now there is police work to do, is there not? Together we *will* solve these crimes!"

Alvin passed the gun to Murphy who turned toward Joe, asking as he held out the weapon, "This is yours—do you want it back, Joseph? I think a man like you should never tarnish it, nor all the lives you saved in France and Belgium. No, Captain JJ Harper will not misuse it."

Joe took the pistol from Murphy. "God bless you, Michael." Ejecting the magazine from the semi-automatic Colt, Joe racked the slide, clearing the bullet from the chamber. The weapon was now empty with the breach locked open. Joe set it upon the dresser, the letter from Martha beneath it. Taking a seat at the kitchen table, Murphy called loudly, "I have yet to interview you, Joseph."

Following Joe, Feherty pulled up his chair close to the table until his paunch pressed against it, his forearms firmly resting there. "If you don't object, I would like to listen."

Murphy nodded approval as he began his questioning. "Joseph, let us begin with the first day in the pharmacy…"

But Alvin interrupted. "Captain Murphy, I suggest you start by asking Joe about Wally's calls from the pharmacy's phone booth."

Murphy considered Alvin's question, but it was not his preferred methodology. "No. Thank you for your suggestion, but I wish to know everything from the first day she walked into Lincolnway. I must recreate this despicable edifice up from its foundation."

Joe began to explain about the broken-down car and her need to call her brother from the store's phone booth. He knew nothing of the boys in the alley or where the car was actually parked.

Alvin interrupted him again. "Captain Murphy, please listen—Joe heard things, I know he did on two different occasions, maybe more. Sometimes I heard bits and pieces, but I was too far away from the phone booth most of the time. But Joe was close. He seemed preoccupied to me the first time, but the second time I realized he was focused on listening carefully."

Raising his voice over Murphy's procedural preferences, Alvin turned to Joe demanding, "Isn't it so, Joe? I am right, aren't I, Joe?" The man remained silent.

Alvin then looked to Murphy. "The second time, after Wally exited the phone booth, Joe manhandled the boy, demanding to know when Martha was returning. I knew something serious was going on for Joe to act the way he did. This must be what you sense, captain."

All eyes now on him, Joe was defiant. "Alvin, they were just whispers—whispers in a phone booth. How could anyone hear them?"

Unconvinced, Alvin challenged his friend. "You could, Joe! I saw you writhe in your seat. Then you accosted the boy. What else could it be? Joe, you must tell Captain Murphy everything."

Again, Joe vehemently denied the accusation. "Alvin, you are imagining things!"

But the pharmacist was unrelenting. "Captain JJ Harper, you must stay true to your code of honor—tell what you know!"

Suddenly convicted to the very depth of his soul, Joe swallowed hard. "Alvin is right, Michael. I did hear many things. I think Wally and Martha plan to meet her...her...friend. A traveling salesman or truck driver I presume, but I don't know for sure." The great man began gasping for air as his face became pale. "His name is Jack. He is coming here from Indiana. They will meet him somewhere on Lincoln. Sounded like he said they should park in front of the National Tea Company store late this evening. I think Wally said something about 10:30 p.m."

Feherty interrupted. "Captain Harper, why that store? Will he be traveling here with others or alone? Do you have any other details?" Even though it had been years since he had been there, Feherty knew every storefront on that block.

"I think the boy asked her about that," Joe answered. He asked something about what happens if Jack is alone or if he has friends with him. It was hard to follow everything without hearing the other side of the phone call."

Feherty looked at his watch—it was nearly 10:10 p.m. Suddenly the old man's eyes lit up like a pair of headlights. "Jack? Did you say Jack? Yes, that's it!" He sprung from his chair with enough force that it tumbled and landed on its back. "Joe, do you have a telephone in your apartment? I need to call my associate, DJ Green, *right now.*"

Alvin answered instead. "No, Mr. Feherty, but there is one in my apartment. It is yours to use."

Racing into Alvin's apartment, Feherty pulled out a note-card from his pocket and dialed like his life depended on it. "DJ, take down this information. Indiana plate 666DC. Run it immediately and call this number back." There was a pause, then he replied to Green. "You can get one of the other agents to help you." Another pause. "I don't care if you have to take your sick baby with you, I need the license plate information as quickly as you can get it. Call me back at this number. Just do it, and get back to me as quickly as you can."

Moments later the phone rang in Alvin's apartment. Mr. Feherty rushed to the phone and answered. "Yes...right, DJ. Are you absolutely sure? Got it. Get word to Sam and Melvin now. Tell them it's confirmed, there will be a car waiting at 10:30. *Code number one* in front of the National Tea Company on Lincoln." He repeated, "Yes, that's right—*code number one*. I only hope there is time." Hanging up the phone the elderly lawyer cried out, "I know where they are and much more! I will explain everything as we drive, Captain Murphy. We have no time to waste. The boy is in great danger."

Murphy, knowing beyond a doubt, that Feherty had found the culprits and so much more, led the way down the staircase. They leaped into Murphy's car. The captain stomped the accelerator pedal to the floorboards as he popped the clutch. They raced off, tires squealing. Murphy sideswiped two parked cars as they peeled out of the parking spot.

CHAPTER 47

After their narrow escape from Sergeant Fitzgerald, Wally and Martha drove to Jack's remote house where they stayed once before—the night she found her runaway nephew. Martha frantically roared up the long driveway, barely able to skid to a stop without hitting the garage. "You stay here, Wally. I'll check to see if Jack's inside or left me new instructions." Martha did not wait for the boy's answer as she ran to the door. She disappeared inside for just a few moments.

Running back to the Oldsmobile, she exclaimed, "He's not here now, but Jack *was* here! He left a note. We have to go back to the city. Just like he planned, we'll meet him outside the National Tea Company. But we must change cars. He wants us to use the Ford. It's in the garage."

"Let's just wait here for him," Wally complained, worried that if they left the Olds there, he'd never get his share of the cash. He immediately realized convincing Martha to stay was futile, so he began negotiating against himself, attempting a compromise. "Fine, but let's take the Oldsmobile."

Now irritated and impatient, Martha screamed at the boy, "No! No! No! Jack said to take the Ford, so we're taking the Ford! It contains things he needs." She shot her accomplice her most powerful don't-even-think-about-it glare. "And, you *are* coming with me! If you ever want your cut, you're coming with me! Listen Wally, you're not getting any more money from me until Jack says it's okay. Got it?"

Sulking, Wally pushed open the garage door. Two cars stood parked, though there were bays for at least three more. Countless large bales of hay were piled up around the perimeter walls of the expansive structure like a fortification of straw. Martha almost hit him with the Oldsmobile as she pulled it inside. Locking the car, she slid into the Ford and started it. The flathead V-8 engine roared to life. Martha ordered, "Let's go, Wally—we have to be parked in the right place by 10:15; I don't want to be late."

As the two rode back to the city, Wally considered how he might wrangle information from his bizarre relative. He had to know more about Indiana and Jack if he was to figure out a way to get the cash and escape! "Where in Indiana do you live, Aunt Martha?" He tried to make his question sound innocent.

Keeping her eyes on the road, she snapped back. "You know, Wally. Gary. Gary, Indiana. Did you ever hear of it, Wally? It's a town in Indiana. I live in Gary, Indiana."

Her tone caused him to fear another psychotic episode might unfold, but he persisted. "What do you do there? What's your address?" Martha did not answer. He continued. "When did you meet Jack? How long ago was it?"

A strange look came across Martha's face as if she had ventured into the world of her sick and twisted daydream. "I work for my friend, Ana. You will meet her tonight. She introduced me to Jack months ago. I think he likes me more than Ana, or any of her other friends. He said if I help him deliver things, I can go on his business trips, too!"

"Oh, that is wonderful," Wally replied. "I'm sure Jack likes you the best. How could he not? You're so beautiful and smart. What kind of work do you do for Ana?"

"I help her, Wally," Martha said, her voice trailing off as if she was now tumbling down into the dungeon of her own insanity. She put her right hand on his upper thigh and stroked it. "Light me a cigarette, my big man. Put it between my lips. The lips you want to kiss so badly. Tonight, Wally, I will show you how to become a man," Martha's pointy tongue circling her lips in anticipation.

Terrified, Wally sat quietly, now certain beyond any doubt she was utterly sick and extremely dangerous. Forcing himself to give her the cigarette, he dared not ask any more questions. They drove on without talking while Aunt Martha, almost childlike in her musical expression, hummed a tune he did not recognize.

Overwhelmed by curiosity about the contents of the box in the back seat—the *things that Jack needs,* Wally twisted over the seat back in an attempt to peek inside. "Don't touch Jack's stuff!" Martha screeched, interrupting her tune. Wally had barely cracked the lid open, catching a glimpse of something metallic before Martha struck him with the back of her hand. "I told you, don't touch Jack's stuff." He withdrew before his curiosity was satisfied, as Martha hummed her strange tune once again.

When they arrived at their destination, Martha found all the parking spaces full on both sides of the street in front of the National Tea Company store. Just a couple of doors south, where the street was interrupted by an alley, she finally spied one open parking spot across the street. "Wally, Jack said to park right in front of the grocery store. I can't. There aren't any spaces. But Jack told me where to park. I have to do what Jack says!"

Wally's mind raced as Aunt Martha started to panic. He took control. "Park there." He pointed to the spot. "There aren't any other spots. Park the car there, *now!*" As she carefully pulled the Ford into the open spot, Wally lowered his voice to reassure her. "Aunt Martha, this will be just fine. The store is just across the street and only a couple of doors north. It will be really easy for Jack to see us here. It's just like parking right in front, only better. Really, there is no difference. Jack will be so happy to see you, and you'll be happy too. Won't you be happy to see Jack?" She just nodded.

Soon focused on her wristwatch, like she was watching a movie, Martha turned from nervous to giddy. "Wally, it's just about 10:30; Jack will be here any minute! You get behind the wheel. Jack will want to leave right away. I will stand outside on the sidewalk and look for him. He knows this car; he knows to look for me. But we are too far away from where I am supposed to be. I have to watch for him." She paused for a few moments, then grew frantic. "What if he doesn't like where I parked? What if he doesn't like what I'm wearing? What should I do, Wally?"

The boy jumped out of the passenger side of the Ford and raced around to the driver's door, commanding, "Slide out and get on the sidewalk, now! I'll drive. You stand there and watch for Jack. Wave when you see him. Call out loudly. He'll be so happy to see you. Don't worry—how could he miss spotting such a beautiful woman?"

Now positioned behind the steering wheel, Wally considered his options. With Martha finally out of the car, he could just take off. He could get back to the Oldsmobile and his cash, then go into hiding before she and Jack could find their way back to Indiana. Suddenly, however, he remembered her threat—if you ever betray me, I'll kill you. After the last few hours, he had no doubt this wasn't an idle threat. He also understood that if Martha didn't kill him, she could tell the police everything he had done. Then he would probably spend the rest of his life in jail. Decision made—wait for Jack, go to the house, somehow get his money, leave the drugs for them, and then run. If he couldn't escape immediately, he could simply lie to Aunt Martha, telling her he was homesick and wanted to go home—back to his family. And if Jack wouldn't give him his money, he would beat him severely like he did his neighbor and Bobby.

Trying to steady his nerves, Wally kept an eye on the passersby and the cars traveling in both directions. But he soon began to suspect something was out of place. Men in fine suits loitered. Men in expensive suits don't loiter, not that many of them anyway, especially when the late-evening temperature was still in the eighties.

"Jack, Jack!" he heard Martha shout as she waved her arms above her head. "Here we are, Jack!"

The man she called Jack waved back and started toward the Ford, leaving his two companions on the sidewalk behind him. A man in a nearby doorway lit a cigar. Suddenly, his pace quickened as he stepped onto the pavement. Jack accelerated to a sprint as he reached in his pocket, retrieving his Colt .32-caliber M1903 Pocket Hammerless Pistol. Before he could raise and aim his weapon, several gunshots rang out. The ear-crushing explosions of gunpowder echoed off the storefronts as Jack staggered and fell in the street near the alley. Wally watched blood spurt like a small fountain from the man's head. Within moments, more men in suits and then uniformed cops swarmed the scene.

Jack's two companions, Ana Cumpanas and Polly Hamilton, now stood handcuffed next door to the National Tea Company, in front of the Biograph Theater under the marquis advertising "A Manhattan Melodrama." Ana operated the place where Martha had been living and working for many years, a bordello frequented by the man just shot by the FBI—the infamous John Dillinger, notorious bank robber and murderer, number one on the FBI's list of the most wanted criminals in America.

In 1933 and 1934, Dillinger's name had dominated the newspaper headlines while he and his violent gang terrorized the Midwest. According to the FBI, in just ten months, he killed ten men and wounded seven others. It is believed he robbed at least twelve banks. He had even escaped from jail three times. On Sunday, July 22, 1934 at approximately 10:30 p.m., his trail of terror ended. Five shots were fired from the guns of three FBI agents, Charles Winstead, Clarence Hurt, and Herman Hollis. Three of the shots hit Dillinger—he fell to the pavement, mortally wounded. A short time later, at Alexian Brothers Hospital, he would be pronounced dead.

As Jack lay covering the pavement in blood, Martha shrieked. She tried to run toward her beloved, but an iron-tight grip seized her arm. She now stood face-to-face with Joe. "Martha, it's JJ. Everything is fine. You're going to be okay."

Oblivious to who prevented her movement, she howled, "Jack, Jack!" Suddenly the distraught woman began to wobble. She let out a gasp, then started to fall. Joe kept hold, preventing his wife from hitting the sidewalk.

"Martha, Martha." Joe softly repeated her name, scooping her up into his arms.

Watching all of this unfold in just seconds, a panicked Wally started the Ford's motor to flee, but Captain Murphy would not have it. He rammed his car into the Ford's fender, blocking Wally's exit. The Irish Giant jumped out and reached for the driver's door, pulling it open before the boy could grind the transmission into reverse. Dragging the young criminal out, Murphy overpowered Wally on the spot, effortlessly pinning him to the ground and handcuffing him.

Fitzgerald also sprang into action, violently snapping handcuffs on Martha as Joe held her in his arms. The sergeant ordered Joe to carry his new prisoner to one of the paddy wagons which had just converged on the scene. Tenderly, Joe placed her inside as Fitzgerald nodded his approval. Joe climbed into the paddy wagon. Stroking his wife's cheek softly with the back of his hand as she regained consciousness, he whispered, "Martha, forgive me for leaving you." He kept repeating, "Please forgive me," as Martha turned her face away.

"No!" she screamed. "You're not my JJ. No!" Covering her face with her cuffed hands, Martha began to cry. "Joseph died in the war. You're not my JJ. He died in the war."

Crushed by the sight of his wife, now lost to her insanity, Joe spoke to her gently. "You will be fine. The police will get you help. You are right. JJ died in the war. Forget about him—JJ died in the war."

Joe slid himself out of the rear of the paddy wagon as Fitzgerald and Feherty looked on, trying not to stare at the great man, now fully broken, as he continued to whisper softly, "I am sorry I left you. I am sorry for what I have become. Please forgive me."

Fitzgerald stepped in front of Joe and locked the back of the cage while Martha peered through the bars of the paddy wagon door screaming "Jack—Jack—Jack!" Joe knew it would be the last time he would ever see her outside of an asylum. Turning his head in anguish, Joe stepped into the crowd and vanished from the scene before anyone could attempt to stop him.

CHAPTER 48

From where Joe melted into the gawking mass of human-ity, Feherty approached Captain Murphy, who still held Wally down on the pavement, his knee on the boy's back. The growing river of warm blood upon the street now reached the boy, the dry fabric of his pants and shirt thirstily absorbing it. "Perhaps we might take him to the apartment above the pharmacy for a discussion, captain."

But Murphy rebuked him. "This boy will be charged as an accessory after the fact, to bank robbery and murder. I will have no choice!"

With Dillinger's blood now soaking his clothes, Wally started to scream, "Get off me! Get off me! Let me get up!" But the two men ignored his pleas.

Feherty would not relent on his plan. "I am certain the boy had no idea who he was dealing with. Think about it. He may be a brilliant thief but why would he knowingly want to join a cold-blooded killer? He is way too smart to embrace such danger. It makes more sense that he was being manipulated by Martha for some sick and twisted reason."

Murphy thought about it, not knowing what to conclude or say as the boy continued to scream.

"You don't have to turn him over to Purvis, captain. He doesn't know anything about him right now. For all he knows the woman calling out to Dillinger wasn't connected to Wally or the car. She was on the sidewalk. We must take him to Joe's apartment before you take him to the can," Feherty urged.

But Murphy objected. "Even if the Feds don't want him, such a thing is highly irregular, my friend. Do you understand what you are asking?" Wally's begging to escape the river of blood was now becoming hysterical.

Ignoring the boy, Feherty continued, insistent. "We must afford the boy the opportunity to confess to Alvin and Lois. It may be the only way to save his soul. I watched this boy grow up in the backyard below my hermit's window. I know his parents well—at one time they filled a hole in my heart. Captain, I am positive he had no idea of who Jack really was. Now that you have found the evil one who was out to destroy him, free of her, perhaps he will find redemption in confession." Feherty challenged him. "Do you have such authority Michael Martin Murphy, Captain of Detectives? More importantly, does your soul contain enough charity for what must be done?"

Captain Murphy could not believe Feherty's audacity. As he considered what the old hermit proposed, in his head a voice called to him as if from the other side of the veil: "You must take him there," was all it said. Murphy suddenly remembered the old man's son, Sergeant Brian Feherty. His entire countenance changed as he gave a smile to the old man. "Sir, such authority is mine, and your wisdom shall be honored this night, if not for the boy, then in memory of your son. But from there, it is up to the Lord God Almighty to save him. I cannot. He must pay for his crimes as the courts and the Heavenly Judge see fit. But Mr. Feherty, I fear your brethren will not look so kindly on your request."

"Yes, they will," Feherty boasted as he walked over to the FBI Special Agent in Charge of the Chicago office, someone whom he knew very well. "Mel, this boy is wanted on two felony burglary charges by Captain Murphy. He was simply at the wrong place at the wrong time. I unequivocally assure you he had no knowledge of *number one*. He must be arrested and held on the charges Captain Murphy has established. Of course, since he was at the scene, you'll have complete access to him for questioning anytime you wish. In fact, I can guarantee you I will gain his full cooperation for you. But it won't be of much value."

The agent, Melvin Purvis, shook his head in disbelief—was Feherty actually out of his apartment? Regaining his composure, he listened with an open mind—Purvis had long been mentored by the legal genius. He also knew the legend of The Irish Giant and had the utmost respect for him. The Special Agent in Charge of the Chicago office consented to Feherty's request on the condition the boy would be kept cuffed and shackled, and under the control of Murphy and at least one other policeman at all times. After all, at that moment he had bigger fish to fry.

The Captain of Detectives agreed as he summoned an empty Chicago Police Department paddy wagon. He hurriedly threw Wally into the cage. "Mr. Feherty, let's get the boy out of here before Purvis sees what's in that box."

With Feherty as his passenger, Murphy jumped in his car and sped through a snarl of police vehicles and cars, headed back to the pharmacy. "Captain, what was in the box?" the old man asked.

"Aye, death itself Mr. Feherty, death itself." After taking a deep breath he continued; "Two Thompson .45 caliber Submachine Guns, each with its fifty-round drum magazine. Somehow the shadow of death failed to cast its darkness upon the lad—why, I do not know. A powerful guardian angel must watch over him, in spite of his criminality."

Fitzgerald and two other cops followed in the paddy wagon carrying the boy thief soaked in Dillinger's blood. Wally frantically rubbed his pant leg against the bench in the wagon, desperately trying, but failing, to transfer the blood from fabric to wood. He vomited repeatedly as he visualized the bullet wounds and felt the dead killer's blood against his skin.

CHAPTER 49

It was almost 11:00 p.m. when Murphy repeatedly rang the buzzer to both apartments. Alvin, exhausted from the tumultuous events of the day but still fully dressed, slowly descended the stairs to see who would buzz for them at such a late hour.

Murphy spoke first. "May we come in for a few minutes? There is someone I want you to speak with." Alvin nodded his agreement knowing the captain's intent, as he noticed two cops pull Wally from the back of the paddy wagon. Fitzgerald was told to guard the apartment entry. Following Murphy and Feherty, the cops dragged Wally, his shackled feet bouncing off the stairs while Alvin led the way up.

Inside Joe's apartment, Lois sat on the sofa, consoling him. He had just told her everything that occurred. She firmly grasped his hand in hers, "You are free now, Joe. You can live your life for who you are, by your code of honor. And Alvin and I will be your family, if you'll have us. Joseph, I am pregnant—we are going to have a child. It is fitting that you are the first to know—we would like you to help us raise our children. *Mon ami,* we would all be blessed by your wisdom. Joe, we love you!" Gently sobbing, his head now resting on her bosom, Lois continued to reassure him. "And your friends John Schmidt and Michael Murphy will never abandon you."

They both turned at the sound of the group bursting through the apartment door.

Regardless of Wally's size and strength, he was now compliant and weak as the two cops threw him onto a chair. Mr. Feherty turned to Murphy and demanded, "His father must be invited to this conference of redemption—for his sake, and for the good of the boy. And the owner of the liquor store, he must attend as well."

"This event is your creation, Mr. Feherty," replied Murphy. "It shall be as you wish."

Murphy pointed at one of the cops from the paddy wagon, tore off a piece of paper from his notebook, and handed it to the cop. "Here is the address. Bring his father, Peter, back here. Tell him Wally is fine, but that Captain Murphy wishes to speak with him. Don't be intimidated by Peter—he is a reasonable and measured man. Just tell him Captain Murphy asks him to join us for the good of his son. He will understand."

Then he called downstairs to the other cop. "Hey, Fitzgerald! Fetch me Thompson. Tell him I require his presence immediately for an interview. Do not take no for an answer, even if you have to rough him up and cuff him. You can beat his sorry ass to within an inch of his life, if you have to."

Wally began to ask questions, but Captain Murphy cut him short. "Hold your tongue, laddy, until we have assembled all participants in Mr. Feherty's production. Then you shall speak to your father and to the others you have hurt as if I am not here. The police will not be the wiser for your words until you are in the station." The others in the room held their tongues as well.

After somehow convincing Helen to remain home, Peter entered the apartment over the pharmacy. At first, he did a double take seeing Mr. Feherty out of his apartment, but quickly noticed the silent and somber group focused on his handcuffed son seated at the kitchen table. Murphy took control as Peter rushed to his son. "Peter, your son has much to confess. It is at the request of your friend, Mr. Feherty, that I have detoured his route to jail. I can explain it all to you, if necessary, but I respectfully request you first let him tell you and the assembled what I hope he will have the courage to say. That would undoubtedly be the best for his salvation. And it may just help reduce the severity of the charges, should the lad confess and cooperate. This conference, shall we say, is more than a bit irregular. The police—that is me—shall treat it as if it never happened. What will occur afterward will be the only official police business. Whatever the boy decides to do once we are at the station, he himself shall determine how the cards of his fate are dealt."

Peter, having anticipated a grave situation, replied, "Of course, Captain Murphy. I knew something serious was going on when he and Martha said they were driving to pick up Helen and did not return." Standing behind his son, hands on the boy's shoulders, Peter commanded: "Wally, it is time to speak with complete honesty—nothing less."

Just then the owner of Town Liquors, stinking of booze, pants pulled over his pajamas, hair mussed up, shirt misbuttoned, entered the apartment. Fitzgerald dragged him in by the arm. "What the hell do you want from me? I was already in bed," he slurred. "Sunday is the only night I close early!"

"Thank you for cooperating, Mr. Thompson," Murphy said. "Tonight, you shall do one good deed at my request. Please sit down." He then directed Alvin and Lois to take the other seats at the table. The thief and his victims now assembled, "Talk laddy; 'tis time!" Murphy barked.

Wally still obsessively rubbed his cuffed hands on the drying blood on his pants as he replied. "I didn't know who that man was, the man who got killed. Sergeant Fitzgerald told me it was John Dillinger. I had no idea, honest. Dad, a bullet blew a gaping hole in his head. The blood squirted high in the air like a fountain. Then it trickled its way to me as that giant cop held me down, his knee on my back, and my face in the pavement. The river of blood kept coming at me, growing. It started to cover me! It all just keeps replaying in my head. I can't stop seeing it!" Wally dropped onto his knees, dry heaving onto the floor under the table, begging, "Dear God, make it stop! Please make it stop!"

With his voice raised, Peter demanded, "Dillinger? What's going on here, Captain Murphy? What does Wally have to do with John Dillinger?"

Murphy answered in a soft voice, attempting to calm things down. "Peter, the man Martha was to meet tonight was none other than that infamous, cold-blooded killer himself. It was Martha who, I am sure, led the boy to that perilous place. Your son saw the gangster get shot by the FBI agents, practically right next to his car door. It was a gruesome sight to behold."

Murphy locked a piercing stare at Wally. "A life of crime ends in only one of two ways—your death or prison. Is this the dark path you wish to tread? Your deeds tell me it certainly must be."

Wally climbed back onto his seat, wiping the spittle off his chin with his blood-stained hands, objecting defiantly. "No, it's not, it's not. I swear it's not. Yes, I beat up Bobby and took the keys from him; I robbed the liquor store alone and tried to frame him. He's innocent. Yes, I figured out how to break into Lincolnway, too." He then explained everything that happened—from running away until Martha found him. Looking up at his father, he confessed the evolution of his first white lie. Next, Wally described in meticulous detail how he, with Aunt Martha's help, finalized the plans for his crimes from the phone booth at Lincolnway.

Peter gripped his son's shoulders more firmly, as the boy continued. "Once she gave me the idea that the robberies would be my key to happiness, I figured it all out. She didn't make me do it—she only encouraged me. Dad, you were never around, so it made me happy to steal alloys from the foundry's sample room to use in the robberies. I wanted to get even with you for hitting me and for always being at work. But I'll never forgive Aunt Martha for what she did to me!"

Growing impatient, the owner of Town Liquors stood up and interrupted the boy's confession. "Murphy, spare me all this family bullshit! You go get my money this bastard stole. Then, put him in jail and throw away the key."

Murphy, shielding Thompson from Peter's advance, called to the boy. "Wally, don't you have something to tell Mr. Thompson?"

"I am sorry I stole from you, sir. All the money except for fifteen dollars is still in the trunk of the Oldsmobile—I can show the cops where it is. The twelve dollars in my pocket belongs to you. I've only spent three dollars. I will pay that back too."

Murphy impatiently glared at Thompson. "You have not yet done the good deed I have asked of you."

Refusing to grant forgiveness, the man shook his head no and moved toward the door. "Come on, can't you see the boy is lying—it's obvious. He's not sorry for what he did; he's just sorry he got caught. Now go get my money and throw the punk in jail!"

Before Peter could attack the drunk, Murphy grabbed the liquor store owner by his throat and slammed him against the wall, fracturing the plaster. Then taking him by the scruff of his neck, he threw him out the apartment's door, sending him tumbling down the staircase.

Captain Murphy, a bit amused at his own indiscretion, called down to the drunk sprawled out at the bottom of the stairs. "Be off with you then, you filthy pig! The department shall remember your cold and merciless heart." Chuckling, he turned to Peter, "Better I than thee—you might have killed him!"

Peter spun the boy around in his chair. "It's over now, son." Wally stood up, accepting his father's hug. But the boy was not done. He shared how Martha convinced him he would be happier with her, describing her evil guidance, including her sexual provocations—the kissing, the touching, the promise of sex.

"Oh, mon Dieu!" (Oh, my goodness), Lois covered her mouth to attenuate her audible gasp.

Joe jumped up from his place on the couch. "Wally, are you telling the truth? What did she say? What did she do?" Pausing his demands, Joe plopped back into his seat mumbling, "No, don't tell me. I don't want to know."

Relieved of his fear of what Joe might do to him, Wally muttered, "No sir, I won't."

Then Wally turned, slowly allowing his eyes to meet Alvin's. "The day we helped you move in all your new stuff, I peeked inside the vaulted sidewalk and saw it was open to the east, to the tailor's shop. Hiding in the shadows across the street, I watched Joe secure your store. I figured if I had any chance, it would be through the vault. As my father spoke of the alloys they were now creating, I realized I might be able to open the door from the vault side if I could find what I needed in the foundry's sample room."

His eyes locked on Wally, Alvin asked, "An ignorant man who refuses to learn makes himself a fool. Do you wish to learn from your criminal ways or become a fool, Wally?"

The boy looked away, now unable to continue eye contact with Alvin. "No sir, I don't want to be a fool. And I am sorry for what I've done to you and Lois. I can easily lead the police to the house in the woods—to the car with your money and drugs. But I had no idea who Jack was, only that Aunt Martha said I could work for him and make lots of money. I was going to be Jack's apprentice. I was going to drive for him and learn how to work on cars. I had no idea, honest!"

Alvin stood up from his chair as if swearing an oath. "The Torah teaches that our forefather Joseph forgave his brothers after all the harm they had done to him. Such is the example we have been given." Pausing, he looked into the boy's eyes without blinking. "Wally, I forgive you."

Lois quickly stood alongside her husband. "Wally, *we both* forgive you."

Peter was compelled to speak. "Your mother and I will do everything we can to help you get through this, no matter how long it takes or what it costs. We will always love you! And we forgive you for what you did. Please forgive me for not being there for you when you've needed me." Wally accepted his father's second hug.

Knowing that not all parts of this tragedy were yet known, Captain Murphy redirected everyone's attention. "Peter, I want you to again meet a man you knew a long time ago." Gesturing toward Joe he said, "Joseph, please forgive me, but the time has come for the truth to be fully honored. I can no longer, in good conscience, participate in a deception that deprives the world of one of its heroes—especially now when he will most need those who love him."

Joe stood silently, painfully dreading the inevitable.

Still staring at Joe, Murphy continued. "Because of his humility and after the heartbreak of failing to find his beloved once home from the war, Captain JJ Harper tried to escape from public notoriety. And lo these many years, he did so with the help of John Schmidt and myself. But I fear I have sinned greatly by repeatedly sending the investigators from the White

House and the War Department on dead-end trails until they stopped looking for him."

Turning his gaze to Peter, Murphy continued. "Peter, this is your wife's brother-in-law, JJ—also known as the famous Captain JJ Harper of the United States Expeditionary Force—now a steelworker toiling in anonymity at Schmidt Foundry under the alias Joe Harpy."

Peter looked at him, shocked, and saddened. "Joe, I had no idea. Oh my God, Joe. Oh my God. You're JJ? The accident at the foundry—I remember it was some new guy's first day. I had no idea it was you. You were Martha's JJ? Oh, my goodness, Joe."

Joseph Jeffery Harper turned away.

Peter raced to his wife's brother-in-law and embraced him, compelled to complete the catharsis. "Captain Murphy says it's time for the truth to be honored. He is right. Sir, there has been a deep, dark family secret kept locked up for many years. It is time to bring it into the light of day. Maybe it will help all of us make sense out of this insanity."

Peter swallowed hard. "The night of your wedding, my wife Helen, despondent with guilt for not being there to celebrate your marriage in person, told me the story about her brutal drunken father—a man who hurt everyone he knew. For the first time, she told me the sordid details of *why* Martha and Helen escaped from under the cruel thumb of an evil monster." Peter gulped again, suddenly regretting his decision to explain all. But he had crossed the proverbial Rubicon. "You see, Joe," he hesitated, "Martha had a…horrible life in Poland."

"What are you talking about Peter? What are you trying to say?" Joe insisted.

"I'm so sorry, Joe. Martha was…uh…uh…defiled by her father when she was only a child of thirteen—God help her. That's why their mother sent them to America—to save the girls from that perilous place. Helen had hoped all of Martha's suffering would be extinguished by finding a new life in America."

Joe stood motionless, trying to summon up all the hero's bravery he could muster. His eyes fixed on Peter as the steel-worker continued, "As beautiful and strong as she appears, I guess we will never understand just how broken Martha is. Joe, none of this is your fault. You were called to war, to unselfishly risk your life for your country and for the people of Europe. I only wish we were here for you when you came home. But Joe, you are part of our family, and Helen and I truly wish to include you."

Joe tried to absorb the heartbreaking realization about the woman he married. He demanded: "How could a father do such a thing? How does a person hurt their own child? Why didn't I try harder to find her? Why wasn't I there to help her? And finally, she was consorting with Dillinger? Oh, my Lord, how could she be so accursed? Why, Peter, why?"

Lois gently took Joe's hand as Peter and the others were frozen in silence, softly repeating again and again, *"Mon précieux ami, tu ne dois pas te blamer."* (My precious friend, you must not blame yourself.) It strengthened him.

Suddenly, as if snapped out of a trance, Joe released Lois' hand. He turned and extended his hand to Peter with the unmistakable firm handshake of commitment. "Thank you for telling me, Peter—and for embracing me as part of your family. We mustn't hide from the truth, regardless of how bitter and ugly it may be. And I must honor the marriage covenant I swore unto death, regardless of the damage done to her by that monster." Weeping, Lois embraced him.

Then Peter turned to his son, "Wally, now you know of the curse over our family. Misfortune and worse has haunted your mother's family for generations. But you might be the one strong enough to end the curse—forever. This family shall not be overcome by perversion, lies, or crimes, nor by the shadow of a monster; at least not without a fight.

The famous army captain who always knew how to determine the state of mind of his troops challenged Wally. "Was it the gruesome wound to Dillinger's head and his blood on your clothes that now make you confess? Perhaps getting caught is too much for you. Tell me Wally, which is it? Or was it both?"

Without even blinking the boy replied. "No sir, I knew better. I wish I could take it all back. But why did that woman keep encouraging me? I'll never forgive her!"

Quickly interrupting Joe as he began to react, Peter spoke firmly to his son. "Wally, if you seek forgiveness, remember you must also freely grant it. You were manipulated by a tortured soul looking to destroy you so she could destroy her own sister. Perhaps it was because of Martha's abuse that she could not bear the happiness your mother and I have found. It must have been the twisted call for help of a tormented soul no one could quite understand. You must forgive her as well, for she was not the first to sin."

Wally resisted. "What she did to me was bad enough, but she wanted to hurt mom even more? I'm supposed to forgive her? Really? How can I do that?"

Joe interjected. "Wally, your father speaks with great wisdom. Everyone knows the meaning of charity, but few understand that forgiveness is perhaps its greatest form." Joe trembled as he tried to maintain his composure. "Now is the time mercy *must* reign in *all* our hearts." Everyone's eyes locked on him. Joe took a deep breath. "Ask yourself Wally, do you want to be like your father, or like Jack?"

Wally hung his head and cried.

Gently gripping his arm, Lois whispered in her husband's ear. Alvin then declared the couple's intention. "Wally, President Lincoln once said '...mercy bears richer fruits than strict justice.' I repeat, Lois and I forgive you! And we will help you and your parents with the costs of your legal defense."

Shocked, Peter replied. "Alvin, your kindness is generous beyond what is fair and just. Thank you, but we shall be responsible for our own. This boy must work to repay you for the damage done and heartache he has caused. He has already cost his victims enough."

Arm in arm, the couple smiled. "Peter, we really want to help, and will, if you will permit it."

Joe then urged, "Peter, do not deny Alvin and Lois their act of forgiveness. Such loving generosity comes from the innermost depths of their hearts. If I may presume to say so, you should respect and consider their offer. It is who they are."

A broad smile turned up the corners of Murphy's mouth, shaking his head in astonishment. "Mr. Feherty, you have the wisdom of Solomon. And you have my eternal gratitude for demanding this detour. The lad may truly have a chance at redemption now." With that, Murphy motioned to Fitzgerald. "Okay sergeant, it is time for our young burglar to begin his way upon the path of justice. I will follow shortly to direct the taking of his official confession—do not start without me. And remember, this little session never took place."

Slowly releasing Wally from his embrace, Peter could only watch with heartbreak at seeing his oldest child led away as the criminal he had become, knowing it had to be so.

As the sound of the creaking staircase reported Wally's descent, Feherty's wisdom was not yet extinguished. "Peter, this is far from done. Helen must speak to her boy tonight!

He must confess and apologize to the one he has hurt the most, and she must hug him as many times as her tender heart requires. Otherwise, I fear the stress of her sister and her son both being arrested tonight may be too much for that gentle soul to bear. Captain Murphy, you must allow them to meet in an interrogation room for as long as his dear mother needs. Please don't traumatize Helen by making them meet in a holding cell. And I will watch over Peter and Helen's little ones this evening, for as long as it takes."

Murphy quickly confirmed Feherty's request. "So be it. I shall see to it myself."

Peter answered. "Yes, thank you, Mr. Feherty. Sir, you are wise and generous. I will gather her up and go with her to the police station, but how in the world can I explain to her everything that has just transpired?"

The old hermit shook his head in sadness. "Peter, there is no way to sugar coat what has happened. Be direct but speak with love—the love you have for her and for Wally. Get it all out, say it fast, leave nothing out—but focus especially on his confession. Then hold her. Assure her of the formidable power that lies in a parent's prayers. Take strength knowing that God's mercy walks arm in arm with His justice. Stand firm and know that I am just a flight of stairs above you, should you need me."

With fear of future trials that would beset him, Peter mumbled, "Thank you, Mr. Feherty."

The old hermit was not finished. "Peter, for all these years I have retreated ever further into my own isolation of self-pity. But I should have been there for you and Helen, and your children; you tried to show me so much love early on, but I rejected it. Well, Peter, finally I am free from my self-imposed prison. Now, I shall be there for all of you, but especially your son—and I still have my license to practice law!"

Murphy chuckled, "No prosecutor will want to see you in a courtroom, Mr. Feherty. Aye, they might offer to plead down at just the hearing of your name!"

The irresistible internal glow of love upon Lois, she quickly turned everyone's attention back to the urgent situation: "Peter, with your permission, I'll join Mr. Feherty to help look after your little ones. They may need a woman's touch. And I think it may give comfort to Helen knowing she has both of us there."

His head still spinning, Peter hastened to leave but stopped in the doorway to address the group. "Mr. Feherty, Alvin, Lois, Michael, Joe—thank you. I should never have thought it possible for one family to be so blessed by so many wonderful neighbors."

Joe exclaimed, "Amen!" as Peter turned to race down the stairs.

But Captain Murphy called after him. "Peter, my work is far from finished. I shall have the honor of driving you and

Helen myself. I shall follow you in short order, after you have a few moments with Helen."

He gave one more order. "Lois, Mr. Feherty, you have children for the tending. We dare not tarry; a mother needs to embrace her son." Alvin nodded approvingly at his wife as Lois dashed into the rear apartment to grab her purse.

From his window onto the street below, Joe watched Fitzgerald shove Wally into the paddy wagon. Feherty stepped alongside the bravest of war heroes as together they saw the door slammed shut and the padlock snapped upon the hasp. Placing a trembling hand on Joe's arm, choking on his words, he whispered: "My boy would have been about the same age as you, Captain Harper."

Joe managed a fractured smile, interrupting the old man, "Please, call me JJ."

"Thank you, JJ. Perhaps we might get together and talk sometime soon. I would like you to tell me about my son during his time under your command. And I would like to share all Brian wrote to me about you."

"It would be my honor and privilege. He was the very inspiration of our company's motto—*only the fierce are fearless.* Men like Brian were the reason we prevailed." Joe drew close to the old hermit. "You know, Mr. Feherty, had my father lived he would have been about the same age as you. Coincidentally, he was a lawyer too."

A wide smile came upon the hermit's face. "I think I need a friend. Perhaps you do, too—now that we are both finally free."

AUTHOR'S NOTES

The following sources were used in the research phase of the creation of this novel:

Bacon, Gershon. 2011. Poland: Poland from 1795 to 1939. YIVO Encyclopedia of Jews in Eastern Europe. https://yivoencyclopedia.org/article.aspx/Poland/Poland_from_1795_to_1939

Wilhelm II, On This Day, www.onthisday.com, https://www.onthisday.com/people/wilhelm-ii

U.S. Merchant Ships, Sailing Vessels, and Fishing Craft Lost from all Causes during World War I, "American Merchant Marine at War", www.usmm.org, http://www.usmm.org/ww1merchant.html

U.S. Entry into World War I – HISTORY, A&E Television Networks, updated August 30, 2022, https://www.history.com/topics/world-war-i/u-s-entry-into-world-war-i-1

Britannica, T. Editors of Encyclopaedia. "Zimmermann Telegram." Encyclopedia Britannica, September 12, 2023. https://www.britannica.com/event/Zimmermann-Telegram

The American Expeditionary Forces, Stars and Stripes: The American Soldiers' Newspaper of World War I, 1918 to 1919, Library of Congress, https://www.loc.gov/collections/stars-and-stripes/articles-and-essays/a-world-at-war/american-expeditionary-forces/

Statue of Liberty, HISTORY, A&E Television Networks, last updated: July 1, 2019, https://www.history.com/topics/landmarks/statue-of-liberty

Wrigley Field History, cubs.com, MLB Advanced Media, LP, https://www.mlb.com/cubs/ballpark/information/history

Global Cooling: The History of Air Conditioning, American Society of Mechanical Engineers, *updated: 10/7/2022,* https://www.asme.org/topics-resources/content/global-cooling-the-history-of-air-conditioning

Prohibition, HISTORY, A&E Television Networks, last updated: April 24, 2023, https://www.history.com/topics/roaring-twenties/prohibition

'Big Bill' Thompson: Chicago's unfiltered mayor, Chicago Tribune, last updated: Feb 05, 2016 at 1:14 pm, https://www.chicagotribune.com/opinion/commentary/ct-big-bill-thompson-trump-flashback-perspec-0207-jm-20160205-story.html

"The Evolution of Fingerprint Technology Through the Years," Grunge Science, Grunge is owned and operated by Static Media Inc., published November 10, 2022, https://www.grunge.com/1096321/the-evolution-of-fingerprint-technology-through-the-years/

The Scientific Crime Detection Laboratory, Chicagology, https://www.chicagology.com, https://chicagology.com/?s=crime+lab

1811 Year of the Comet, Cognac-ton, https://cognac-ton.nl/en/, https://cognac-ton.nl/en/homepage/other-topics/1811-year-of-the-comet/#

The Harrison Narcotics Act (1914), Schaffer Library of Drug Policy, StoptheDrugWar.org, https://www.druglibrary.org/Schaffer/library/studies/cu/cu8.html

"City Streets: How Chicago Raised Itself Out of the Mud and Astonished the World," Gapers Block (website) www.gapersblock.com, May 5, 2005, https://www.gapersblock.com/airbags/archives/city_streets_how_chicago_raised_itself_out_of_the_mud_and_astonished_the_world/

Vaulted sidewalk, Wikipedia, The Free Encyclopedia, last revision: 28 September 2023 20:59 UTC, https://en.wikipedia.org/w/index.php?title=Vaulted_sidewalk&oldid=1177672515

History, Famous Cases and Crimes, John Dillinger, www.fbi.gov, Federal Bureau of Investigation, https://www.fbi.gov/history/famous-cases/john-dillinger

"The Guns of John Dillinger, The Arsenal of Public Enemy Number 1", Guns Magazine, An FMG Publications Production, August 2020, https://gunsmagazine.com/guns/handguns/the-guns-of-john-dillinger/

ACKNOWLEDGMENTS

Special thanks to the following individuals and organizations who helped make possible *Whispers in a Phone Booth —A Depression-Era Tale of Danger and Deception:*

Publisher Barbara Reed of Terra3 Communications, who guided the completion of this work in countless ways with boundless skill, patience, and determination. It is because of her that I recognized the need to edit and reedit more times than I thought was possible.

New York Times and WSJ bestselling business author, Rich Horwath of the Strategic Thinking Institute, who vigorously encouraged me to explore writing fiction when I first contemplated doing so.

Zvi Noy, for whom French is his first language, and Mary Beth Medley, a native English speaker with an advanced degree in French, both of whom reviewed the accuracy of the French dialogue.

Cover and graphic artist, Rafael Andres, who created the unique cover design giving the visual impact needed to bring this work to life.

Copy editor Michele Aschkenase, who guided me in how to communicate more artfully and clearly.

My awesome beta readers: Chris Charnas, Andrew Hochberg, Hugh McLean, Jill Rossol, Tony Rubino, and Donna Tropp, who helped to identify my gaps and blind spots.

Reedsy.com—the writers' online ecosystem, especially its vendor marketplace and tutorials.

www.ingramcontent.com/pod-product-compliance
Lightning Source LLC
Chambersburg PA
CBHW021337310726
48971CB00001B/169